The Journey From Ennuied

a novel by
Donald Braun

◆ FriesenPress

Suite 300 - 990 Fort St
Victoria, BC, Canada, V8V 3K2
www.friesenpress.com

Copyright © 2015 by Donald Braun
First Edition — 2015

Edited by Dr. Greg Tweedie

All rights reserved.

No part of this publication may be reproduced in any form, or by any means, electronic or mechanical, including photocopying, recording, or any information browsing, storage, or retrieval system, without permission in writing from FriesenPress.

ISBN
978-1-4602-7239-8 (Hardcover)
978-1-4602-7240-4 (Paperback)
978-1-4602-7241-1 (eBook)

1. Fiction, Visionary & Metaphysical

Distributed to the trade by The Ingram Book Company

That which is belittled in plain speech finds the respect it warrants in the subtleties of metaphor.

—D. Braun

Preface

This book is dedicated to you. In my work as an educator, psychologist, and spiritual seeker, I have come to view life as a journey full of purpose and mystery. It is my sincere wish that you will enjoy this book as a fantasy story on its own, but more than that, I hope that you will come to understand your own life as a journey of unfathomable significance. I am convinced that there are spiritual dimensions at work in this world that have much less to do with religious ritual, rules, and dogma than with orientation of our hearts. Having worked with many thousands of people, I am also positive that the spiritual—that which is good, pure, and full of life—is near each and every human being regardless of race, faith, culture, and place.

The Journey from Ennuied is intended to be a mysterious text, an invitation to spiritual connectedness that is unique to each human being. It is my hope that by reflecting on the meaning of the text, you will be drawn into the wondrous purposes in your own life. The book relies heavily on the language of metaphor. I chose this way of writing because there are many things in life: difficulties, joys, painful experiences, and wonders that are belittled through plain speech. Like that friend who seems to hear what you say but seldom listens to your heart, discussing life's most intimate experiences recklessly is seldom what we need.

Some of the metaphorical language in *The Journey from Ennuied* is written to be understood easily, while other passages may remain cloaked in mystery, triggering images, feelings, and perhaps memories of your own. This novel is best read by paying careful attention to those events and settings that trigger emotions, understanding, and even inner conflict.

The book is divided into four sections describing how the experience of pain may be needed to launch us into important journeys, the journey within ourselves, the journey beyond ourselves, and matters of wisdom. In *The Journey from Ennuied,* you will find a pathway where down is up, up is down, and the experience of darkness, pain, and even death itself are more than endured, with the potential to bring us closer to unspeakable wonders, though likely not in the way we would expect. Prepare yourself to encounter a message that contrasts starkly and pleasingly with much that is conventional.

On the surface, much of our lives seems to be a choice between two paths. On the one hand there is what I call the way of competition and strife. We are under great pressure to take this path through life, so much so that we regard it with great reverence and often without question. We know we are on this path when our thoughts are consumed with desires to be stronger than others, happier, thinner, more talented, more beautiful, and more successful. Sadly, in circles of faith, this same way is paved and clear. A path where being "righter" with the best rules and practices sets one person or group above another. All of us have found ourselves on this path from time to time. Sometimes we reach off this path through kindness and generosity, but it can quickly draw us back into its gravity. I like to call the other path we can take the way of the beaten. When we perceive failure on the path of competition and strife, we find ourselves on this wide roadway. When life's difficulties are simply too much and we lose the will to resist, we are there. Of course, every person experiences the difficulties of this path, but should we journey here too long, we will taste the darkest of emotions and find ourselves harmed by others and lacking in the will to live life fully.

In *The Journey from Ennuied,* you will find a third way, what I call the way of love and lowness. It is a way that is both fresh and old. The wise among the ancients discovered this way, yet each person must journey to this place for him- or herself. It is a place of connection to the great power behind the cosmos. It is a place of tremendous strength and a full experience of both sorrow and joy. In the way of love and lowness, just one thing remains and rules over everything else—the primacy of union and selfless love. I hope that in *The Journey from Ennuied*, you will find yourself drawn closer to this third way and that you will find much in your life drawing you there already ...

Prologue
San Francisco, USA—2059 C.E.

My name is Jack Burchell, and I have a most unusual story to share with you. Let me explain, working at home was supposed to be the great panacea. Uninterrupted access to information, the ability to communicate with partners around the world regardless of time zones, and non-geographical networking through technology were supposed to restore our American competitive edge. Plus, they said, we could do all of this and have so much more time for family and leisure—the best of all worlds, we were told. The reality of it all was something quite different. Truth be known, the demands of it all had begun to take their toll on me, and I was not sure how long I could maintain my pace. A nagging thought arose in the back of my mind, barely perceptible, and I doubt I could have put it into words; I had a growing fear that I was about to unravel from the inside out. I dismissed my unease as a symptom of my advancing age. Not old yet, no longer young, the desires of youth still alive in me, yet facing the reality of strength's demise.

As a youngster, I recalled a very different life. My parents worked very hard, and while life was challenging, there were breaks and many fond memories. We took holidays at national parks, camped in the wilderness, and played at the amusement parks that used to surround all of the big cities. My favourite place to visit was a large park with rides that were based on magical fairy tales. I can still smell the scent of the water and feel the cool mist blow on my face as the rides took me to imaginary worlds and on mysterious adventures. I enjoyed talking to my father about the old days, a time of primitive computing machines, heavy televisions, and cars the size of yachts. My dad told me of how he spent hours memorizing facts at school and described how the teachers insisted that his handwriting meet their exacting standards.

The world is a different place now. The wars of the 2040s changed everything and set the earth on a new trajectory. The advances that brought a semblance of peace came with a cost, and the dividing line between mind and machine had become blurry. Each advance seemed to make life simpler and more connected on the surface but was more restrictive and arduous as well. The reduction of sickness and the home-based data centre, while convenient, led to the seven-day work week and an end to what was once called retirement. The advances also led to the formation of global partnerships that were never before so productive. Competition and intrigue within the world of commerce and trade reached new heights, leading to the near constant industrial surveillance that was now part of my daily routine. But all of that is part of another story.

The nostalgia of the day led me to search my storage space for the one box of mementos I could afford to keep at my small flat. My manager, really just a link in the long chain that comprised the multinational where I worked, would just have to wait. And while my Duty Director would track my movements away from the home workstation data centre, I doubted she would berate me with any more vigour than usual. With a touch from my forefinger, the locking mechanism on the stainless steel locker read the information from the chip embedded in my hypodermis, so small as to be almost invisible, should I remove it. The door clicked and the small storage closet was open. I scanned the plastic containers for the one I was looking for. Inside a sealed green polyethylene case was a traditional cardboard box with worn flaps and tears in the corners. Here was all I had left of my family history. I placed the box on the floor and sat down on the white tile to review the contents. I pulled out the family photo album. There were many pictures of my parents, uncles, and aunts and a few of me as well.

While I was looking through the familiar documents and mementos, I saw a simple hardcover notebook, well-worn yet undamaged, like a book that was used all the time but treated with care and respect. I opened the cover and saw my granddad's name written in his own vaguely familiar cursive. I wondered aloud how I could have missed this book before, sure that I had never detected it in the box. The tattered cardboard box was more than familiar to me. It was the box I had used to collect seashells when I was twelve years old, and it was the place where I stored my most treasured belongings during the many moves of the war years. I knew with certainty that I had not put the mysterious volume in the box myself. I reasoned that perhaps Mother added the book to my collection without my knowledge, though even this seemed unlikely. It was at least ten years since the last time I saw her. Intensely curious about the contents, I opened the book to a random page near the beginning. Underneath a date long before I was born and when my father was just a child himself, I read what appeared to be a journal entry from Granddad's pen.

January 28, 1986

I am so tired of it all. The pressure, the work, the disappointments. Sometimes I wonder how much longer I can continue. I feel like something is twisted inside me and I can't untwist it.

I turned a few pages and read more of Granddad's heartfelt words.

April 26, 1986

Home, home, home.
A house, family, nation, people?
Where is my home?
Emotions shaken, fearful of lost control
Something is amiss

As I read Granddad's mysterious journal, I felt a most uncomfortable mixture of emotions: relieved in one sense that my granddad, who lived in what I thought was simpler time, felt just like me; and intensely anxious on the other, worried that such timeless tensions might never find resolve. I took the journal and the box to my sleeping console, sure now that

I would hear the digital voice of my director urging me back to the work station. I had to learn how things turned out for Granddad; I felt that my own life might hinge on what I discovered that day. I sat on the soft mattress, choosing not to activate the sleep acceleration rhythms, and I read every page of what I now surmised was Granddad's secret memoir.

While the first half of the journal was filled with longing and regret, the second was very different—it was filled with stories about his family and friends and many a stranger as well. I knew from my father that Granddad loved his cars, waxing, polishing, and cleaning them with a legendary commitment to detail. Apparently, a young man out celebrating with his friends crashed into Granddad's prized Buick (a common luxury motor vehicle of the era) while it was parked on the street. Granddad barely mentioned the car but filled pages with descriptions of this young man, who became his close friend and my godfather. Granddad left his well-paid position in sales and worked for many years in a home for children with all kinds of disabilities. The stories he wrote about these children were astounding, describing the personalities, interests, and needs of even the most profoundly disabled. I tried to pinpoint where this change began, and my mind led me to one very simple entry somewhere near the middle of the memoir:

> *I found a book yesterday and when I touched it, a strange wind blew through my window. I smelled lavender. Time seemed to stop. I had no thought of food or drink. I have read the novel from cover to cover. The air itself is filled with life.*

Strangely, Granddad never mentioned this mysterious book again, but from that day forward his journal entries began to change. If Granddad experienced relief from his inner turmoil, he never mentioned it; rather, he seemed to simply forget about it, becoming immersed in the problems and needs of others. The latter half of his journal filled me with a sense of pride—Granddad, it seems, was a great help to many people—yet I was left unsatisfied. I wanted to find out about him, not all of these other people. I mused that the mysterious book Granddad read might help me understand his life.

At this moment I heard the familiar drone of the Duty Director's dry, lifeless voice questioning why I was away from the data centre console. With a conditioned response that would make Pavlov proud, I hurried back to my endless work, but an idea began to form in my mind. I had never seen Granddad's journal in the old box before, and I wondered if it was possible that the mysterious book was there as well. I thought it unlikely; I had never even heard of the book until just a few hours before. Nevertheless, I snuck away from the data centre one more time and emptied the box's contents onto my sleeping console. I recognized everything, save one, and it was indeed a book.

I have to say at this point that reason is a useful tool. It keeps the power of imagination in check and grounds the mind to the earth. But reason alone is insufficient to describe the strange world we inhabit. I have no idea how this book made its way into my box of family mementos, but I suspect that you too can recount your fair share intrusions into the world of reason if you only look.

The book was crimson red and appeared to be covered in some kind of fabric rather than thick paper. The Duty Director's shrill and unfriendly voiced pierced through the implant near my cochlear nerve, questioning me again and urging me to return to the data centre. Conflicted, I was drawn to this strange red book yet compelled to return to my duties. Sometimes life's most momentous decisions take place in a split second, and it was at that moment I chose to listen to a part of me that had remained silent for far too long. I reached out to pick up the red book lying on my mattress. As soon as the tip of my forefinger touched the peculiar fabric, something like electricity swirled around my head and, though it sounds impossible, inside my head. In a moment, the Duty Director's voice was silenced, and I knew that the strange energy had destroyed her implanted chip. I grabbed hold of the red book, determined to experience its enigmatic contents for myself. On the cover, in faint print a somewhat lighter shade of red, was a strange saying. In time, these simple words would come to mean the world to me:

The Dolor Door
The Way of Humilis

Gaudium Exigo
Journey from Ennuied

    There in my sleeping console, far into the night, and without thought of sleep or distraction, I read the mysterious book from start to finish. The hours passed as minutes, and I experienced for myself the same subtle thunder as my granddad those many years before. I don't speak of this experience very often; it is so often misunderstood. Perhaps the most important things in this world are difficult to express with words. I have not been the same since that fateful day. With some hesitation, I have chosen to share this book with you in the pages that follow, asking only that you read it with timeless eyes. Please prepare yourself to meet dozens of people, some of whom you will come to know well and others you will encounter as acquaintances who come and go. I simply ask that you sit back and enjoy the story I am about to tell. Perhaps some deep part of you, deeper than the thoughts that scurry about your brain this way and that, will find agreement or conflict in its strange and wonderful twists and turns. Join me in the mystery of this quest to find meaning in that which defies simple explanation.

The Journey From Ennuied

PART ONE
The Pain Is Awakened— The Journey Begins

Chapter One
Trapped in Ennuied

I suppose I always knew there was something more. So many years ago, when I was walking along the path to my house, the strangest thing happened. It was getting dark, and I was returning from a long day of work in the fields. That is how I had spent much of my time, by the way—working in the fields of fodder grass, the staple grain for almost all of our food. As a teen, I spent most of my days tending these fields of fodder grass, going to school to learn about fodder grass production, or attending the many festivals and celebrations—always about fodder grass.

As I walked along the familiar path, the dry winds that plagued my village quieted just a little. From a distance, I heard music. It seemed a great distance away yet close enough to send shivers down my spine. It was not the harsh music of the fodder grass festivals, with their pounding rhythms and screeching tones that demand one's full attention. It was soft and gentle music and, as uncanny as this sounds, though I had never heard this music before, it was strangely familiar.

If the stars at night could sing to each other or the sun hum a tune just before rising in the eastern sky, it might sound like this music. All the other music that I had heard before had gone into my ears and sometimes even around my mind, but this music did something else. It entered my heart and made me feel strange and wonderful things, happy and lonely, hungry yet full of good things. I heard one instrument above all of the others. It was the sound of high strings, tender, yet each note striking with the force of a hammer, cracking my heart and giving me hope all at once. For the briefest moment, I felt a surge of hope that goodness surrounded me and that goodness ruled over all.

As I stopped to listen, terrified that the soft sounds would disappear, I was sure I smelled something as well. To this day, I find it hard to describe; the smell was like lilac blossoms, pine needles, and the water of the sea all rolled up into one. It was a lovely scent. I would have been happy to stay in that spot forever, but the wind quickly returned and I heard nothing but its roar in my ears and smelled only the fodder grass dust that coated my skin and hair. When I arrived home, I told my mother all about what had happened to me. Fear flared in her eyes, and she repeated what I had heard all my life: "Eloy, you must avoid The Pain. Do not awaken The Darkness." She told me to stay focused on my studies and the toil in the fields and broke into one of her lengthy tirades about applying myself to what was important.

Deep down, everyone in my village knows there comes a time to leave. You see, nobody grows old in my village, Ennuied, where I was born. It is where my journey began. Ennuied was a strange place, full of secrets and mysteries. As a child, I knew none of this, but with time, as you will see, the secrets and pressures became a weight I could no longer bear.

"Avoid The Pain. Do not awaken The Darkness." That is what they said endlessly in Ennuied, for there was great fear of pain and darkness. Even then though, I was drawn to them with a tormenting ambivalence, intuitively aware that there was somewhere I needed to go, somewhere only they could bring me.

My father used to say the same things. I remember walking and talking with him when I was young. Papa was a leader in the village and often carried me on his shoulders during the walk to the village council. As we strolled together, he would speak to me about the great traditions and festivals and how we were better off than people in other lands because of the soil, sun, and land that gave us the gift of fodder grass.

One winter, I noticed a change in my father. He seldom spoke to me of the fodder grass and spent his time wandering alone, deep in thought. I discovered, years later, that there had been serious conflict in the council chambers. Some in the village wanted to do away with the supremacy of fodder grass. They argued forcefully that the land would produce just as much if we allowed the planting of fodder nut trees in the valleys. They even said they had stopped eating fodder grass and preferred the flavour of the nuts. Papa knew that fodder grass was the greatest plant the world had ever known, but he reasoned that if others wanted to grow the fodder nuts, they should be allowed some land, away from the main fields of course. Hardened in tradition, bound by notions of right and wrong passed down by those who came before, and with little thought given to wisdom or kindness, the council refused to listen to Papa. Many of the fodder nut believers were sent away, never to be seen or heard from again.

My father, so I have heard, began to feel The Pain. I only know this from overhearing the soon-to-leave ones whispering, and it is only now that I can properly put into words what I heard and saw. It was, for Papa, the pain of becoming disillusioned, of no longer trusting the institutions, beliefs, and important others that had been his bedrock. It began with a loss of belief in the village council who had acted with such cruelty against the fodder nut lovers. I suspect that Papa also became curious about the fodder nuts themselves. Perhaps he wondered whether the nuts were in fact better than the fodder grass. Why had he never tried a fodder nut? My father's heart turned to the banished ones, many that he had known well, and he became a hero of sorts to the soon-to-depart ones. He even left the village lands searching for the believers in the fodder nut. My mother urged him to stop thinking of these things.

"Avoid The Pain. Do not awaken The Darkness," I heard her plead with my father, but it was too late. The Pain had become too powerful, and The Darkness visited my home.

That day in my twelfth year, the air felt strange and full of murky energy. It was as though the whole natural world knew there was something about to happen, something terrible. The skies were grey and windy, but this is often the case in Ennuied. This was something different, as if all that was good and peace-loving had gone away on a trip, and a treacherous presence came in its place to set the world on edge. I have heard that The Darkness takes many forms, and that night it took the form of many.

As I sat in the small wooden entry to the house, I knew I was being watched. It was as though I wore no clothes at all and something terrible could see my innermost parts and read my thoughts. Before I saw anything, I heard the voices—whether it was in my mind or through my ears I don't know, but I heard them hiss in a low and sinister tone. "Leave, leave, leave, never return. Leave, leave, leave, never return."

It seemed like an eternity that I heard the words slithering through my mind, though it was probably just a few minutes. I was frozen with fear and could not move. Then I saw lights in the distance, glowing in red pairs against the night, and I realized to my horror that the lights were, in fact, eyes.

The lights were attached to bodies, and those same bodies were coming out of the woods walking toward our house. I would have called them animals, except every animal I had known had some quality about them that made them alive; these creatures were most definitely not from the world of the living. Their bodies were blacker than the night, contrasted by the crimson glow emanating from their eyes. Each creature had legs, but I could not discern whether they walked or glided on the air like phantoms.

As they moved closer to our house, the voices grew louder, and I heard the same words over and over again. "Leave, leave, leave, never return."

I heard a bang from upstairs, and my father came crashing down the stairway. He was wearing his bed clothes and nothing on his feet. He came out the door and was about to run past me when I called to him.

"Papa, what is happening? What are they? Help me!"

Papa looked like he was going to run past me and away from the approaching creatures, but he hesitated for a moment and stammered, "Eloy, I have to leave, I have to leave. My time has come. The Pain … The Darkness!"

And with that, my papa ran away into the dusk wearing nothing but his nightclothes. He was never again seen in the streets of Ennuied. As he left, the creatures followed him and the chanting grew fainter. I realized then that the voices in my head were not speaking to me; it was for Papa that The Darkness came that night. We rarely spoke of Papa again, because in Ennuied everyone leaves, except, of course, for those who turn.

Another great secret in Ennuied is The Turning. I have said that no one grows old in Ennuied, but not everyone is chased away by The Darkness. By keeping fodder grass as the centre of life, some seem more able to avoid The Pain and never seem to awaken The Darkness. I think Mother is one of these, but she too will never grow old because of The Turning. Those who can successfully avoid The Pain and are never visited by The Darkness have an even stranger fate. They never leave Ennuied at all and come to care little about what may lie beyond its borders. Over time they begin to fade, barely noticeably at first. They may be difficult to see in the dark, and sometimes their voices wane mid-sentence; it is as though their very being loses its depth. The condition always advances, and without the person knowing, The Turning becomes more apparent until one day he or she disappears completely, never to reappear. Mother always said with a smile that to turn is better than the dark, but even then I was not so sure.

Chapter Two
My Sister Dalia

Before introducing you to my sister Dalia, I should tell you a little more about fodder grass since it is so important in Ennuied and because I came to find it so revolting. The people of Ennuied believe that fodder grass is the centre of life, the most important thing. I suppose all people have something like fodder grass, those most important things they grew up with and were told will meet their needs. We called it a "grass" because the stalk is very grassy and green for a short time in the spring. After the grass has grown five or six inches, it turns into a brown stalk with a greyish grain growing on top.

I was always quite certain that "fodder" referred to foodstuffs fit for livestock. It seemed strange to me that the townsfolk used this word to describe their most important food source—the very thing that consumed most of their toil and attention. Perhaps, though, when people make anything not bathed in love their priority, "fodder" is not such a bad word after all.

Fodder grass grows very quickly and spreads with incredible speed. At the festivals, we praised the fodder grass because even in the tough, rocky soils and harsh winds of Ennuied, it is able to grow—it is said that fodder grass saved the village and gave the people the food they needed to survive. I was told that in times long ago, there were other crops and foods with names that sounded unnatural and had mostly been forgotten. These crops required constant care, the right amount of water, ample sunshine and warmth, constant attention. Not so the fodder grass.

Fodder grass was discovered quite by accident. Even the village elders do not know who sowed its seeds in the fields. One day, a kindly man discovered fodder grass spreading through his crop of something or other, no longer recalled. He tried to pull up the fodder grass and even dug it out from the roots, but no matter what he did, the fodder grass advanced when he was not looking, and soon all of his old crops were overrun by this new plant. Fodder grass will not share the fields with any other crop. The kindly man's fields were not the only ones affected; the fodder grass spread throughout the region, and there was great panic, sadness, and worry. Hunger also advanced, and many of the old and infirm were close to death. An elder in the village, considered wise by all others, suggested eating the grey fodder grass grain. Being brave as well as wise, he ground the grain himself, made it into a paste with water, and ate. Apparently, once he started eating, he felt power return to his body, and he continued. He ate for hours before stopping to rest. Following his example, others began to eat, and they too were slow to stop. The rest is history. The villagers found many ways to prepare fodder grass, in stews, breads, drinks, and desserts. The rough stalk could even be used to make clothes and bedding, though quite honestly, these always leave one itching just a little.

There are some intriguing things about fodder grass that everyone in Ennuied thinks of as a normal part of life. The first, and most obvious, is that it takes a long time to feel full when eating fodder grass. This is why the fodder grass festivals go into all hours of the morning and include every type of entertainment imaginable. The amusements make the time pass quickly until all feel satiated for a while. Another curious aspect is that when eating fodder grass, one's stomach often begins to hurt. It would seem to be that to help with this problem, one should stop eating, but just the opposite is true with fodder grass. If you eat more and push through the discomfort, it gradually disappears and is soon forgotten.

It was when the people of Ennuied began to eat fodder grass that The Pain and The Turning arrived. It was considered irreverent to speak of this, and even thinking about such things made the people of Ennuied feel ill at ease.

Given Ennuied's penchant for secrecy, I told just one other, my sister Dalia, about my encounter with the wonderful smells and the haunting music. Dalia and I were very close. She was older than me, and I always thought she was a little smarter. When I told Dalia what had happened to me, her eyes lit up. She told me that she too had smelled something incredible, twice! But for her, the fragrance was different. She expressed to me that that it reminded her of freshly cut grass, wood, and springtime cherry blossoms. I asked Dalia what the smell meant. She said something about imagining another place, a land of colour and life where everyone experienced peace and joy that started in their core and bubbled out for all to share. But my sister's life in Ennuied was far from the beautiful land she dreamed about.

Dalia was not the prettiest girl in Ennuied, but she was far from unattractive. She had sandy blonde hair, thinner than most, and freckles on her nose and cheeks. Dalia loved people and was gentle at heart; she seldom criticized others, and she forgave quickly. Dalia had always liked boys and as a young girl enjoyed flirting, playing with the schoolboys, and even stealing the odd kiss in secret. That awkward stage where a girl becomes a young lady was hard on Dalia. She was slow to take a woman's shape, and her skin developed unsightly blemishes from time to time. I don't know what happened to her exactly, but I know she came back crying from more than one fodder grass celebration, and she sometimes pretended she was sick so she did not have to go to school. I knew this because as soon as Mother left the house in the morning, Dalia did not seem very sick any more. Still, Dalia believed in love and destiny; with time, she left the wobbly days of adolescence behind her. Dalia met a young man named Danny from the other side of the village. Danny was also soft of heart and quick to laugh, and he had rugged good looks. Dalia was smitten, head over heels, and more than a little infatuated with Danny. They walked through the fields of fodder grass together, and they sent notes and messages back and forth when they were busy at school. I could see Dalia's face flush pink when Danny entered the room.

I think Dalia thought she had found the one with whom she would gladly fade away, but Danny and Dalia were on two sides of fate. Danny often told Dalia that they could not remain together unless she left her home and joined him on the other side of the village. I know Dalia thought nothing could be better than joining Danny, but she was bound by duty and honour to her family home and to her studies. She felt that one day the time would be right and she would happily move to the ends of the earth to be with Danny.

As the daughter of a respected village councillor, Dalia grew up believing in the wonders of fodder grass. She had simply never imagined anything different. Danny—at first without Dalia's knowledge—was drawn to the life of the fodder nut lovers, who were less traditional in their approach to love. They had spoken about these matters of course, and even Dalia acknowledged curiosity about the illicit food. Danny began to eat the nuts, the odd nibble at first, followed by binges where Danny would gorge himself on fodder nut dishes. Dalia's love was strong enough to look past these indulgences, but Danny's interest quickly waned. As though he had forgotten his promises and the blending of his heart with Dalia's, Danny immersed himself in the fodder nut world, where he met another.

Dalia was grief-stricken at the turn of events, which were the direct opposite of what she had dreamed and planned. I suppose Dalia was shocked and dismayed that Danny imagined he could replace her love with another's. I watched my sister withdraw into herself, no longer reaching out to friends, seldom even speaking to the young men of the town. Dalia did not talk much to me about what was happening inside her, but I found myself able to feel what she was experiencing.

Dalia felt naked; she had exposed her inner self to another in the deepest way she could, only to have that deepest part of her rejected. This rejection began to colour her inner life like black ink in a pail of water. In a strange twist of reality common to the rejected, Dalia now spoke about her childhood and schooling, which were not all bad, as though immersed in the same rejection that she experienced with Danny. Her dreams for the future were equally tainted by rejection. Boys came calling at our door, never staying long enough to share their hearts with Dalia, as though pushed away by an invisible force emanating from her. Dalia now lived in the despair of someone facing a world of unyielding loneliness, without another soul who cared to look at her or into her.

When I was fourteen, The Darkness was awakened in our home through Dalia, and once again, I shared in the terror. Long after the sun went down and the moon was shining, I lay in my bed. I had been fast asleep, but something awakened me. It was a light tapping on my window, as though dozens of tiny fingernails were drumming a secret message. I felt a wave of nausea pushing its way up from my stomach and the same darkness I had felt when Papa ran away, never to return.

I did not want to look out the window, but I could not help myself. I left my bed and slowly made my way across the room to the outer wall. I cautiously pushed the brown fodder grass-weaved curtain to the side.

Before I continue, I must explain that I had always feared spiders. I considered them the most cunning and ruthless creatures in the animal kingdom, their many eyes constantly on the lookout for the weak and vulnerable, trapping the unsuspecting and defenceless in their webs, poisoning their prey, and dissolving them from the inside out. I had watched spiders at work in the gardens and fields, amazed at how their meals looked fully intact—healthy, in fact—and ready to walk away on the outside but were melted, rendered, and liquefied within. A more accurate image of the damage that rejection wrought upon Dalia and inflicts on so many others I could not have found.

As I moved the curtain further, I saw to my horror that black spiders covered my window. They were covered in eyes, which were even darker than their bodies and encased in tiny hairs. Their silvery fangs glistened in the moonlight, and their webbing seemed to pour from their fleshy abdomens. The fibrous strands coated much of my window, and I could not see the rest of the house, the yard, and certainly not the distant woods that I had seen through my window all of my life. I raced back across the room, into my bed, and under the covers, willing myself to wake up from what I hoped was a horrifying nightmare. One of my feet was partially uncovered and exposed to the night. I felt something tickle my foot, then a sharp pain. I pulled my foot back under the covers, but something came with it. I felt it crawling up my leg. Then I felt another on my back and one on my stomach. Soon I felt them all over my body, their legs crawling and fangs stabbing. Too afraid to even scream, I jumped out of my bed and down the hall to the door, rubbing my skin everywhere to rid myself of the hairy legs and the fangs. With fear consuming my senses, I did not even see Dalia struggling to open the outside door.

I ran into Dalia at the front door. In the dim light I could see that she was covered in spider bites and webbing. The wounds were something I don't like to remember. They were larger than the bite of any spider or insect I had ever seen, pinkish at the base, becoming increasingly red and angry toward an opening at the top where they slowly bled. Along the body of each sore were what looked like small red veins branching upward and down into the flesh below. With each beat of Dalia's heart, the veins grew large, gorged with venom spreading through her blood and to every part of her.

I knew immediately that The Darkness had come not for me but my sister. Whether it was the venom or the fear I do not know, but Dalia took no notice of me. She managed to open the door despite the swelling on her hands and the fibrous webbing clinging to her fingers. Outside, the world around our house was transformed. It was as though a billion spiders had toiled a year to cover the grounds in a sticky grey web.

Dalia dashed out of the house like her father, in her bedclothes and nothing on her feet. I followed behind, desperate to find a way to help. Dalia ran in circles, blocked at every turn by a wall of webbing as strong as the trunk of a tree. Both of us seemed to spot a gap in the webbing at about the same time. The webbing formed sheets that overlapped one another, making it hard to spot, but with careful observation I could see that that a gap opened into a pathway of sorts. The path led away from the centre of the village, to the lands outside our knowledge. Dalia exploded toward the gap in the webbing, pushed her way past the hanging sheets of web, and ran onward, leaving Ennuied and her family home forever.

I ran back to my room and jumped under my covers. The spiders seemed to have left with Dalia, but I remained awake in my bed until the first light of morning, fearful of their return. Cautiously, I poked my head out from under the sheets. All had returned to normal in my room. I walked to the window and peered outside to the lands around our house. I saw no more sheets of webbing and no spiders at all. The only evidence of the events of the night was a few grey strands of web hanging from the trees, burning away quickly with the light of the sun. My mother did not notice Dalia was missing until the morning. In the moment she realized that her daughter was gone, I saw a flash of pain in her eyes and felt a wave of darkness in the air. As quickly as it came, the feeling was gone, as my mother forced The Pain into some deep recess of her heart.

She said, more to herself than to me, "The Pain awoke The Darkness. There is nothing more to say." And with that my mother returned to her daily work, preparing a fodder grass stew.

Chapter Three
Beginnings

But enough about my village and family. I want to tell you about my journey and how I came to know my time had come to leave. I was born helpful and have never been described as lazy, at least not that I know of. I was always wanting to assist Papa or Mother, building things, and constantly asking questions about fodder grass. This made my parents very proud, and my mother used to voice her hopes for me. "Eloy will surely live long and fade away in peace."

I did not realize it at the time, but others viewed me as clever. At ten years of age, I could memorize lengthy passages of fodder grass lore. I could read and write well and had a voracious appetite for work in the fields. I assumed that I would follow in my father's path one day and become a leader in the village. I got along well with others, but I would not say that I ever felt close to the people in my village, save my sister Dalia and one friend.

I can't remember a time when I did not know Khalid. He lived close by, and when I was little, we were inseparable. We explored the woods together, made up games, swam in the streams, and ate and laughed together. When I started school, things changed a little. Khalid was never that excited about the fodder grass lore or the work in the fields. As a matter of fact, even when we were little, I can't recall ever setting foot on a field of fodder grass with him at my side. Khalid just seemed to like people. Though I spent less time with him with each passing year, Khalid never made me feel bad about it, and when I was with him, I felt the ease and freedom to laugh that we had known as children. Khalid was one of those amazing people whom many probably thought of as their best friend. When you were with him, you felt like you were the only important person in the world.

By the time that I had my first experience with the indescribable—the music and the smells of a distant land—I was spending very little time with Khalid. I was far too busy with my studies and my work. It is common for the villagers of Ennuied to join guilds dedicated to fodder grass in some way. At the age of eighteen, I was drawn to the Youth Harvester's Guild. We believed that the older villagers lacked enthusiasm and fresh thinking about production. Full of youthful idealism, we also believed that they did not truly understand the wonders of the grass in the way that we did. I became even more dedicated than the others in the guild. Though I studied and worked in the fields every day, I somehow found the time to attend activities with the guild three, four, or even up to six times a week.

Looking back, I think I thought that if I was this dedicated to the fodder grass, I would experience the full benefits of the grass and have a great life in Ennuied. I imagined that my life would be full of what really mattered: fodder grass! And that seeing my love of fodder grass and perseverance, the villagers of Ennuied would be drawn to me and I would never lack friends and company.

I don't know exactly when I began to change inside. Gradually, the excitement of youth and the guild began to fade. I was getting rather tired from all the work and the meetings, and as I watched life in Ennuied, nothing really seemed to change. The Pain was awakened in many, even in my guild, and others that I knew simply faded away. I remember the moment that the first mark appeared on my body. While working in the fields, painstakingly digging around the fodder grass roots to ensure the flow of the rains would be quickly consumed by the plant, I had the thought: "What if all of my toil, sweat, and hard work are for nothing? What if I will not benefit in any way from my efforts and all my time has been wasted?"

The thought was very disturbing, and I quickly dismissed it from my mind. I reminded myself of the songs we sang at the guild and how we encouraged each other that our hard work would be worth it in the end. A curious thing the Harvester's Guild was. We lived with two messages, utterly incompatible. The first was that we were working ceaselessly, solely for the benefit of others and for Ennuied, and the second was that we ourselves would someday benefit enormously from what we did. I would come to learn that altruism was a rather solitary thing that mixed very poorly with self-interest. While I was strengthened again in my resolve, that day a blemish appeared on my body. It was just a small one, a pink bump on the left side of my chest. While it hurt a little, it did not seem to grow, and I reasoned it would go away in time.

My life with the Harvester's Guild lasted for three years, and during that period I met hundreds of my fellow villagers. It was during my third year that my body changes became pronounced. I was spending much of my time in the guild with a couple of companions. Amser was a fast mover and quick thinker. At first, I felt I could keep up with him, but he seemed to move more rapidly every day, and it was difficult for me to match his pace. Sansig seemed a good friend initially, and we had great fun out in the fields of fodder grass. The problem I found with Sansig was that he always talked about the same things. I saw other people in the village, probably close to fading, who were a lot like Sansig, still discussing the same stories and doing the same things they did in their youth. Endless tales about how they could celebrate the harvest better than anyone else, and about their plans for the next festival. Some of the older villagers, like Sansig, spent their days constantly finding new cohorts who would join them at the festivals.

Time ... the people of Ennuied describe time as a great enemy, an evil force beyond any power to slow or stop. My work in the Harvester's Guild taught me the power of time. It marched on like a runner who never tired, slowly gathering speed—much like Amser. I became exhausted trying to keep up with my companion. Amser always had new ideas and different ways of doing things. There was the time he suggested that we increase our crop yields by sleeping in four-hour intervals so that someone was always working the fields. I agreed and joined the effort. I found it demanding, but with youth on my side, I adjusted to the shifts and kept up with Amser and the others.

Every week though it seemed that Amser had another new idea, each one taking more energy than the last. I spent less and less time with my family and rarely took time to enjoy the trees and fresh air. By the third year, I could scarcely keep up and felt fatigue gnawing at my bones at the mere sight of Amser and his ceaseless energy.

Chapter Four
The Darkness Comes for Me

It was in that third year that all of this began to make me weary, though I justified this as the fatigue that comes from a life well lived. During this time my entire body began to change. The blemish on the left side of my chest had remained there for some time; one morning, I noticed that in place of the original spot there were now three. I was alarmed, having never heard of such a condition before. Within a week of the additional spots' appearing, I found more blotches, painful wounds really, on other parts of my body. Red, puffy blotches surrounded my eyes and nose, making it difficult to see clearly and even to smell the fresh fragrance of the fodder grass. A reddish, translucent substance dripped from my ears onto my pillow at night. Even my private places were not immune to the fiery lesions. I explained away these increasingly debilitating sores as a symptom of my hard work and dedication rather than considering that the priorities I lived by were actually harmful to myself and others.

The Darkness around me was building, but before I describe my chilling encounter under the grip of its hopeless clutches, I want disclose a little more about the place where I began. As you know, there are no truly old people in Ennuied. They all awaken The Darkness or fade away and disappear. From time to time, pain of some sort came to visit everyone, and those who were successful in suppressing its power lived on in progressively lessening significance. For us, this was simply an everyday truth.

Ennuied, like anywhere, had its fair share of youthful games and dangerous entertainment. For some, The Darkness held great allure as the great unknown, driving unending curiosity. Before my time, there was a cluster of youth who sought to conjure The Darkness. They knew the Ennuied lore and hunted The Pain to awaken The Darkness. Some in the group tried to bring forth The Pain by thinking and imagining painful thoughts. Many of the young ones believed that by reading books about the pain and experiences of others, it would become their own, and The Darkness would arrive in some daring and amazing form. Still others simply pretended to be trapped in the trauma of pain. Most of the time, nothing at all happened, despite the best efforts of the young villagers. The pain that awakens darkness and journey cannot be borrowed from another.

For a few of the more soft-hearted, those with great empathy, a whiff of darkness occasionally appeared. Stories are told of the appearance of strange black creatures speaking about journeys and life beyond Ennuied before vanishing with a gust of wind. This pseudo-darkness, I surmise, was just a glimpse of the horror and never actually caused anyone to leave Ennuied. It is my belief that there is really no way to mimic The Pain. The Darkness that drives one to journey comes from a deep and hidden place, more real than life itself. It also seems that those who seek The Darkness that drives the journey seldom encounter its terrors. As well as I could see, The Pain and The Darkness came only to those who sought to live their lives in light, only to find there the demise of hope.

My father was awakened to the pain of the disillusioned whose foundations decay from within. My sister learned the horrors of rejection and the meaning of being alone. For me, The Pain was different still. I had unknowingly stumbled into the pain of wearying, meaningless, and self-full toil. All that I did, even the kindness I showed, was in some way designed to promote my own interests, leading to a superficial yet exhausting kind of existence. This was a pain that led me into every bit as much darkness as Papa or Dalia.

The Pain and The Darkness visited the people of Ennuied in many different ways, but it always drove them to journey.

I have heard of many who suffered the pain of the guilty, for instance. A friend of mine from the far side met the pain of regret. A caring and giving person, she realized that she had given away her most precious possessions, even her very self, at the fodder grass celebrations, and she could not get them or herself back. While less common, I have seen some feel The Darkness through an awakening pain of hunger. These few never seemed to stomach fodder grass at all and were desperate for a different kind of food. Often the hungry ones left the village when they were still very young.

Regardless of the reasons for The Pain, The Darkness always followed. There were rumours and stories of some who left Ennuied of their own accord without the prevailing pain and darkness. I personally doubt these stories were true. I have learned that there are many kinds of pain, and The Darkness appears in forms unknown. I suspect that even those who began their journeys with smiles on their faces had tasted The Darkness in some shape or form.

The Darkness came for me as I lay in my bed at night, drifting between the waking world and the land of sleep and dreams. I came to experience a thought in my mind. This thought was not a passing idea drifting through my consciousness; it was a firm conviction, a certainty that quietly took residence in my centre. My hard work, perseverance, and dedication served no real purpose at all. I felt the sores on my chest begin to pulse even more than usual. What began as a stinging sensation soon became something altogether different. It was as though someone was pouring the acid we made from fodder grass leaves straight into my chest. The Pain was unbearable, and I cried out to someone, anyone for help. No one answered my cries, and I felt the strangest sensation; perhaps it was the approach of death. My heart within my chest felt as if it was shrivelling, shrinking down to nothing. My head felt light, and my legs and arms began to tingle. I crawled out of bed toward the mirror hanging on my wall. I could make out my face in the dim light of the room, as pale as the white of my bleached fodder grass sheets.

Though thinking purposeful and clear thoughts was becoming increasingly challenging, I came to realize that The Darkness was visiting again, this time for me alone. Though I was yet to comprehend the source of my pain—that of the weary struggle after meaningless pleasures and futile accomplishments—The Darkness had come. Unlike for Papa and Dalia, it seemed as though my pain and darkness would not afford me the chance to run and escape the dread of Ennuied. My strength was almost gone, and I was sure my heart would shrivel to nothing at any moment and the blood in my veins would reach a deadly standstill. The Darkness itself began to enter my eyes, and my sight began to fade.

When playing in the woods, my friends and I had invented a game where we held our breath as long as we could before our brains forced us to gasp for life-giving air. Sometimes when played this game, I heard a rumbling in my ears, something like the rushing of swift water. At this moment, I experienced something a little like that game from long ago. I heard the rumbling and smelled the faintest scent of the forest and the sea. Impossible as it sounds, the fragrance seemed to penetrate the walls from the outside. I heard a quiet hum of that most peaceful music; it danced around my body, and in the very depth of my centre, I felt the faintest sliver of hope.

At that moment I knew I had the choice to rise up and follow that tune, the music from another place, or to die in the spot where I lay. Some strength returned to my body, not enough to stand but enough to crawl. I shuffled down the hall and out an open door. Through dirt and gravel, rocks and sand, I crawled with bowed head, passing under the gates of Ennuied. For hours, I crawled, days it seemed, until Ennuied was nothing but a faint glow to my rear. With each mile I put between myself and Ennuied, I felt some strength return until, at last, on shaky legs, I managed to stand.

And so my story really begins—my journey from Ennuied.

Chapter Five
A Surprising Companion

I found myself standing on a path with Ennuied and the light of dawn behind me and the unknown in front. The trail was nothing special, made from packed earth and rocks where many feet had passed before. The sun was shining, and a light south wind blew just hard enough for me to feel on my cheek. Ahead, I saw the path wind around some large boulders that appeared to have fallen from the sky. Beyond this, the path disappeared into a small ravine, and I could not see far beyond the boulders. I was amazed at the silence of the spot where I stood.

The quiet was so complete that it seemed to roar in my ears, but my thoughts were far from silent; the peaceful place where I found myself contrasted directly to the disturbance I felt within. I thought of the pain and the sores and my agonizing journey out of Ennuied. I cautiously rubbed my hands over my skin to review the status of my wounds and was disappointed to discover that all of my sores remained. When I touched them, I felt the pain immediately, though perhaps it was just a little less intense than before. I also noticed that some strength had returned to me. While I cannot say I felt energized, I was confident that I could walk for at least a little while.

I looked closely at the lands around me. There were the boulders on the path which disappeared into the ravine. Tufts of grass grew in patches close by, but I could see very little to my right or left because of the summertime haze. I did not hear the sound of birds or the buzz of insects or hear any animals at all. In my heart, I wondered what had become of those who left Ennuied before me—there was certainly no sign of them here in this barren place. Deep in thought, I was startled suddenly, sure that I had captured movement in the corner of my eye near the fifth boulder down the path. Yes, something was moving.

Fear returned as I thought to myself, "I can't run back to Ennuied! I have nowhere left to go!" I resolved to place one step ahead of the other to face whatever came next.

Cautiously, I moved ahead toward the colossal boulders. I wondered what might happen to me if another stone came crashing to the ground while I walked along. As I approached the first boulder, I stumbled, banging my head into the solid granite. No worse for wear, I looked ahead and was able to make out a few more details down the path. I thought that perhaps I saw branches waving in the wind; however, I could see no evidence of trees growing anywhere nearby. As I moved closer, it became obvious that I was looking at the shape of a man. I could see his head, and what I had thought were boughs blowing in the breeze were, in fact, his waving arms. I could see the man now, sitting on the rock; he jumped down and began walking toward me. To my utter astonishment, it was Khalid, my childhood friend. I ran to greet him and embraced him warmly.

I stammered, "Khalid, you must have faced The Pain and endured The Darkness at the same time as me! What an amazing coincidence."

"Coincidence I do not know, but yes, I have felt The Pain and walked in The Darkness like you."

Strangely, I felt no need to ask Khalid for the details of his exit from Ennuied. I could tell that we both understood what had happened to each other and words on that topic would seem to belittle the depth of the experience. As I looked at my old friend, I was struck that he had not changed that much over the years. Dressed in simple trousers and a white shirt beneath his grey jacket, Khalid had the same sense of ease and sparkle in his eyes that I had loved as a child.

Like me, Khalid was small in stature, with simple, dark brown hair and unimpressive features. He was not someone the girls would notice right away, but he had honesty and charisma in spades. I was pleased to see that Khalid carried a sack of bread and held a skin of water; we set out to walk this part of the path together, passing all of the grey boulders and proceeding down into the ravine. As we sauntered along, Khalid looked at me knowingly and passed me a small bag that contained a simple brown jacket, much like his own. While I was not chilled in the least, I accepted the jacket as a thoughtful gesture. The path followed the gully downward for some time, lower and lower. I thought to myself that this was likely the lowest I had been in my life. Eventually the path levelled into a flatter land, a land that was different from any I had known.

Near mid-day, Khalid and I stopped to look at our surroundings. For the first time, I began to ponder where I was going. To this point, all I knew was that I was getting away from Ennuied with its pain and darkness; I knew for certain I could never return to that land. I recognised that my journey was away from there, but the destination remained unknown. I would say that it was then that I began to feel where I was going. I could not have put it into words, but I was searching for a place where I belonged, some kind of home that was unquestionably not my house in Ennuied. My heart was drawn to the strange and wonderful music I had heard in the distance and almost tasted as well. If I could think of anywhere I was going, it was to the place where that music and the wondrous smells came from.

Chapter Six
The Edge of the Forest

Ennuied had its share of trees. There were wooded patches, mostly poplar, and expanses of brush everywhere, but what I saw in front of me was nothing like the woods of Ennuied; it was the greatest forest I had ever imagined. The trees were a variety I had never seen before, larger and grander than the poplars of Ennuied. The trunks of the trees had an amazing girth, and I doubted that I could put my arms halfway around very many of them. The lower parts of the trunks had just a few twigs, with most of the branches appearing randomly above the level of my head. I saw that these trees had needles in place of the broad leaves I was accustomed to. The land surrounding the forest became wetter and greener the closer to the forest I looked, and on the floor of the forest there was a green carpeting of mosses, ferns, and grasses with dark dead wood contrasting with the jade-like floor. There were a number of pathways entering the forest, and ahead I could see a row of simple houses on the edge of the forest.

"Khalid, what do we do? Where do we go?" I asked.

"Friend, we enter the forest and travel its paths without fear!" he replied.

I was not sure where Khalid's confidence came from. I was yet to tell him about the music and the smells, and I wondered how he knew where we should be going. I was curious about those who lived in the houses and what they had discovered, compelling them to settle where they did. I explained my need to investigate the settlement, *border houses* I began to call them, to Khalid. As was his custom, Khalid grinned and told me that would be fine just with him.

The path that we travelled led directly to the border houses. I was apprehensive about knocking on the doors or talking to the inhabitants directly; thus, I decided to watch from a distance. The houses along the forest were better described as cabins, perhaps rustic cottages of sorts rather than houses. They were small and simple, with fenced yards and paths leading into the forest. Each house had barrels to catch rain water, and I could see equipment piled up in the yards such as traps, rucksacks, tents, and other gear that could be used in the forest. Interestingly, each home had a pet dog in the garden. The dogs looked wild and unkempt, as though they were accustomed to doing whatever they wanted as they ran about their tightly fenced yards. After only a short wait, the door of one of the houses opened and a man came out, a large fellow with a scruffy beard and strong-looking arms. He stood in his yard and stared at the forest with both longing and fear. Shortly afterward, another man entered the yard of the house next door. He looked almost exactly the same as the first man.

I heard the first man say, "Yep, my boy Earh—the finest dog in the world. No fear at all. He explores the forest like it is a walk in the fields!"

The second man was not to be outdone. "Babble here loves the woods. I reckon he is half wolf himself, and he runs circles around those trees like he is on fire!"

The first man smirked a little and began packing up some gear for what I guessed would be a trek into the forest. I thought to myself that this would be my opportunity to follow an expert from a distance and see for myself what was in the forest. I invited Khalid to join me. He declined the offer but let me know that he would catch up with me later on.

The man heaved a pack full of equipment onto his shoulder and sagged beneath the weight. He grabbed a walking stick, a map, a canteen, and a bag that looked to be full of bread. Under the afternoon sky, with his dog Earh, he set out into the woods, following the well-worn path behind his small lodge. I tailed the man and his dog, a little worried that Earh would smell me and alert his master to my presence. I had no desire to confront anyone, especially someone who seemed so much stronger than me. I need not have worried. Earh, the amazing explorer dog, took no notice of me, distracted as he was chasing the plentiful insects and forest sounds.

The man walked for what seemed like just a few minutes. I could still see the edge of the woods behind me, and the safety of the man's house was never far away. He stopped at a small clearing in the woods where there was a pond. The water in this pond was very shallow, not deep enough to even discern whether the water was clean or dirty. The man made his way to the far side of the puddle where a path led deep into the forest. His dog by his side, the man took off his gear. He set up a tent and built a fire, cooked and ate a dinner of some kind of stew, and then did the strangest thing. He stood completely still, almost as though he were a tree himself, and stared into the woods. He stood and stared for what seemed like hours. Then suddenly, without warning, he stopped staring, packed up his equipment, and walked the path back to his house. I was incredulous. I had thought the man I followed was a renowned explorer of the woods. I arrested my thoughts and corrected myself—perhaps I had misunderstood and this was some kind of retreat or rest period prior to his trek. I followed the man back to his house and watched him talk to his neighbour again.

"Friend," he stated, "I have been deep into the trees today. My mind was still, and I saw and heard much. As I stilled my mind, I heard the howl of a wolf, and I sensed the size of the trees blowing in the wind."

The neighbour replied, "You are a great seeker, a man of the forest. You see what others don't. You understand the deep places of the world."

The man, looking far weaker and more like me, retorted, "The more I look, the slighter I feel, neighbour."

"Yes, it is the way of the woods, my friend. We will look again tomorrow," the neighbour comforted. "We will consult the writings from old to now, and if we understand the forest, trees, and sounds, our lives will feel the warmth and be complete."

After listening to their discussion, I was very tempted to approach the men and ask if I could build another dwelling in the area. If these men remained afraid of the forest after all this time, who was I to think myself brave enough to explore its depths? There were many, many older cabins, obviously abandoned, belonging to others who had come and moved on from this place; perhaps I could set up with Khalid in one of these.

My thoughts were interrupted, and for the third time in my life, I began to hear lovely songs in the distance. The sounds crept upon me as I considered staying and joining these men in their noble quest to understand the forest. The melody sounded almost mournful, as though it was calling me and was unsatisfied until my heart joined the song. Difficult to explain with words, the song I heard was once again played with a stringed instrument, but it included deep reverberations that sounded as if the earth and sky joined in.

I turned to see if the border dwellers heard the song. Startlingly, the neighbour was scratching his ears as if something was bothering him, and the man I followed into the edge of the woods looked tired and forlorn. In that moment I realized that those who are curious about the forest and think they know much, but who explore only its outer reaches with the security of their home nearby, are in a perilous position. For the border dwellers, resisting the music and avoiding the journey seemed to require more energy than they could muster. I focused my senses on the direction of the music. There was absolutely no doubt that the melodies were coming from somewhere deep in the forest, or perhaps even beyond in some unknown land. In a flash, I knew that this meant I could no longer stay with the border dwellers who observed without risk. The thought occurred to me that they were a little like the villagers of Ennuied, and I wondered if some darkness appeared here from time to time, chasing the terrorized border dwellers deep into the woods with only the clothes on their backs.

PART TWO
The Forest Lands Within

Chapter Seven
Into the Woods

I looked around for Khalid to let him know of my decision to follow the music into the woods, but Khalid was not to be found. I waited and waited for him there on the edge of the great forest. The light turned to darkness, and still no Khalid. I felt deeply hurt that he would leave my side so soon into our journey and wondered where he had gone. I walked along the path that cut straight into the forest and waited still longer for my friend, hoping against hope that Khalid would return. I fell asleep while waiting, but it was not a deep sleep. With the setting of the sun, the temperature dropped considerably, and the tree I leaned against was covered in sharp bark. I awoke with the first light of dawn, feeling chilled to the bone, sore from my wounds, and itchy from the shards of tree bark that penetrated my clothing. As I sat up on a large flattened rock, I noticed a piece of wood with dirt and plants obscuring some kind of writing. I approached the wood, and realizing it was a sign, I cleared away the plants and cleaned the surface as well as I could. The sign read as follows:

Traveller
The journey is beyond control
Its paths are set and worn
With strength and will, you have begun
Weak and frail to come

The contents of the sign bothered me immediately, and I wondered who would write such disturbing nonsense. Undoubtedly, I was in control of my journey. I decided where to go and when. The worrisome message seemed to imply that it was inevitable I would become weakened and frail. Where was Khalid? I wanted badly to speak with him and ask him what he thought of the sign. I was also getting hungry and thirsty and would have loved to share some of Khalid's bread. With great resignation, I reminded myself that I had been chased from Ennuied alone and that my journey was my own. With these troubled thoughts swirling around my mind, I stepped forward into the woods.

As you know, the trees were very tall and the majority of the branches began above the level of my head. The floor of the forest was covered in green plants that seldom rose higher than my thighs. The result was a small area where I could see at least a little into the forest, which, as far as I could perceive, continued endlessly with very few changes. I walked along the trail for some time and noticed the path began to narrow. I reasoned that the lane was not as wide here because some travellers probably turned back at this point. Seeing that I had no other place to go, this was not an option for me. The narrowing of the path did not stop as I hoped it would, and I soon encountered a part of the forest where the tree branches grew lower on the trunks, and I found myself rubbing along the dry branches and sharp needles as I walked. It became very difficult to move forward, but I pushed onward, hoping desperately to reach some kind of clearing.

It seemed to me as though the canopy of the forest had lowered itself right to the ground. In my heart, I decided that this path was completely untrustworthy and dangerous, and I made a decision to try to move forward off the path. It seemed a little easier at first because I could pick and choose my way around trees and obstacles of every kind. In my heart, I mocked the silly sign which implied I would not be able to control my own movement through the forest. I soon realized though that there were some problems with my plan, the first being that I had no idea where I was going and the second that the topography of the forest seemed set against me. When I moved one direction, feeling it to be the most agreeable, I encountered such thick undergrowth that I had to turn. The undergrowth was just as bad to my left, so I spun to my right and was able to make what felt like excellent progress again.

Throughout my foray into the forest, I heard the sound of rushing wind through the tops of the trees, and the sound became louder as I hiked along. I soon realized that what I heard was the sound of rushing water as well as the wind. I came upon a roaring stream, more like a small but swift river, with steep rocky slopes on either side. I pondered jumping into the stream and riding the water where it took me. I would have jumped in, but I realized that the stream would take me out of the forest and away from the sweet music. Instead, I followed the rushing water upstream as closely as I could. The forest became thick once again, and the branches pressed hard against my body.

With great dismay I found myself back on the path where I had started, and ahead of me the forest canopy still crowded the path ahead like a vast green wall. I did the one thing I knew how to do: once again, I faced the undergrowth and its pain and put one foot in front of the other, pushing my way into the tangled foliage. This was one of the toughest choices that I ever made. The needles felt like knives as I trudged slowly forward. They cut deeply into my chest from the front and into my back and shoulders from above. I felt the wetness of blood on my skin, and I could see it begin to drip and flow onto my feet and the ground itself. The pain I felt would certainly have awakened The Darkness had I been in Ennuied. It was a throbbing agony. I can't exactly explain it, but the ache went deep, and it was as though parts of me were literally dying from the pain.

I somehow had the strength to move forward, and by keeping my head low and letting the needles rub over my body rather than fighting them, I was able to move more quickly. I must have been going too fast, because I tripped over something unseen and fell face first to the ground. I felt something pierce my chest. I had fallen on a sharp piece of dead wood, and to my horror it was still embedded in my chest, the left side of centre. Whether wise or foolish, I pulled the skewer from body and watched in awe as the blood flowed. I did not know my body carried as much. With a growing numbness, I continued, and gradually the forest canopy began to rise and the painful needles moved to my sides.

Though I guess it was now approaching mid-day, I could not perceive time and somehow continued to walk until I found myself at a small pool of what looked like the cleanest, purest water I had ever seen. I collapsed and rested, wondering if I would have been much better off if I had jumped into the river pouring out of the forest or at least stayed with the border dwellers and enjoyed the forest more safely. After catching my breath a little, I turned my attention to the pool of water. It was small enough that I could easily have thrown a stone across, but it was deep. I would have guessed that eight of me, end on end, could have stood on the deepest part and remained covered. I could see the rocks and sand at the bottom of the pool with a clarity that seemed better than the air itself. Even individual pebbles, some of which sparkled in the sunlight coming through the tops of the trees, were visible at the bottom of the pool. As I stood at the water's edge, the light of the sun was at a perfect angle to create a mirror-like reflection on the surface to my right.

I was incredulous at what I saw when I looked at my own reflection. All over my body, the blemishes that had come upon me during my last days in Ennuied had been scraped away by the needles and branches. Most surreal and morbidly fascinating was the wound over my heart. I felt reasonably strong in my body and I knew my heart was working, yet I was keenly aware that a part of my heart that had been with me my whole life had died when pierced by the wood. I felt different, a bit like something had been taken away from me that made me who I was, yet I felt a strange freedom as though unencumbered by some sickened part of me beyond repair.

Needless to say, I was extraordinarily thirsty, and given the presence of a crystal clear forest pool, I bent over for a drink. The water refreshed me greatly and seemed to bring me nourishment as well as quench my thirst. The water felt so pleasant on my lips that I decided to plunge my entire head into the water and found myself diving in head first. Though the aches remained, the water caused my wounds to tingle, and I sensed something was happening to them, something wonderful. I took a breath at the surface and propelled myself deep into the pool. As I swam deeper and deeper, I began to hear the beautiful music again. Sounds travel differently in the water, and I had the oddest sensation that the melody was entering my body through my wounds, particularly the large one in my chest area. As I heard the music, my thoughts turned toward Khalid, and I felt saddened that I had let him journey alone. I also felt compassion for the border dwellers and my friends and family back in Ennuied, who all suffered in their own way. The compassion seemed to enter through my wounds and mingle with my own pain in an amazing way. If not pleasurable, it was certainly a profound experience. The music and compassion formed some kind of energy that I was quite certain somehow passed beyond me to those in my contemplations. Soon though, I felt the need for air and was forced to rise to the surface of the crystal pool. As I rose, the music faded and then disappeared altogether. Standing once again at the side of the pool, I shivered just a little, not nearly as chilled as I expected, alone and wet in the forest shade. The pain from my cuts had certainly lessened, and I felt as though I had the determination to continue my quest.

Chapter Eight
The Dark Water

Following the path beyond the crystal pool, I passed another marker on the side, a sign with writing on it. As before, I needed to clean the dirt from the wood. I thought to myself that these pathway markers were easy to miss, hidden in plain sight. This sign read as follows:

> Clean and unclean, malevolent and selfless
> The forest covers all
> The man of the forest knows the paths

The sign was difficult to understand, and I was close to dismissing the message when I recalled the last sign and the path through the needle knives. I shuddered. It had hinted that I was facing a path I could not control and that the way forward would leave me weakened. None of this was news I wanted to hear at what could be the beginning of a very long trip, yet now I could not argue with the message. The first two lines on the latest sign seemed to state the obvious, that good and bad things lived in the forest. The last line left me stumped completely.

As I reflected on the signpost messages, the pain I felt, and of course the music that spurred me on, I become conscious of the fact that I did not miss Ennuied at all, and the mere thought of eating the fodder grass I had left behind made my stomach turn. It was now approaching dusk, and in spite of my distaste for fodder grass, hunger rumbled in my stomach.

I combed the forest floor, looking for anything that looked edible. I found some fibrous plants that looked soft enough to eat growing around the trees. The plants were golden on the outside and a softer yellow within. I ate a few, hoping they would not hurt me, and found they tasted quite good, almost bread-like. I found some shelter beneath a fallen log covered in moss and settled down for another cool forest sleep.

I awoke early, sore, hungry, and chilled yet grateful that I seemed to suffer no ill effects from the yellow plants. The way forward was free from the daunting branches and needles, but it was difficult to see the path. Grasses and moss covered the forest floor, and I perceived that fewer people had walked here than the wide paths at the edge of the forest. I sauntered along at a relaxed pace for some time, listening hard for the music that might lead me to the land I sought. I did not hear the music, but I heard a good deal of other sounds—rustling in the undergrowth, birds singing, and occasionally a most unnerving growl. I soon forgot the refreshing vitality of the crystal poor and felt fatigue creeping up on me. In the distance I saw another clearing and hoped in my heart I would find another refreshing pool. Perhaps they were spaced so that weary travellers like me could find regular strength. As I came closer to the clearing, I could see that there was water and someone sitting close by the edge of the pool.

The person sitting by the pool greeted me with a smile when I arrived. "Traveller, stop and drink. The water awaits you!" the woman said.

The woman was attractive, dressed in dark colours with a hood around her head. I felt strongly drawn to her in the same way I was drawn to the night sky, fire, and smoke at my first fodder grass celebration. The woman smiled at me with slightly squinted eyes, and I thought for a moment I saw rather large eyeteeth between her full rosy lips. I asked the woman her name.

"My name is Kakawangwa," she replied. "I am of the forest. I have seen your path and welcome you to my pool. My wisdom is accurate, and my quest is fair. You will find that my waters bring truth and awaken the quest for justice within those who travel."

With that, Kakawangwa walked straight into the woods and disappeared. I heard a howl in the distance and trembled.

Who was this strange woman, and how did she get there? I thought about the sign and wondered aloud whether she was of the malevolent or selfless variety of forest dweller. I turned my attention to the pool of water. The scene before me was certainly striking. The roots of the green trees stretched to the edge of the water, which sparkled on the surface. I could not see into the water; its greyish blue was dark and mysterious. I was thirsty and the water was inviting, so I crouched down for a drink. The water tasted good. It was cool, and I could feel it doing something inside me as I swallowed. I chose to drink deeply. The water seemed to spread from my throat to my chest and then through my limbs.

In place of my weakness, the water left me feeling strong and powerful. My thoughts were drawn to my situation and the circumstances that had brought me to this point.

In that moment, almost all at once, I recalled my childhood. The incessant lectures from my mother, which I now felt lacked even the most basic wisdom; all the nights when my father was away at village council while I sat at home with so many worries and questions—I remembered all of these. I thought about the many rejections I had suffered from those who I thought were friends, the times I was ignored, misunderstood, and misrepresented. The more I thought about these things, the more powerful I felt, and much anger entered my body. I found that my memory was sharpened from the dark water. I recalled more tragic events that had impacted my life. I had forgotten about the times when an older friend pressured me to join him in the fields at night. He manipulated me to touch and eat fodder grass long before harvest, and I knew that each bite stolen would never grow to maturity.

My heart felt it might explode as I recollected the loneliness that had contributed to my journey. I keenly felt the injustice of numbing isolation in a village and world full of people. With each memory my anger multiplied. I had to stop swallowing the liquid for fear that something in my body might not withstand the intensity of emotion.

Kakawangwa, it would seem, knew what she was talking about. I felt a concentrated accuracy in my memories. I remembered far more things that bothered me deeply than I had ever realized, and I required retaliation. In my quest for the beautiful music, how could justice be turned aside? I wanted badly to confront those who had eaten away at my dreams and sent me on this dreadful quest into the wild forests and wilderness.

I thought that my best choice of action may be to head back to Ennuied and oppose as many of those who had injured me as possible. Many had already faded away, and quite a few had awakened The Darkness themselves, yet I reasoned there would be some that I could find. With the dark water still vibrating inside me so differently from the kind and gentle feelings at the crystal pool, I walked quickly to find my way back to the path by which I had come and return to Ennuied. Walking around the pool, I could not find the path back. It was as though the plants and trees closed in on me from every direction. I spent the better part of the day searching not just for the way back but any way at all. Try as I might, I could not find any path, and with self-defence and retribution strong in my mind, I journeyed into the open woods in the direction I thought best.

Chapter Nine
The Lady of the Forest

I plunged through the trees and undergrowth with implausible speed for someone who had not been eating much and was still covered with wounds. The light began to fade, and night approached. No longer able to find my way, I stopped and sat under a very large tree where I drifted into a cold, restless, and disturbed sleep. I don't know what I dreamed that night, but I remembered snippets. There was running and hiding, climbing and falling, hope betrayed, and rescues thwarted. It was with tremendous relief that I awoke to the light of dawn and the sounds of the forest. The relief was short lived. While the intensity of the anger had left me, I now felt a deep sadness that sapped the very life from my bones. I slowly set out, trying to find a path and perhaps food. While my journey continued, I could not say whether backward or onward.

The sounds of the forest gave me some comfort. There were birds singing, and the haunting tune of the hermit thrush echoed through the trees. The small creatures continued to rustle in the undergrowth, and even the odd unnerving growl left me feeling a little less alone. As I scanned the woods, I still saw no sign of the path I had walked, or any path at all for that matter. I regretted going on my journey at all and told myself I would have been better off in Ennuied than here, all alone in the vast expanse of the desolate forest.

Self-pity aside, hunger began to drive my search, and the need to survive surpassed my desire for justice and my initiative to find the source of the music. Perhaps it was an ancient instinct from long before the days of fodder grass that led me to search for colour. I gave my eyes the full power of my attention to find any fragment of a colour that was not a shade of green or brown. Far to my right, I thought I saw the faintest hint of red. I made my way toward the colour, and as I approached, I saw that there was, in fact, red as well as many other colours. I found myself in a beautiful berry patch, though like so many of my experiences, it was unlike any I had ever seen before.

I desired to pick and eat the berries right away. I would certainly have done so had I not felt a drop of rain land in the centre of my forehead. The raindrop brought to mind my experiences with the waters of the forest, which I knew carried tremendous powers. I pondered whether the foods of the forest too might have some effect on me. I recalled the last sign marker and its message of both good and ill, and I wondered where I should begin or even whether I should eat any of the berries at all. Thinking back to Ennuied, I reminisced about Mother sipping the fodder grass stew a little bit at a time to see if the flavour met her expectations. I supposed that I could employ the same strategy with berries in the woods. I would taste just a little and see what happened before eating more.

I spotted a reddish berry covered in a yellow-orange exterior. It smelled a little like a tomato, a plant grown but rarely eaten in Ennuied. I tried a little of the berry, just enough to let the juice run onto my tongue and down my throat. The taste was scarcely tolerable, but I still wanted to eat more to satisfy the hunger that I felt. At first I felt nothing, and then there was a burning in my throat, and nausea. I was very glad not to have eaten more, as this fruit was clearly not healthy or helpful. I tried some of the other berries, some blue and some red, that both tasted sweet and brought peace to my body, much like the clear water I first encountered in the forest. I tried still others, some which tasted sugary and others, bitter, both of which left me feeling unsatisfied and hungrier than ever. The next berry I tried was one of the strangest, growing into an oblong shape with multiple berries coming from a central spot between long green leaves with thick veins. This berry had the curious effect of making all other the berries I tasted afterward seem much sweeter than they actually were. As a result, I consumed far more of the bad berries than I would have otherwise.

My stomach hurt for some time, and I lay down in the mosses until the pain passed, determined not to touch the harmful berries again. Afterward, I gathered as many of the good berries as I could carry. I chose the ones that left me feeling strengthened and better off on the inside; after eating them, I felt happier, and I had enough strength to take care of myself and perhaps even to help any others I might meet in the forest. I forgot, for a time, the feelings that arose when I tasted the dark water reflecting that the quest for personal justice would bring me no closer to my destination and the beautiful music. It seemed to me that the more good berries I ate, the more will I seemed to have to avoid the harmful berries, even the ones that looked inviting.

This experience taught me a very important lesson about the forest. From this point forward, I learned to judge the plants of the forest by the fruits they produced and, to survive, I had to develop my skills of observation and attune my senses to discern subtle differences among them.

As I walked forward under the midday sun, I saw a line that ran nearly parallel to the ground in the distance. Though I could not make out many details, my mind told me that someone or something had made that line and that it was not a natural part of the forest. I continued moving toward the line in the distance. It became clearer as I approached, and I saw that it was some kind of wall or fence. Yes, it was a dark fence, iron, with tightly knit bars, and it was very tall. I tracked the fence and noticed that it followed a gentle angle curving toward my right. I came to a break in the fence where there appeared to be a gate, a doorway. The gate was very wide and strong looking with thick iron bars and massive hinges. I tried to open the gate, but my hands could not fit around the latching mechanism, and I could not budge the heavy metal. I tried digging under the gate and even climbing it. It was not that I wanted so much to get to the other side; it was more the fact the gate and fence stood in my way that made me want to breach the barrier.

I gave up after hurting myself in the effort to go through the gate. I followed the fence around and around for the better part of the day until I found myself back at the gate where I had started. Somehow I was now not only off the path but encircled by a gated fence beyond my ability to cross.

My attention was drawn to an alarming noise. It was not unusual for me to hear growling and other angry noises in the forest, but this time what I heard was worse; there was growling, barking, howling, and whining coming from more than one animal. Stealth did not seem a big concern to whatever creatures were making the noises I heard. Cautiously, I moved toward the ruckus, from tree to tree hiding behind the tall trunks for my own safety. When I came close enough, I saw a beautiful woman in the throes of a snarling pack of wild dogs and wolves. The woman had dark hair and chestnut eyes, and from the state of her clothes, I guessed that she too was on a long journey. She wore a white blouse covered with a black vest trimmed in gold coloured lace. Around her neck was a black band with golden medallions hanging below. On her head, a loosely tied scarf of white and gold partially covered her long raven hair. While her outfit was worn and damaged, it was clear to me that this woman was some kind of royalty. I was drawn to her and wondered what could have happened in her life to set her on a course to bring her to the same place as me.

There were two wolves running around the woman with tremendous speed. The first seemed a little bit playful but included a good measure of small bites that left the woman with visible wounds. When the first wolf tired of prancing around her, the second took over. To my horror, this larger wolf jumped on her back and dug his powerful teeth into the bands of muscle connecting her arms and neck area. The woman did not seem to notice; she just sat down where she was and stared into the distance. After a while, the first wolf began to run around the woman once again, causing her to get up and walk quickly from one place to the other. Meanwhile, there were a few smaller wild dogs tearing about, barking and nipping at her body. I saw one bite the woman's left hand very hard, leaving bright red marks that I guessed were caused by fresh blood. I was astonished and dismayed as I watched. The woman bent down to pet the wild dogs and play with them. I could not comprehend how or why this royal young woman thought these animals were friendly, or even pets. I named the first wolf Restive and the darker second wolf, Despair, and I came to learn to that both were enemies of the true journey.

Where the bravery came from, I do not know. These wolves were powerful beasts that I knew I could not subdue. I decided to move closer to the woman, and as I did, the wolves and dogs stopped briefly and focused their eyes on me. I was alarmed and concerned now for myself as well as the lady. While I was present, the smaller wild dogs ran off into the woods, but the wolves stayed close by, even intensifying their efforts to torment the woman. I approached and began to speak with her.

"Greetings, young and brave one," I called. "Do you not notice the wild beasts who seek your end?"

"Why, hello, traveller. Pleased to meet you. I don't see many others while I walk. As for these animals, who is to say whether good or ill? They are my long-time companions, and I know no others. The smaller pups are amusing, and I wonder where they will take me as we romp and play."

While far from knowing my own way, I was concerned for the woman. I told her a little of the crystal pool and what happened to me there. She seemed interested in the deep pool, and I decided to try to find it with her. I was concerned that the mysterious iron fencing would prevent me from locating the pool and anxious that my troubled sense of direction would make it difficult to find. After all, I had been off the path for some time now. We walked for a time together, and I learned that pain had also awakened in her a desperate journey. A band of evil men had invaded her land and caused her family to flee for their lives. They were settled in a new village that sounded a lot like Ennuied, but the woman was deeply dissatisfied there. Surprisingly, it was much easier to find the crystal pool when looking with another person than on my own. We stumbled upon it quite by accident while we discussed our journeys openly and honestly.

The pool looked the same as it had earlier: sparkles on the water as the breeze upset the surface ever so slightly and the striking grains and pebbles on the bottom. I was astounded once again at the clarity of the water. As the woman stood by the waters, her reflection formed as had mine. In the reflection of the pool, her clothes were clean and pressed, as though she had been dressed by a team of servant girls. I encouraged her to have a sip of the water, but she would not. It was almost as though she did not know how to drink from an open pool. As I knelt down for a drink, she did too and sipped a small amount of water. The water seemed to awaken something in the woman. I noticed the gashes in her back from Despair were becoming smaller, yet this seemed to make her more restless than ever, almost as though the awakening of hope brought with it many unpleasant and uncontrollable emotions. After I drank of the clear water, the way I felt after the dark water seemed like a distant memory, and a softer set of thoughts once again took root in my mind.

Chapter Ten
The Gate

The woman and I walked together for a short time toward the large metal gate. I settled down into the grass and mosses to wait and think. While I was deep in thought, I looked up and saw that the woman had passed through the gate. I was shocked that she was able to do this when I could budge no part of it myself. In the distance, I heard the barking and whining of dogs, and most chillingly, the howl of the wolf. I approached the fence to talk to the woman and warn her of the impending attack. She looked like she wanted to come back. I tried to dig under the fence again but to no avail. I spoke with her for a time through the fence, but it was getting late; shortly, the dogs approached from her side, and she followed them deep into her side of the woods. I returned to my spot on the grass and pondered what to do next.

I was lost in thought when I felt something on my shoulder. I turned around quickly, worried the wolves had come for me. To my delight and surprise, it was Khalid's hand on my shoulder.

"Friend!" I exclaimed. "Where did you come from? Where have you been? I am so sorry for going separate ways!"

In his usual easy-going manner, Khalid replied, "I have been close by. It is good to see you too, my friend. Why are you sitting here in this spot?"

I told Khalid the story of the pools of water, the berries, the woman, and the gated fence. He nodded with understanding, and I assumed he had visited and seen some of the same things on his journey. I asked him what he thought of the massive iron gate that the woman had passed through so easily and that I could not budge. Khalid walked over to the gate and stood thoughtfully for a time, as if listening to wisdom coming from the silence of the forest.

He turned to me and said, "You could not pass through this gate, my friend, because it leads to a place you are not going."

I explained to Khalid that actually I had very little idea where I was going. Khalid spoke to me sternly, stating that beyond the trees I saw across the fence was a path, a path that would lead me not toward the music but straight back to Ennuied by the quickest route. I was taken aback by the firmness in Khalid's voice and the solemn look in his eyes, having seldom heard him speak in anything but a pleasant tone. I asked Khalid if he thought there was any way we could help the woman.

Again Khalid was firm with me and said, "Eloy, do you not remember the crystal pool?" Did she not drink from its waters? The journey is beyond your control. Its paths are set and worn. It is not for you to decide the course this woman will take."

Khalid and I began to walk away from the gate together. I was perplexed with him, as it was not like Khalid to appear so unconcerned with the plight of another person. He was silent for some time, deep in thought.

He said to me, "Friend, I too did not like those dogs. Had I a boot with a strong toe and the opportunity, I would show them the meaning of fear. Yet she is taking her path. For many, the path winds and turns, backwards, forwards, this way and that. Her path may yet bring her to the music one way or another, one day."

I was astounded that Khalid knew about the music. I asked him if he, too, had heard the music.

"Yes, Eloy, I hear the music. I am sure that it calls to everyone."

"If all people hear the music, and their paths may one day take them to the lands you and I seek," I replied, "why should we care what the dogs are doing? Why would we seek to help this woman and others we meet on the path if they must go their own way?"

Khalid responded, "Friend, answers to some questions are like the mist of the morning: impossible to grasp with your hands, but there in front of you nonetheless. What happened when you dove deeply into the well? Did you not feel the pain and longing in the music? The suffering on the paths is beyond measure. Do you think the music will find rest before all have made their way?"

Khalid and I spoke together long into the night. I was unsure how he knew so many details about my experience in the crystal pool. I assumed he had also been swimming in its waters. For the first time in a while, I slept comfortably next to Khalid under the thin but surprisingly warm blanket he carried. We rose early to continue our trek, and as we walked along, I saw that Khalid's face had changed and the unflappable Khalid I knew had returned. We ate berries, bread—which somehow Khalid had always had—and some tender, tasty roots that he taught me to identify.

We walked along the fence, talking and joking with one another, until we came to a small gate. When passing this way earlier, I had missed this gate completely. If Khalid had not been with me, I am certain I would have overlooked it on my second pass as well.

Khalid stated nonchalantly, "Gates are important, Eloy, because they permit the movement to what is next. Narrow gates are sometimes the most important, and fewer have led the way through them."

The gate blended into the background almost completely. It was the same height as the fence itself, and the bars followed the same pattern. The hinges were small but deep-green coloured, providing one of the few clues that there was a gate there at all. The green reminded me of fresh plants peeking through the spring soils. There was a small latching mechanism, scarlet red, and the gate itself was exceedingly small—I was not sure if I could fit through it. I put my right hand on the gate latch. I should not have been surprised that things in the forest were never as they seemed. As soon as I touched the fire-red latch, I felt acutely all the pain from my journey: the pain of the meaningless toil that first chased me from Ennuied, the loneliness of the journey, the wrongs done to me brought to my consciousness by the dark water, and the pain of watching the beautiful lady.

The latch began to ease forward as I experienced the realness of these things. It became too much, and as I was accustomed, I began to force these dark thoughts from my mind. When I did this, the latch became more difficult to move, and soon I could not budge it at all. As I let my mind and heart return to the suffering, the latch began to move once again, ever so slowly. I wondered how long I would have to revel in these unpleasant emotions. Unlike the feelings that had arisen after I drank the dark water, there was little feeling of power here.

I felt much more resigned, as if finally understanding that these things were terrible and there was nothing in my power to change them and no benefit at all in revenge or personal justice.

Just when I thought I would be stuck with my hand on the latch forever, I felt it click, and the gate popped open. I took my hand off the latch and immediately felt relief from difficult experience, though a residue of dark emotion remained, a reminder that my journey toward the music remained incomplete. I stared at the open gate and looked at Khalid for some help and advice. The entry way was even tinier than I had imagined, and I did not think it would be possible for me to get through.

Khalid was silent as he watched me try to pass through the gate. There was no chance I could walk through it normally, so I tried to push through sideways. I got through partway and became stuck between the iron bars. Had it not hurt so much, it might have been funny. I was like a person stuck between two worlds—who, I imagined, looked ridiculous in either one. I tried moving my hips back and forth and shifting my shoulders, but I only became more completely stuck. I saw Khalid looking at me with compassion and more than a little amusement.

He said to me, "Eloy! Turn toward the music—it is the only way to pass through the gate!"

I replied, not without some irritation, "Khalid, I can't just hear the music whenever I choose. I have only heard it a few times all the days of my life."

"You are closer now. Still your heart and listen," he responded.

Though very sceptical, I did what he said. I stilled my mind. I stopped all the efforts to drown out the pain and simply listened carefully. This kind of listening was not only with my ears; it was as though my heart itself was focused intently on discovering the beautiful sounds. Ever so faintly, barely distinguishable from the silence, I heard a few very high notes and, in the distance, pounding bass.

"Now turn to the music, friend. Face it and turn away from this place."

The music was not very loud, and if I allowed my thoughts to wander, it was difficult to hear. The sound came from somewhere in front of me and to the right, to the south and the west. I turned my head that direction, but I could still not move forward even a little.

"Not your head, friend!" exclaimed Khalid.

I did not understand how I would face the music, if not by using my head. I aimed my sideways feet awkwardly toward the direction of the music, but that did not help. After struggling for some time, I thought I might finally understand the instructions. I slowly began to turn my chest, and the heart within, toward the music. I found my body turning around the bars, and with almost no effort, I moved through the gate, with Khalid smiling from the other side.

I had learned another powerful lesson about journeying through the forests. It was not enough to attune my head to the music; it was a matter of the heart.

I thanked Khalid and encouraged him to pass through so we could be on our way. Khalid told me for the second time that he would see me later, and without further explanation, walked away from the gate and on into the distance.

I was upset for a few moments before telling myself that Khalid was on his own journey and must know where he needed to go. I easily found a packed dirt pathway beyond the gate, and turning to the right, I ventured forward along the gently sloping track. The air smelled fresh, and the sounds of the forest brought me great pleasure. It was not as though I had forgotten what I'd experienced at the gate, but the powerful sting of the memories was certainly less intense. I came upon a large hill with a thin path leading to the top and reasoned that it might be a good spot to get the lay of the land. I scrambled up the hill with more energy than I thought I had and was astounded at the vista before me. I could see farther than I had ever seen in my lifetime. As far as I looked, in every direction, were slopes, valleys, and flatlands, all covered in a deep green matting of forest.

I could see no end to the forest, and it dawned on me that the forest was not a place to pass through on the journey; it was the entire location of the journey. I sat down on a large rock and reflected on my first foray into the vast forests of this world.

I took a look at the wounds on my body, the ones I could see anyway. They were all there still, and while I could not see discharge indicating any kind of infection, they remained bright red. In addition to the wounds where the sores of Ennuied were scraped away and the large puncture in my chest, I had a few new ones from my first days in the forest. They all hurt. The forest was a place like none other I had experienced and certainly not what I would have guessed lay before me in my quest.

The Border Dwellers seemed to think that every creature in the forest was a beauty to behold, yet I was becoming convinced that there was as much in the forest to harm as to help, and it was sometimes hard to tell the difference.

The dark water, to name one, was full of honesty and accuracy, yet it led me off the path and caused me great exhaustion. I also noticed that some of the berries that looked the best were harmful, and others that looked rather ordinary brought me comfort and strength. The clearest good seemed to have been the crystal clear water that led me to the great music. My heart felt a fresh stab of pain as I thought of the beautiful, royal young lady. I wondered why the wolves and dogs did not take the time to battle me, or if they somehow had without my knowing.

My reflections were also turned toward my dear friend Khalid. I could not have made it through this part of the forest without his guidance and concern. What a friend he was turning out to be.

Chapter Eleven
The Abyss

I walked along the path for many days. There were no forks in the road and no opportunities to change direction, so I kept on going. I gathered berries—the ones I knew were safe—ate more tender roots, and found another food source by cracking open the shell of large brown seeds and consuming the somewhat bitter but sustaining meat inside. I stopped during the night, sleeping under the trees and gazing at the stars, surprisingly warm in the brown jacket Khalid had supplied.

I was becoming accustomed to the smells of the forest. The needles from the trees gave off a pungent smell that was most pleasant, a little like the smell of rosemary. I loved awaking to this fragrance with the first light of morning. There were also the odours of tree sap and the smell of fresh green from the mosses, ferns, and saplings in the undergrowth. I thoroughly enjoyed the fragrance of moisture in the air just before the rains, though I could do without the drenched clothing that usually followed.

For perhaps a day or so, the path had been moving steadily downward. As I moved downward, I began to smell something quite different. It was the faint hint of smoke. Not the kind of smoke that I smelled from wood fires at the fodder grass celebrations. This was the odour of something that ought not to burn; it smelled unnatural and brought dark thoughts to my mind. That night, as I lay under yet another tall tree, my dreams were troubled. In my sleep, I saw myself climbing stairs to the entrance of an ancient crypt. Inside there was a vast room with vaults descending downward, farther than I could see—eons of death. It was a desperately dry and desolate place. I awoke to the smells of the forest mixing with the new sour smell and walked onward, down toward what I feared might be the source of the bitter scent.

The slope of the path I followed became gradually steeper, and soon I was struggling to keep myself from running. There were some small plants on the side of the path, and I tried to slow my descent by grabbing them. All of these plants broke off in my hands, and I kept moving downward, quickly. I did not like what was happening at all, as the smoky smell was getting thicker. I tried to run side to side to slow down; this helped a little, and my momentum gradually slowed, and finally, I stopped. I thought about Khalid and wished he were with me at that moment. I began to climb back up the hill slowly, with my feet sideways and my arms out for balance. The ground was dry and dusty with loose rocks across the way; my feet slipped on flat rock, and I fell. My face slammed into the dirt, sending a piercing pain through my nose and into my head. I did not have time to assess my injuries, because I was falling, rolling and tumbling down the slope at an uncontrollable speed. The trees rushed by my side, and the rocks crushed into my flesh as I rolled.

It was dark, and the smell of the forest was only a memory when I awoke. I was in a dreadful place with a weight on my chest like nothing I had imagined possible, and it hurt to breathe. It pained me to even think of anything but the dread that surrounded me; there was heaviness in the wind swirling above my head.

It was as though all the hope and joy had been drained from the air and all that was left was regret, consequence, and sorrow.

My thoughts were full of The Darkness once again. In my mind, I rehearsed the painful events that had brought me to this point, reliving each and every one. The journey I had started with hope now seemed little more than a harsh joke with tantalizing rewards, always up and out of reach.

I believed, almost completely, that my journey was finished, and the end was more terrible than I had dreamed.

I had very little energy and wanted to sleep. Food lost its appeal, and it felt unlikely I would be able to enjoy anything again. These thoughts and many more travelled around my head in circles without pause. Like a rut formed by the rains or the track made from countless hooves in the forest, my thoughts were walled and channelled, binding me to the dark, reinforced every moment by powerful emotions I felt in body and soul.

I now understood that after rolling down the hill, I had plummeted into some kind of dark hole, or pit—no, a better word was *abyss*. Looking below me, I could not see the bottom of the hole into which I had fallen, and it became darker and darker as I looked downward until everything became completely black. The abyss must have been a wide hole because I could not see across it through the thin layer of smoke coming up from the depths. The ground on which I lay looked like it must have once supported life. There were stubby plants with no green left and an occasional stump from a long-departed tree. The ground now supported no living thing, and I was lying on a combination of rocks and exceptionally dry dirt. While in this abyss, I saw no other human being or living thing at all; it was simply me without any help in a dreadful, lonely hole.

Looking upward, I thought that perhaps I could make out the surface somewhere at the top of the pit. It took tremendous energy and all the will that I had left to begin to climb. There was no path before me, only the knowledge that I needed to move upward. I tried to get up and walk but slipped on the loose rocks and fell deeper into the pit than I had been before. This happened to me repeatedly.

I was now at the point where I seriously considered jumping into the depths of the abyss. I thought of many ways I could do this. I could simply jump from where I stood, certain that my head would hit one of the larger rocks below and that I would keep on tumbling until my bruised and battered body finally surrendered to The Darkness. Perhaps, I mused, I could lie down where I was, without food or water, and expire within a few days. I wondered if I would be missed by anyone outside of my hole.

I cannot say how close I was to my end, but I know that it was close enough to have been a real possibility. Instead, I tried something a little different. Rather than standing up and trying to walk up the hill, I crawled on hands and knees. It was a dreadfully slow process, and the rocks and dirt were ground deeply into my arms and legs. As I climbed, it felt like the hole itself had a will of its own and sought to drag me backward into my ruin.

The climb was, to that point, the most difficult act of my lifetime, even surpassing the pain that had propelled me away from Ennuied many days before.

At long last, the surface at the top of the abyss came into view above me. Unfortunately, my strength was gone, and try as I might, I could go no further. Still on hands and knees, I waited in the silence, feeling sorry for myself, wishing Khalid was nearby to rescue his friend one more time. As I drifted into unconsciousness, I felt a sharp blow to my rear side, propelling me upward. Using the momentum provided from the jolt, I fought the hill for every foot and somehow made it to the top of the abyss. I crawled away to the cover of the nearby woods.

I took stock of the state of my battered body. I imagined that I must be a sight to behold, adding to my list of injuries a flattened nose and more cuts and scrapes. I wondered if anyone alive was as sorry a sight as me. I removed many stones that were buried in my hands and knees, counting each one until forty. Though invisible to any onlooker who might happen by, there was now a searing pain in my right hip, and I knew somehow that I would carry this ache for many days to come. The mysterious wallop that had propelled me up and out of the abyss had left its mark on me that day. Were I not in such rough shape, I would have questioned this mystery more deeply. Where did it come from, and did it mean me harm or good? I found some berries and pleasing plants nearby, and with some nourishment in my body, I turned my attention to the hole, the giant pit in which no light is seen.

Chapter Twelve
Anger

I walked slowly back toward the abyss, smelling the pungent odour of destruction and death. Moving close to the pit filled me with great dread and fear; hence, with all my strength, I determined that the abyss should be filled. It was a strange obsession that consumed me—what began as a somewhat rational decision to protect myself from the hole became a frenzied crusade, and the more I thought about the abyss, the more irrational I became. I started by grabbing nearby rocks and throwing them into the hole. After exhausting the supply of rocks in the vicinity, I hunted for deadwood in the forest, throwing each and every piece I found into the abyss.

Soon I had cleared all of the wood within walking distance from where I had climbed out of the pit, and I applied all of my mental energy to find other ways to fill the abyss. I found pieces of tree bark that were straight and strong and used them to scoop earth into piles that I pushed into the pit with my bare hands. I did this over and over again. I was driven by a great fear that the pit would swallow me yet again, and so I seldom stopped to eat the fruits of the forest and rest. When night fell, I slept briefly, dreaming of being chased and threatened, only to awake and continue my efforts to fill the giant hole.

It was many days later that I saw something familiar in the corner of my eye. In some far recess of my mind, I knew that I should stop working and pay attention to what I was seeing, but I remained driven to fill the giant void in front of me. I heard someone call my name, and I turned to see my old friend Khalid smiling at me with something that resembled pity in his eyes. Though I had not seen anyone since before my tumble into the hole, I was more annoyed than glad to see Khalid with his merciful eyes. Could he not see that I was in the midst of serious and important work, filling the dreadful hole that stood in the way of my travels?

"Eloy," Khalid said calmly, "what are you doing?"

"Khalid, greetings," I said in a panicked voice. "I am filling this dreadful hole, and I must work with haste. It aims to take my life."

Khalid inquired how the hole might be able to take my life. Without slowing my work, I explained to Khalid how I had fallen into the pit and could not get out. I told him about my brush with death and the treacherous journey out of the abyss.

"I would never have emerged from this hole had someone or something not landed a blow on my rear end, but the pain is with me still."

Khalid responded, "I thought you said that no living thing was found in the abyss. How then did you come to experience this push that brought you relief?"

I could not answer Khalid, because the truth was that I had no idea what had happened in the abyss to rescue me. I only knew I had to fill the hole before it swallowed me alive. Surprisingly, Khalid did not speak to me about how ludicrous the idea of filling this hole would be to any thinking person.

The abyss stretched farther than I could see, and as far as I knew, it had no bottom. During this time, Khalid did not leave my side while I worked. He sat down and relaxed most of the time, looking like he was enjoying a story that only he heard in his mind. Occasionally, Khalid threw a pebble or a clump of dirt into the hole and smiled at me, and every once in a while, he invited me to walk. After declining many of his invitations, Khalid suggested that we could walk a little way around the rim of the pit and I could continue filling the hole there. This made sense to me in my dishevelled state of my mind.

We slowly made our way to the left and around the side of the crater rim. I walked for a few minutes before returning to my abyss-filling work. There was fresh earth to move here and more trees and rocks. After a good day of pit-filling and forest foods, Khalid once again convinced me to walk for a while. The acrid smoke from the hole did not allow us to see very far along the ridge we walked, but I noticed some kind of movement through the swirling mist. Khalid cautioned me that we should move slowly. Before I could see clearly, I heard a man yelling, "I'll show you! Think you know more than me, do you? Arrrrhhhh!"

I heard a swooshing sound followed by the pounding of boots on the earth, moving quickly and plunging into the woods. I was ready to walk forward, thinking the danger had passed, but Khalid put his hand on my chest and suggested we wait. Before Khalid had finished speaking, I heard more screaming. The crazed man was back, cursing and yelling obscenities into the abyss. It was a near constant tirade. I could not make out everything he said, but it included rants at people who had been rude to him by passing by him while he walked on a path. I also heard him complain about those who disagreed with him, even when he knew he was correct. He screeched something about wealth and not getting his fair share from someone or another. The man evidently did not like people telling him what to do and saved some choice vocabulary for those who attempted to direct him. After every verbal outburst, I heard the whooshing sound. The man's voice became even louder, and I heard the next words clearly. "Ohh, so you think he is better than me! He is nothing but a scoundrel! You chose to cross me—now it's your turn!"

Of course, the man used many other words to express himself, and following his outburst, I heard the loudest whooshing sound yet. I was so intrigued by what was happening in front of me that I forgot about filling the abyss for a moment. Khalid and I moved closer to the disturbance and hid behind a large group of stones to see the man behind the ruckus. I was expecting to see a large, rough-looking brute of a man, but the fellow in front of me was strikingly normal in his appearance. He was slim, with a clean-cut face and short brown hair, and he wore simple dark trousers with a khaki shirt. Khalid and I watched as he cursed and yelled some more and threw a piece of wood into the abyss. I could now see that there was a pile of wood pieces beside him. They appeared to be lengthy branches from the trees nearby, but the ends had been sharpened. I realized then that the lengths of wood were in fact spears with lethal looking tips.

Khalid surprised me by standing up and walking from our safe zone toward the man. "Sir, have you filled the canyon before you with your rage?"

The man looked at Khalid and yelled back, "I will, I will. I will not stand for this. I do not deserve any of this!" And with that, the man continued yelling and throwing his spears into the pit. I came out from behind the stones and stood with Khalid.

"So you two mean to do me harm, do you?" he accused us.

"No, sir," I said. "It is simply nice to see another on the journey. We will be on our way."

"So I am not good enough for the likes of you? I had food and water ready fit for a king, but you want none of it!" The man made an unearthly sound as he yelled through tightly clenched teeth.

And with that, the man threw two spears faster than I thought possible. One hit me on the edge of my nose as I turned, and another hit Khalid in the leg. I was incensed with this wild and senseless man. Without thinking, I picked up one of the spears and threw it back at the man. The spear missed and tumbled into the abyss nearby. I picked up another piece of wood and threw it toward the man, again straight into the abyss. As I searched for something else to throw, I noticed that Khalid was not preparing to attack the man at all. He took the spear that had grazed his lower leg, snapped it in two, and threw it into the woods. He said to the man, "Come walk with us a little. We are making our way around the rim of this dark hole."

The man replied angrily, "I will not leave this place until every last inch of that hole has felt my rage!"

Khalid looked saddened but not particularly surprised. Personally, I was still angry and did not want the man to come with us anyway; I thought it just as well that he stay and continue throwing his silly sticks into the hole. I asked Khalid what he believed was wrong with the man and whether the man really thought he could fill the abyss with his little pieces of wood.

Khalid responded, "I suspect he does not think this way at all, friend. He only knows that throwing the spears gives him temporary relief, and he seldom reflects on the hopelessness of his efforts. He cannot see the futility."

Khalid and I continued to talk as we walked through the misty air. It was hard to tell where the rage in the man originated. There was nobody with him at the moment, so I assumed he was reliving past events as he cursed and threw the spears. Clearly, the past affected this man in the here and now; my stinging nose was a testament to this fact. I carefully reviewed the man's rants and searched for some kind of meaning. It seemed to me that the man believed that virtually every action taken by another was meant to harm him and he truly believed he was defending himself with his weapons. Khalid offered me a drink from his skin of water. As I drank, I felt different, strangely peaceful and able to see a little further across the crater.

"Khalid! Is this water from the crystal pool?"

Khalid smiled and said, "I have found no better water yet, Eloy."

As I drank the last of the clear and cool water and thought about the angry man, I felt a lump grow in my throat, and I felt a heavy weight on my chest. I believe that I saw the angry man as he really was for just a moment. In my mind's eye, he took the appearance of a boy, asking the world for what he needed and getting little in return. I saw both that he needed what he asked for from the world and that nobody could give him what he sought. Khalid and I talked about the situation further. In one sense, the man's anger was completely justified, and in another, it was an exercise in utter futility.

Chapter Thirteen
Self-Pity

While Khalid and I conversed, I remembered my own need to fill the hole and began pushing dirt over the edge, amazingly seeing no similarity between my actions and the crazed man close by. After a few hours of busy, dirty work, I was ready to keep walking, and with Khalid, I moved a little further around the lip of the giant crater. I have to say that I was more than a little anxious about meeting another violent man; Khalid and I were both limping now, and my face hurt. To my alarm, it was not long before I heard noises again, this time the sounds of a woman's voice. I was beginning to realize that the abyss—this place of great difficulty on the journey that I had thought of as a lonely place devoid of all others—was becoming a little crowded.

The sounds from the woman in the distance were desperately sad. Sometimes, we heard noisy wailing and at other times, quiet sobbing. I remembered my dip into the crystal water early in my journey into the forest and the life-giving berries that had a similar effect. While under the waters, I had felt great mercy and compassion for the dejected and lonely as well as the strength to absolve all those who had made me feel that way. I wondered, almost out loud, why I did not feel the same way about this woman, obviously suffering appalling torments.

Khalid and I walked closer to the woman. She appeared dangerously close to the abyss, and it looked as though she was staring down into its depths. We moved still closer and were able to see that she was not staring at all—the woman was weeping and letting her tears fall into the canyon below. Could it be? I reached the conclusion that this woman was attempting to fill the void below with only her own tears. A more hopeless sight I have seldom seen. All the sadness in the world might not create the tears required to fill this hole, and instead of sadness, I felt profound frustration.

"Woman," I cried. "What are you doing here? Do you know realize how close you are to the great pit below you? You could fall!"

The woman replied, "If you had walked my path, you too would weep at the crater's edge. It is my fate to suffer, and I will fill this pit to the brim with my tears."

I looked over the edge of the abyss, incredulous at her plan. I saw a damp patch in the dirt below her, but despite her incessant tears, there was insufficient liquid to even flow a small distance down the slope. I asked the woman to tell me what had brought her here to the edge of this cliff with her tears. She told me a lengthy story filled with pain, anger, and regret. The narrative culminated with the story of her marriage and the birth of her two children. Her husband had been killed in an accident, and her firstborn child had been missing for years. It was clear that this woman had reasons for her tears, more reasons than any other I had met. Yet I could not help feeling troubled by her hopeless plan to fill the abyss with her tears. I wanted to find out more.

"What is your name, dear lady?" I inquired.

"My name is Likhapa. The world is bent against me."

"I understand the reasons for your tears, Likhapa, but why this plan to fill this crater with your sadness?"

The woman replied, "Like the vast expanse below me, my pain is without end."

"Have you never heard the music from the other place, Likhapa?" I asked. "A land so different from our own. I am on a journey to discover the way to this place. I heard sounds from there that brought hope to my heart."

Likhapa looked at me with both confusion and recognition in her eyes but seemed to quickly dismiss her conflicted thoughts.

Feeling frustration rise within me, I probed Likhapa further. "Why do you remain at the crater's edge? With such an ocean of sadness, why have you not plunged into the depths of the abyss before you? I myself came very close to doing so."

The woman was silent for a time; her tears slowed for a moment and were replaced with a wrathful look in her eyes. "I wait at the edge of the abyss for rescue. I wait and I wait, and none come for me."

She looked at me hopefully for a second and turned away when she realized I had absolutely no way of liberating her from her plight. Khalid, who had been watching with interest, motioned to me, hinting that it was time to move along. I sat down on a rock and thought deeply about Likhapa. The more I thought about her plight, the more I wanted to get back to work filling the hole myself. I pushed some more earth into the abyss until I tired and joined Khalid, who was waiting for me patiently. We walked together again, and I remained lost in my thoughts.

I said to Khalid, "There is really very little difference between the two, isn't there—the angry man and the tearful woman? One vents his anger at others into the abyss and the other, at herself, but also into the abyss."

Khalid nodded slowly in agreement and waited with me while I cleared more earth and stones into the abyss. As I moved further along the crater's rim, the acrid mist cleared a little. Khalid and I could see to the left and the right and saw that there were indeed many others, hundreds in my line of sight, all attempting to fill the void below in their own fashion.

Chapter Fourteen
Control

The abyss was awesome in size, many miles from rim to rim. My eyes were drawn to another woman not far away. She was scurrying about, busily throwing rocks and pieces of wood into the abyss below her. She threw clumps of dirt into the hole, and then I saw her do something that hit me in the chest like a physical blow. I saw her move on her hands and knees and begin to push dirt over the edge of the crater just like I had been doing for some time now. Amazingly, this was the first time it had crossed my mind that my actions were as ridiculous as the actions of the others busy with their abyss-filling work. I felt ashamed and embarrassed at the insight.

I turned to Khalid. "She ... she is just like me. Do you see it? Khalid, I do just what she does."

Khalid nodded calmly. "Yes, Eloy, she is like you."

I felt a tremendous compassion for this woman rise up in me, and sadness filled my heart as I saw the hopeless task at which she toiled. Khalid urged me to join him in trying to help this woman.

Khalid and I approached her along the crater's edge, and we introduced ourselves. The lady let us know that her name was Rafa. She described falling into the abyss and barely escaping its clutches. As I listened to her familiar story, I felt the abyss pulling me toward it. It was a dreadful feeling of separation, as though the whole universe was merrymaking and I was not invited. The isolation I felt coming from the abyss was familiar and seductive. Had not Khalid reached out his hand to steady me, I may as well have ended up back in the hole. Rafa noticed the effect the abyss had on me, and we discussed the need to fill the hole before it swallowed us into a bottomless pit of *alone*. Khalid actually cracked a smile as Rafa and I stared at each other with a dawning realization about the contradiction in our thoughts and actions. We were tirelessly at work filling a pit that had no floor!

Khalid asked, "Is it not time to put down this endless burden? This abyss in front of you was established void, and void it will always remain."

We both decided that we would stop trying to fill this endless abyss, wasting our time and energy, and with that decision came a measure of relief from the crater's incessant pull. I told Rafa about the beautiful music, and she was inclined to listen for herself.

Feeling deeply satisfied that my own difficulties in the abyss had been a great help to someone, Khalid and I left Rafa and approached yet another person working hard along the rim of the pit. We stopped to watch. Incredibly, this woman was actually descending into the abyss and returning with something in her hands. Over and over again, she walked into the abyss, climbing over the ledge and sliding down the slope over the rocks and dirt. I could see her struggle to climb back up on to the level ground, doubly so because her arms were full of debris from the hole. After bringing up a load of rubbish, the woman set to work ordering and organizing the materials. Small rocks went into one section; medium-sized, another; and the largest rocks were stacked neatly farthest from the edge and closest to the woods. The dirt from the hole was even organized by colour and gradient. This woman was very strong and a hard worker. I chuckled to myself about how the villagers of Ennuied would have loved her working the fields of fodder grass.

Khalid and I approached the woman. She walked to meet us in a very business-like fashion, stating, "Well, I see you will do nicely over here, and you belong in this part. Come along!"

I was taken aback by this woman but too dumbstruck to resist her guidance. She led me to a pile of light brown dirt and informed me, as though giving a reminder, that I should further sort the earth by the size of the grains in the dry soil.

The woman tried to size up Khalid to find his place. For some reason or another, she determined that Khalid would be suitable for sorting the large rocks near the woods. Khalid walked to the rocks and sat down to wait with an unenthusiastic grimace. I tried to do a bit of sorting for the lady. As I did so, I felt a strange sense of safety—the security of knowing exactly what I should be doing—but it came with a deathly hollow sensation, as though I were betraying my quest for the beautiful music. I stopped sorting and took a long and careful look at my surroundings. I noticed footprints in the ground moving away from many of the piles. I was alarmed to see that other piles had bones beside them, human bones! I had a growing suspicion that those who stayed at their pile of rubbish with their assigned duties were destined to fade into death, with only their dry bones remaining. I decided that it was time to walk away from my pile. When I took my first step away, the woman was there with the speed of a gazelle fleeing a lion.

"Where are you going? There is work to do. This is your spot!"

I explained to the woman, with us much bravery as I could muster, "I must leave to find the music. This is not my place."

Panic filled the woman's eyes like she was facing the world's end. As I moved away from my spot, she stood in my way. When I tried to move a different direction, she was there again. I called to Khalid to give me a hand with the situation. When he left his pile of large stones, the woman looked at him immediately but turned back to me as if knowing intuitively that there was not the slightest chance of keeping Khalid at his pile of rocks.

Khalid approached and called out with tremendous authority, "Stand aside, stranger! It is not yours to choose the destiny of another."

Seeing herself overpowered, the woman took a step backward. Her face was pale, and her eyes, saddened. She took a sip of a beverage in a skin and stared at Khalid and me.

"I am the glue. I keep things together in this mixed-up world. I am the master of my own play."

I responded, "But, woman, don't you realize the materials you are piling up so neatly all come from the abyss, the smoking pit? Put them back! We are not part of your play, but we will gladly help you return these things to the pit from which they came."

The woman looked lonely and confused for a moment and then angry. "If you are not part of my play, you are no use to me. Be gone like the rest. I will finish the work myself!"

Chapter Fifteen
Around and Out

Khalid and I walked on and settled on the summit of a small hill to rest for the night after foraging in the nearby woods for fresh berries, tender greens, and more than one variety of rich-tasting white fibrous plant. Looking out over the lands around the abyss, I saw many more sights. A poor, guilty-looking man was carrying boulders on his back, walking round and around. Once in a while, he tossed one into the abyss, only to select an even bigger stone to carry on his shoulders. Another was emptying his pockets into the abyss, every last piece of lint and sand, leaving nothing for himself or others. There were more reasons people were drawn to the abyss and more ways of trying to fill it than I had imagined, and all of it was as fruitless as spitting into a gale force wind.

I had to get away from this place. I thought about the path that had brought me to this ghastly valley and wondered if there was another path to take us out. I decided that I would do some investigating in the morning. Khalid and I enjoyed each other's company until long after dark. We discussed the people we had met in our walk around the abyss, and I chose that night to let go of my anger, excusing those who had wronged me here. Surely this was a dreadful place where choosing what is foul is the most natural thing. As I slept that night, I dreamed of much of my past and the people who had caused me harm throughout my life. In the mystery of sleepy dreams, all of my enemies became mixed and mingled into one, and with a sharp knife's slash, I cut the rope connecting us and released them from all need for sense and justice.

I awoke with the first light of morning to see Khalid sitting quietly in the sunlight. He was staring happily toward the south with his head tilted just a little. I walked over to him and sat down quietly. As I sat looking across the smoke of the abyss and the masses of human beings hard at work in their meaningless efforts, I heard the faintest hint of music in my ears. It was a haunting, reassuring melody with strings causing quiet yet powerful vibrations in the air. The music was both mournful and inviting. It was as though the music understood the trauma and suffering of the abyss yet remained completely separate from it. As I listened, the songs became louder and louder, and I wondered how the people at work below could not hear the sounds and feel the vibrations pounding though their bones. In truth, there were a few who seemed to notice that something was going on. Some increased the speed of their abyss-filling work for reasons I did not understand. A couple of others stopped to listen, looking confused and upset, as though the world they had come to understand was in jeopardy. The music continued for some time; as I have said, it is difficult to measure time when the music is heard. Eventually it faded away, and I was left sitting quietly with Khalid. There was no need for us to talk, because we had both heard the sounds that brought more understanding than words could ever bring. I felt cleaner and better than I had in a long time.

The separateness of the music from the noxious fumes of the abyss was a tremendous relief to me. It meant that my journey was not to the abyss or even through it; it was around it. I decided that I would climb one of the nearby trees and see if I could find any way around the dreadful pit. I found a tall one close by, and Khalid gave me a boost so that I could reach the first branches and begin climbing. I have always been a little afraid of heights, and my knees knocked together as I reached the highest limbs of the tree. From my vantage point in a tree on a hill, I could see far around the crater of the abyss. It was larger than I had guessed, and there were even more people surrounding the pit than I had realized. Through the mist, far away on the south side of the crater, I saw a path leading up and away. I knew immediately that this was where

I must go. Unsurprisingly, it was in the same direction as the beautiful music.

Khalid was pleased with this plan, and together we walked around the abyss in search of the path I had seen, making excellent progress. It was startling how quickly we moved around the abyss when I did not need to stop every little while to try to fill the hole with piles of earth and stones.

We passed many more people as we ambled steadily along. A woman was digging in the abyss in search of water to drink. I shuddered. Close by was a man who may have had the most upsetting abyss-filling plan. His work provided a stark warning for all to avoid groups of people who use power and control to accomplish fruitless goals. This man had assigned many strong pit fillers to work while he sat at a table with piles of scrolls at his side. The workers lined up at the table and watched while he wrote something on the scroll. Afterward, they took the scroll and read it together in groups led by some kind of lead pit-filler. Following this, the workers, looking enthusiastic and excited, joined crowds of other pit-fillers in their work, and together, they looked to be making incredible progress. They had cut down many trees and excavated the land beneath to create massive piles of earth and clay, which others dutifully pushed into the abyss. Once in a while, one of the workers would collapse or hurt him- or herself. The others quickly picked up the worker and threw him or her into the abyss with the rubble and debris. It was a sad sight to see because I had learned that filling a pit without a bottom was a project going nowhere. Khalid noticed as well, and I watched him run with lightning like speed into the crowd of workers, right into the upper reaches of the abyss itself! He came out shortly, carrying a young boy over his shoulder. He carried the boy far away from the busy work and placed him in a berry patch.

"He will be fine there. The berries will keep him going and revive him. Then he can make the choice to stay or go."

Leaving this mass of activity behind, we met a strange lady blocking our way.

"Travellers, I see you are weary! Come and drink. I have water for you and food to eat."

The lady led us closer to the edge of the abyss and had us sit down on tree stump seats she had prepared. The lady offered us water to drink from some simple cups. Looking at the water, I was not sure I wanted it in my belly. It was a light shade of brown, and when the sun shone directly into the cup, I thought I could make out a hint of an oily sheen. Khalid set the water down, but I drank it, a little bit anyway, grateful for at least some refreshment. After I finished drinking, she returned with bread for us to eat. Once again, it was not the best bread I had seen, but having grown up on fodder grass loaves, I did not think it looked that bad. I ate the bread as well. After I finished, Khalid and I observed the lady acting strangely indeed. She smiled at us warmly, almost too warmly, and took our dishes in her hands and held them behind her back. She walked backward slowly, toward the edge of the pit. When she was close by the lip of the crater, she subtly threw the plates and cups into the abyss below.

Returning to us, she said warmly, "How else can I help you, dear travellers?"

When we replied that we would require no further help, the lady became cold and uninterested. She returned to her spot, waiting for other travellers to walk her way.

Taken aback by what we saw, I spoke to Khalid incredulously. "She was using her acts of service as a means of trying to fill the abyss, wasn't she?"

Khalid looked at me and nodded with a grim smile on his face. "Her service was tainted by her motives. This is a great pity."

Eventually Khalid and I found the area I had seen from the top of the tree on the hill. Initially, we could not see the path leading up and away because it began a little ways into the woods, but by looking carefully into the forest from the clearing near the crater, we were able to spot the pathway and reach it by climbing through some thick undergrowth. I expected that climbing up the path would be the end of my struggles with the abyss. Still feeling the dark pull coming from the depths, I realized rather quickly that this was not the case and that going around the abyss was a different process from what I had imagined. As I walked up the slope away from the crater, the dark presence diminished but did not leave altogether. Even after I had climbed a long distance, I knew that should I turn my eyes and heart to the abyss, it would try to swallow me again.

Conversely, by turning away from the abyss and choosing to leave my attempts to fill it behind, and by choosing to understand that no person could fill the abyss for me, its gravity within my soul began to weaken. Of course, I cannot discount the hope that came from the music in the story of my ascent away from the abyss. To be sure, though pain and suffering below were completely real and something I had experienced intimately, a small part of me held a hope and trust that there was a land where the abyss held no sway over the lives of people. And it was to that place I journeyed.

Walking around and away from the abyss toward the land of the beautiful songs resulted in some changes in my body, most of them wonderful, just one disappointing. By the time I had arrived at the abyss, I was already covered in wounds, and in the last few days my nose had been further damaged by a spear and my hip had sustained that ghastly blow which propelled me out of the hole. As I walked upward and away from the abyss, the wounds, sores, and scabs began to fade—not all at once, but I noticed differences on the hour. After climbing for the better part of a day, resting for the night, and eating plenty of berries, we reached some sort of summit. Almost all of the wounds on my skin had faded, not completely but enough that even a close friend might not notice them. My nose felt much better as well. It was an incredible relief.

Two conditions remained with me, though. While the sores on the skin of my chest had all but disappeared, my heart still felt strange and not entirely complete. Back in the forest—it seemed like a long time ago now—the wood had pierced my heart and, I am sure, part of it had died at that time. I thought that perhaps one day, in the land of the beautiful music, my heart might be fully reclaimed. The other part of my body that was not the least bit better was my right hip. It was as though I had wrestled with the abyss and though I overcame, I would walk with a limp the rest of my days as a grim reminder of my weakness.

Khalid and I took an entire day to rest there at the top of the slope leading down to the abyss. He took my hand in his and said, "Friend, it is time for me to go once again. Our paths will cross soon, I know."

And with that, Khalid walked off briskly down the path. I thought of running after him and convincing him to follow my wishes, but I was coming to learn that Khalid marched to his own tune. I was sad to see him go, but as I looked down the vast path leading back to the abyss, I was overwhelmed with grief. Having left the scent of the acrid smoke behind, I now perceived the depth of my own pain and the suffering of the many in their futile, meaningless, and hopeless efforts to fill the abyss. I wept and wept until my tears were transformed into a peaceful sorrow. I pondered returning down the road from where I came and showing others that the path away was around the abyss and toward the great melodies in the air. I suppose, though, I knew that I could not return to that place for a time, lest I fall back into the great hole myself. I vowed that if I ever could, I would lead as many as I could far away from that grim and hopeless place.

Chapter Sixteen
The Approaches of Heureux

It was at mid-day when I came to a split in the path I travelled. Thus far on my journey, I had experienced very few choices, as though compelled in one direction in spite of my freedom. Now two alternatives lay before me, and I could discern very few differences between the paths. Perhaps the one to the right seemed a little less difficult than the one straight ahead. While I sensed my ultimate destination was straight in front, I turned to the right out of curiosity and followed the track a short distance, stopping just before the path stretched steeply downward. I was more than a little disturbed because the trajectory of the path seemed to lead dangerously close to the abyss. Hearing human sounds in the distance, though, I wondered if I might meet someone who would help me on my journey. I walked quickly down the slope to the source of the sounds.

I have always been a fast walker, and I caught up to some others on the road walking in the same direction. Everyone in the group was young, save a couple of older folks who looked strangely out of place. None in this group were dressed for a journey; their clothes were attractive looking but did not appear to be durable or warm. I was so grateful for the comfort of the simple brown jacket I wore during the cool forest nights. The men in the group all sported an interesting kind of footwear with a sponge-like sole and a low collar. They looked better for speed on paved roads than exploring the forests and rocky ground I was now used to from my travels. The women all had long hair, beautiful, if a little unkempt. In truth, I thought these travellers looked a little silly on the forest paths.

"Halloo, traveller," a young man said. "How are you? Where are you going? What is the meaning of it all?"

The questions were weighty, and as I prepared to answer my fellow traveller, I discovered he was no longer listening to me at all. I turned my attention to others in the group and introduced myself. Everyone seemed friendly, happy, and easy to get along with. I asked them where they were going, and they looked at me with pity, as one who is ill-informed about important matters.

A lady named Sunny answered me. "We are walking toward Heureux, of course. That is where everyone goes—or wants to, anyway!"

I tried to speak with Sunny a little bit about my journey. She looked enthusiastic when I spoke of the fodder grass festivals, and she was intrigued to hear about my sister Dalia, but her eyes glossed over when she heard how Dalia's story turned out. I perceived that Sunny was no longer engaged in the narrative, or perhaps she just didn't understand much of it. I joined the group, and we walked together toward Heureux. As we approached the town, I felt increasingly uneasy because it seemed we were moving dangerously close to the abyss, and I wanted nothing to do with that place. My suspicions were confirmed when I saw wisps of the putrid pit smoke blowing in the direction of the town. When I pointed out the smoke from the abyss to my newfound acquaintances, they again looked at me strangely, as though I was speaking the unknown language of a people from a distant land. I remembered my promise to help anyone I could avoid the terrors of the abyss, and accordingly, I pressed the issue further with the others.

"Be careful of the abyss," I warned. "That smoke we can see in the air is from a dreadful place, and we are close by. It looks like Heureux is on the borderlands of the great pit."

A girl whose name I did not know responded, "This abyss place might be real for you. It is not real to me. If it makes us happy to live in Heureux, then that is the right thing for us! I don't believe in darkness."

I countered to the girl and the entire group, "It is great to be happy. I am on a journey to a happier place! But I am worried about the smoke. I have fallen into this pit myself. It happened suddenly and without warning when I drew near the abyss. Would it not be wise to find a happy place to live a little further away from this hole?"

A strong and burly young man said, "We control our own fate. If I chose to stay out of deep, dark pits, I will never have to worry. Destiny is mine to mould, and I plan mine to be pleasing and agreeable!"

I was starting to realize that I was alone in my concerns. Perhaps this group of travellers was correct, I thought to myself. Maybe I was the fool for my caution. I wondered if The Pain and The Darkness and the difficult travels were not in fact necessary, and I could enjoy pleasures and delights instead.

Sunny entered the conversation. "Traveller, we all know that we simply need to follow our heart! My heart feels excited and pleased when I think of Heureux."

Another unknown youth piped in, "Why would we delay our amusement? It is here in front of us. Let's go, everyone!"

With that, the group began to walk more quickly toward Heureux. They still permitted me to walk beside them, but the people in the group no longer made any attempt to speak with me; rather, they prattled on to one another about their plans to do this or that in Heureux. As for me, I could smell the smoke of the abyss clearly now, but I chose to enter Heureux with an open mind. I had been wrong about many things in my journey so far, and perhaps it was not really all that dangerous to live and seek happiness close by the abyss.

Walking down a final slope, I was now able to see the great city before me. Heureux was nothing like the forests as I had been travelling. The roads were wide and organized; trees and plants were kept tidily behind fences and gates, and some kind of artificial lighting stood on every street corner. A small plaque indicated that the city had been established untold centuries ago, yet everything appeared shiny and new. When I looked closely at a few of the buildings that were nearby, I noticed that fancy new façades seemed to be placed on older structures. The approaches to Heureux were filled with signs and banners advertising the wonders within the city gates, and I have to admit that I was more than a little excited. Quite a few of the signs discussed the pleasures, companionship, and camaraderie found there. I had my good friend Khalid but really nobody else to share my joys and sorrows with, and the idea of finally having some amusement was appealing. Soon we came to the gate itself, a stunning archway towering over the widening road, covered with ornate pyrite and zirconium dioxide. Above the entryway hung a sign with a promise:

> WELCOME TO HEREUX,
> FIND HEREIN THE DIVERSION YOU SEEK
> LOOK TO THE WEST

Chapter Seventeen
Plaisir Street

The first part of the welcome sign made sense to me. A diversion from the difficulties of the journey would be welcome. I was less clear about the second part of the sign until I saw a fresh wisp of smoke from the abyss waft overhead, from the east, and I decided that looking westward was just fine with me. The crowd with whom I entered Heureux had dispersed, and I found myself alone once more. I followed the road toward a section of the town with bright lights, and as I drew closer, I realized that these lights were bright indeed. I found myself on a street full of buildings, all freshly painted and inviting.

The first building had a large window on the front through which I saw a number of beautiful women and strong, tall men. I was both intrigued and nervous about entering the building, so I decided to sit down and watch for a time. I saw many people come and go. As the men and women entered the building, I noticed the oddest thing—they all wore jewellery around their necks, usually chains with medallions covering their hearts. Some had two or three medallions, while others had dozens or even hundreds. The medallions seldom seemed to match the bearer, and they must have been heavy; both men and women were slouching under their weight.

I was torn about whether I should enter the building but decided I would give it a try and see what happened; after all, the men and women in the window were fine-looking, and the idea of joining them was intriguing. I strolled up the walk to the house, feeling self-conscious about the absence of jewellery around my own neck. My only medallion seemed to be the scar where the forest-wood had pierced my chest. I reached the front door and opened it, expecting to be greeted with smiling beautiful faces, but in the foyer of the building, I noticed very little activity at all. There were some mannequins near the window, beautiful people, dressed well and with beckoning looks on their faces. Disappointedly, I construed that these mannequins were the people I had seen in the window from a distance.

I chose to investigate the house a little more closely. I had observed many people walking in and out, and while I could not see another living person in the building now, I knew that the people had gone somewhere and done something. Looking around the foyer, I spotted a wide hallway and walked down the corridor. There were many doors on either side of the hall, and pictures of beautiful people wearing very little— or no clothing at all—hung on the walls. I enjoyed my walk in the hallway and tried to enter some of the rooms. The doors were all locked, but there was a small placard above the lock on each door. In fancy writing, they all said the same thing:

Enter the room, pleasure within
Enjoy freely, the smallest price
For a medallion, a bit of your self leave behind

As was becoming my new normal, the sign puzzled me. I understood the *enter* and *pleasure* parts, or at least I wanted to understand them badly, but the second and third lines were unusual. The text about enjoying freely and paying a price, even a small one, seemed incongruent, and the third line was still more baffling. What did it mean to leave a bit of your *self* behind? In my heart, I decided that it would be worth this little bit of my *self*, whatever that was, to find out what was inside the room. As I made that decision, I heard a click coming from the locking mechanism on the door. I grabbed the doorknob, turned it slowly, and was met with no resistance. I pushed the door open slowly, caught sight of a bed, and saw a flash of someone inside the room. At the same moment, I heard a small buzzing sound in my ear. I could have dismissed the buzzing very easily as nothing of importance, but I remembered the sign and was very concerned that a small portion of my sense of hearing would be lost if I entered the room.

I stopped immediately, knowing that I still had a choice. Though I wanted to enter this room and try out many of the other rooms in the corridor, I could not live with the thought that this might hinder, even a little, my ability to hear the music. Sadly, I turned around and walked back up the hallway, through the foyer, and outside the building. I paused under the archway, wondering afresh if I would find a medallion for myself. Returning to the street, I felt a wave of relief and maybe a hint of the music I sought in the distance.

I thought it prudent to find out a little more about where I was. I noticed that I had missed yet another sign when I had entered this part of Heureux. I walked backward to peek at it and was pleasantly surprised to see that this one was a simple street sign. Apparently, I was walking on Plaisir Street, West Heureux. Looking at the buildings lining my side of the street, I noticed that they all faced in a westerly direction, full of windows with pleasant breezes wafting gently by. On the far side of the street, the structures had no windows at all and offered no opportunity to look to the east and the direction of the abyss. The pillars, wide eaves, and sprawling porches were dreamy and romantic. I walked back in the direction of the building with the beautiful mannequins and proceeded past it, feeling a fresh wave of ambivalence.

I did not have to walk far to reach the next building, which was clearly a place of entertainment. Like the last, this place seemed pleasant to me, and inviting; consequently, I ambled up the wide sidewalk leading into the building and took a closer look. The entryway was full of pictures and signs discussing the distractions found inside. There were pictures of men and women in love, people on incredible adventures, fighting and making up, conflict, war, and so much more. It was a little overwhelming.

I opened the door to the building and was met with a blinding array of colour and numerous entertainments selections. I chose to enjoy a story about a man who took on the world all by himself and defeated a large and dreadful army. After that I moved into an outdoor courtyard and jumped off of platforms in the trees into a foam-filled pit below. Though I was getting tired, I also went into a room where I could trade something

I had for a chance at gaining a hundred of them. I lost one of my socks. Finally, I walked out of the building feeling both spent and exhilarated and lay down in warm breezes on a bench to rest for the night.

In the morning, the exhilarating feeling was gone, and I felt alone and hungry. Fortunately, I spotted what I could only describe as a house of food with signs and pictures describing the culinary delights within. I began by eating a breakfast complete with rashers of bacon, eggs, toast, and fruit. While I felt no better than after eating the good kind of berries in the woods, I was satisfied and no longer hungry. I attempted to walk out the door but was instead led to a room of desserts, where I ate cakes and pudding. Before escaping out the front door, I was given all kinds of sugary drinks to satisfy my thirst. I was utterly stuffed full of food and drink and needed a long rest at the side of the road before I could continue.

Looking down Plaisir Street, I saw more buildings. There was one with all kinds of bottles and tiny round wafers as well as mushrooms. Yet another building had a flashy sign saying:

Tomorrow House:
Forget about Today, Live for Another

I noticed a perplexing thing about Plaisir Street. As I walked further up the road, the buildings began to repeat themselves, but they were just a little bigger each time. I was quite tempted to experiment with what was inside the larger buildings of West Plaisir Street, but I wanted to continue exploring the town. I took an east-facing road and walked on, frustrated because I could not see far ahead due to the trees and buildings which had been planted and constructed in such a way that my view was blocked. It was not too long, however, before I found myself walking through the entrance of a park.

Chapter Eighteen
The Ocean of Love

The entrance to the park was covered by an arching banner with the words "Ocean of Love" carved into the wood. It was eerie for me to enter somewhere called the *Ocean of Love* when I was this close to the abyss. It was, however, a beautiful park. There were large deciduous trees providing shelter and shade, and many smaller plants and flowers. Other people entered the park at the same time as me, so I sat down on one of the many benches that seemed designed for two and observed. I noticed that the park visitors walked toward the outer edges of the gardens where there were many stalls and tables set up. They stopped at these tables before heading deeper into the Ocean. Curious, I moved closer to see what was happening.

At one table, the visitors appeared to be unloading household chore items, including dirty washing and dishware. Another table must have been reserved for children, because people were dropping young ones off there to be cared for by others. Still another table seemed to have something to do with currency. A few people dropped off sacks of coinage, but far more people dropped off pieces of paper that appeared to be causing them a great deal of stress.

I will now describe what was perhaps the strangest of the many tables and stalls that I saw that day. At this table, people appeared to be leaving other people locked up in large cages. Some of the people who were behind bars looked sad, and others, very angry. I supposed these people must have been causing problems or that they were deemed unsuitable for the Ocean of Love.

Having finished their duties at the tables, the park visitors began to walk toward a small but reasonably pretty body of water: the Ocean of Love, I assumed. I surmised that to enjoy the park, the people needed to keep the normal everyday problems of life separate—hence the tables and stalls around the edges. The water itself was calm and colourful with hues of green and blue, yet it was strangely opaque, making it impossible to see beneath the surface. I wondered what would happen next, guessing that visitors would swim in the water together or sit on one of the many benches for two and wait for the sunset. I could not have been more wrong. I took a much closer look at the park visitors. They were dressed nicely, yet I could see through their clothing that there was something out of place with each person.

One woman had an arm that was badly misshapen, a man had a large dent in his head, and still another had some kind of festering wound in her abdominal area. There were leg injuries, stiff necks, and even people with pain in their rear ends! As I watched, the people mingled and walked around each other near the water's edge. They began to form couples, often with another person with a similar abnormality though sometimes different. There seemed to be someone for everyone among the injured, sick, or maimed near the Ocean of Love.

As I watched the newly formed couples, I listened as well. They spoke to each other with words that seemed kind: "Your leg is not broken. It is perfect!" or "I love your strong arm. It's faultless" and even "That is not blood coming from your abdomen. People just don't understand you."

In one sense, I was happy for the people at the Ocean of Love, but in another, I could not understand why they were lying to each other. Perhaps they did not even realize that they were being dishonest. I certainly did not hear any of them saying things like, "You have a stiff neck, and my ribs are broken—let's get better together" or "Help me out with my crippled arms. I can't even tie my shoe."

Once the couples were formed, they usually turned from the east to face the west, away from the abyss that they likely did not even know existed. They walked back and forth near the water's edge in awe of its beauty. Personally, I thought the water was all right, but after swimming and tasting the crystal waters of the forest, it was not all that impressive. As night approached, some of the couples began to walk out of the park. Many tried to sneak out without gathering their belongings from the tables and stands. The stall operators ran after them with the speed and perseverance of champion athletes. Inevitably, each person was forced to carry his or her load out of the park. Some couples separated immediately with the return of the household chores and problems with their papers. Others stayed together with grimaced smiles on their faces.

I stayed a while longer at the Ocean of Love and found some scraps of food left by the couples and their merry-making. It was good enough for me at the moment, and I settled down on a bench to rest for the night. There was still a little bit of activity among the park visitors, and I was sure I recognized one of the young men. It was the fellow I had met on the way into Heureux, the one who had stated that he planned to enjoy all the pleasures available now. I noticed that he had an interesting strategy for finding partners. He pretended to have one injury and found a partner with a similar problem. When the woman looked like she wanted to leave the park, he snuck away and pretended he had a different ailment, which led him to someone new. He did this many times, and watching him made me sleepy. I decided that if I saw him in the morning, I would ask him more about his time at the Ocean of Love.

At first light, there was almost nobody left in the park. I was a little stiff from lying on a bench built for two for the night. I stood up and took a short walk toward the water to stretch my legs. I found the fellow from the night before sitting by himself under the shade of a small tree.

The young man looked up at me and smiled. I introduced myself to him and asked him his name.

"I am Injud," he stated. "I must be on my way—so much to do, so much to do!"

I asked Injud about his lady friends and where they were now, but he just looked at me as though he did not know what I was talking about. I watched him walk away and decided I should continue exploring Heureux myself. I left the gates leading to the Ocean of Love, under the watchful eye of those who operated the stalls and tables; they had nothing of mine, however, and I left without being accosted.

Chapter Nineteen
The Secret of Heureux

I followed a nicely paved road that led in a south-westerly direction and sauntered along, wondering what I would discover next in this strange place. It was not long before I spotted a tower, perhaps two or three stories in height, seeming to grow larger as I continued down the road. Once I was much nearer, I realized that it was not a tower at all but the soaring gnomon of a massive circular sundial. Fascinated, I approached the device to examine its design and operation.

It was a magnificent piece of work, obviously built with tremendous care and attention to detail. It took me close to a minute to walk across the circular face of the dial. The numbers were etched into massive plates of marble, and the gnomon looked as though it could be made of pure gold. Something troubled me, though, about the numbers. They were in a funny order, with the morning hours to the right and the afternoon to the left. In my travels, I had paid some attention to the cardinal directions, and I noticed that this sundial was facing the west rather than the north, as a sundial should. The net result of these apparent errors was that this beautifully crafted masterpiece was completely useless for telling time.

I had assumed I was alone at the giant sundial, but there was one other person sitting at a table much like the stalls surrounding the Ocean of Love. I approached the stall and saw a man sitting on a simple chair. In Ennuied and even during my travels, I had met many people who were attractive from a distance but did not look nearly as good close up. This situation was exactly the opposite. From a distance, the man at the table looked dreadful. I could see that his head was misshapen, very large on the bottom half, small and narrow on top. He also stood at a strange angle, as though his right side was much shorter than his left. His clothing looked outlandish—something like a little boy might look playing dress-up with his father's fine clothes. I should also mention the pallor of his face, which was a ghostly white with a bluish tinge around his mouth and eyes.

Though I was taken aback by his appearance, I walked toward him for a closer investigation. When I was close to the man, I found that he started to look much better. His lopsided head now looked like a strong jawline and pronounced chin. I saw that he stood at an angle which emphasized his left hip at the expense of the right. The deathly hue of his face now looked sophisticated and modern. Even the clothing looked elegant, perhaps tailor-made. While I felt ill at ease and distrustful of the odd fellow, I decided to speak with him. "Greetings," I said warmly but with some reserve. "Who might you be, and what can you tell me about this town, Heureux?"

The man flashed a grin showing all of his teeth. "My name is not important. I am what you might call the mayor of this town."

I shared with the man how my father had been part of the town council of Ennuied and asked him how the council of Heureux operated. The man smiled again. "We don't have a town council here. Don't need one." His voice turned low as he continued. "We have found a secret."

The man reached under the table and produced a small paper bag. "This is for you," he stated. "Everyone who spends any time in Heureux needs one, and you will understand why we need no town council."

And with those words, the strange man rose, turned away from me, and slowly walked into the distance. As he moved away, he once again lost much of his appeal, and if I had not just seen him up close, I would have taken him for a beggar or lifelong wanderer. I turned my attention to the brown paper bag I had received from the man, opened it, and peered inside at a shiny metallic object. I removed the object and gave it a good examination in the light. It was a metal disc with a line running around the circumference. As I played with the object, I discovered that twisting the top part of the disc against the bottom caused it to pop open. Inside the metal container was a simple compass much like others I had seen in the past. I had already developed a good sense of direction on my journey. I knew the music was coming from a south-westerly direction and the abyss was directly east of Heureux. In spite of this, I thought it would be useful to have a proper compass and decided to figure out how to use it.

I sat down on the ground and investigated the compass more closely, noting some unexpected differences from other compasses I had seen in the past. The most obvious difference was that the "S" was at the top of the compass. The other and far more serious difference was the way the compass actually worked. I held it out in front of me and turned my body in a complete circle, trying to find magnetic north or, for that matter, south. As I moved, the red arrow on the compass needle stayed in the same position, pointing directly at my chest.

My first thought was that the man with the toothy grin had given me a dud of a compass. I threw it on the ground in disgust and walked a few feet to pick up the brown bag to check if there were any descriptions included. As I walked away, out of the corner of my eye, I noted some kind of movement in the compass. I watched more carefully and was dumfounded to realize that the compass needle always pointed to me. It was as though the "S" meant *self* rather than *south*. No matter how I held the compass or adjusted the compass rose, it always pointed to me.

I guessed this was the secret of Heureux. Whenever direction or decisions needed to be made, the people of Heureux must have consulted their compasses, which always pointed back to self. I played with the compass for a while but lost interest, finding it of no useful purpose.

Chapter Twenty
Strange Sights in Heureux

I continued my exploration of the town, thinking more about the compass as I walked. There was an appeal to the way the compass pointed back to me. My journey thus far had been painful and costly, and perhaps I should have considered myself more in the decisions I had made and the paths I had followed. I wondered where this compass would have led me had I used it in the forest when I was separated from Khalid. I suspected it would not have helped me much at all, though, because the path I walked had seemed unavoidable.

Deep in thought, I found a road heading eastward from the giant sundial. The road I travelled was wide, flat, and hard as stone, making progress easy. In a short while, I came to another building with many people coming in and out, including Injud, who appeared to be leading a group of people. This building looked like some kind of temple or place of worship. On the front were statues of young, beautiful people. A sign on the front read:

> *We honour the young*
> *We bow to youth*
> *The hands of time our enemy*

I realized that this was some kind of group dedicated to worshiping youth and being young. Adjacent to the place of worship was another building. I observed many people going to this other building before entering the Temple of Youth, as

I came to call it. The sign in front of this building said "The Parlor." Both young and old, men and women, were entering the building and then exiting some time later. When they left The Parlor, they all looked a little younger than they had when entering the building. The youngest people who visited The Parlor appeared both fresher and healthier when they left than when they had entered. They exited wearing nicer clothes and with fine hairstyles and transformed faces. One young lady in particular had looked like quite an angry and bitter person before visiting The Parlor, but when she left after about half an hour, I could no longer clearly tell that she was angry and bitter, though knowing the price of change, I suspect she was little different.

The older people who used The Parlor did not fare quite as well. It was more difficult for them to mask their flaws, and the results were faces that looked ghastly tight, with puffy lips and cheeks and clothing that only half succeeded in covering up the sags and shapes that inevitably arrive with time.

Many of the people who left The Parlor went straight to another building—a less interesting, flat, cavernous structure made of white bricks. The people entered with nothing but left with more baggage than they could carry. I had to investigate and take a closer look. Pretending that I was a citizen of Heureux as well, I walked into the structure with the crowds and found myself in a very plain and ordinary place that was dressed up to look impressive on the outside. The building was full of shops selling all kinds of goods, some of them useful, others seemingly ridiculous. One store sold only decorations for the inside of closets, a place that people seldom see, which is supposed to store important things. As I watched the people peruse the endless supply of goods, I noticed some extraordinary things.

The first was that people did not seem to have the gold and silver needed to purchase the wares. Instead, they signed contracts of labour with the vendors and their financiers, some of them far into the future. Another strange observation was that many people bought products near the entrance, only to throw them away when they came to another shop with shinier items. After so much time in the forests, I found this building stifling and overwhelming. I was not sure if I felt that I, too, needed something from every shop or if in fact I needed nothing at all from this place. Regardless, I had neither money nor plans to sign on to a life of hard labour, so I ran out the door from which I had entered and back on to the road.

I left the flat building, The Temple of Youth, and The Parlor and made my way in a northerly direction. I had now traversed much of the city, and I wanted to see the rest. In a chilling reminder of where I actually was, I saw more acrid smoke drift over from the abyss. The scent of the fumes reminded me of my time in and around the deep hole and all the people stuck in its grasp. I did not blame the people of Heureux for looking to the west and using the compasses that pointed to self. Anything seemed better than moving closer to the pit I knew was next door.

The smoke became much thicker as I approached the next landmark and a sign pointing east that said "Heureux Trash Depository, East." Looking down the road that led eastward, I saw a lot of activity but quickly moved along the street I was on, heading northward. I told myself that I needed to investigate the final corner of the town and resolved I would visit the trash depository later. The truth was that I was rather uncomfortable travelling that close to the abyss.

I soon found myself in a very different part of Heureux. Looking to the west, I could see the entrance to the town and the sign I had passed under when I first arrived. I had not noticed this part of the city then, perhaps because it was much less developed. There were houses all around me but also many, many construction sites in various states of progress. In Ennuied, when a new part of the village was built, the workers usually constructed many new houses close to each other and connected them with roads and pathways. I wondered what these town planners were thinking, before correcting myself that there probably were no town planners in Heureux. Here, there did not seem to be much of any planning going into where the houses were built or in what direction the development would expand.

In front of me was a sturdy little house with a white picket fence and a little dog in the yard. Next to it was a house that looked halfway built, and next to that were a couple of empty plots of land. In spite of my closest observations, I noted no discernible pattern to which plot of land had an established house and which was empty or, for that matter, which was an active construction site.

I detected movement a little further to the north and moved forward to take a closer look. By entering a neighbour's yard and crouching behind their fence, I could see what was happening clearly. Even from a distance, I recognized Injud as one of the workers in my field of vision. It was astounding how this fellow made it around Heureux; he seemed to be everywhere and trying everything. Injud was armed with some kind of sledgehammer and was hammering away at an existing house. I watched with fascination. The house may have been a little dated, certainly not in need of demolition, yet clearly it was being destroyed. Injud attacked the windows first, smashing them with the massive sledge, and moved on to the doors next. He did not seem to work with the forethought of a master builder; rather, he appeared driven by rage and emotion. His face sometimes expressed fear and hurt, which turned to rage and vengeance before returning to the same fear and hurt. It was a cycle that repeated itself over and over again. Injud and a few others attacked the structure of the house next, and timber by timber, brick by brick, they reduced what was a pleasant, cosy home into a pile of rubble. Then they left.

As I continued to watch from the neighbour's garden, I heard the sound of rustling on the ground and through the grass. It reminded me of the sounds I might have heard in Ennuied when The Pain awakened The Darkness. Then I saw the first rat. It was a much larger rodent than I had seen before, greyish black, with red eyes and a long tail. I froze where I stood, petrified of facing attack with nothing to defend myself. The rat was not that different from the night creatures my father had faced so many years ago. There were many rats; some ran close to where I sat, though none paid me the slightest interest. The rats descended on the pile of rubble that had been the pleasant house. With incredible speed, the rodents carried off the materials that had been the home—pieces of brick, scraps of wood and furniture, even broken plates and tattered clothing. With the wreckage in their mouths, the rats ran to the east and disappeared into the grass and trees. I could not count how many rats there were, but the lot was writhing with them, and it was not long before there was nothing left where the house had stood but plain, bare ground.

Chapter Twenty-One
Enough of Heureux

I was stunned by the ferocity of the destruction. I left my hiding place in search of more information. I turned around, looking carefully for movement in all four directions, and quickly spotted activity to the south. Once again, I walked over carefully, and this time I took cover among a number of fruit-bearing trees providing shade to another pretty house. I took a close look, and to my astonishment, I saw Injud again. This time he was carefully helping to build a house with a young lady. This process was going much slower than the destruction had, so I grabbed a bite to eat from the nearby fruit trees and settled down to watch.

Injud and his partner seemed very caring and affectionate with each other. It brought hope to my heart that perhaps there was deep love to be found in Heureux, and I wondered if I might actually hear the beautiful music again in this place. I listened carefully but, alas, was unable to hear any music from the beautiful lands; consequently, I turned my attention back to Injud and his partner.

"Dearest, where should we put our bedroom?" the lady chirped.

"I only want you to be pleased, darling," drawled Injud.

The couple talked on and on about their new life together in the home they were building. They conferred about where the walls would go, the trees in the yard, colour schemes, furniture, dishes, and more. As they prattled on, I noticed that a few things never entered their conversation, things that I supposed were important when building a house. There was, for example, no discussion of any heat source to keep the house warm or to use for cooking, nor was there any thought given to identifying and planning the water source. I saw no wells nearby. Injud and his partner made sure to talk about all the things that would make their house beautiful and comfortable but failed to discuss the design of the doors and windows and, most importantly, the roof. As I watched, I remembered afresh the commitment I had made to help others after my escape from the abyss, and I decided to make some suggestions to the couple.

"Greetings, Injud. It is good to see you again!" I called. "I see you are hard at work planning and building a house."

Injud looked at me with some disdain, as though I was an unwelcome intruder. "Yes, of course we are building a house. We know love, which you obviously don't, standing alone as you are."

"Yes, I can see you must love this lady, and it is true that I am alone, but have you considered how you will build your roof, and need water and warmth?"

"Such things are of no consequence. We have the heat within ourselves, the compass has told us. This is Heureux! We have no worry of storms or troubles, and such things take time which is ours to enjoy at once!"

I returned to my spot among the fruit trees to watch as Injud and his partner went back to work building. They made rapid progress and were finished before the day was done. I observed them sit down on their front step to admire their handiwork. The couple had not been sitting for long when the small breeze turned into a wind. I could tell that the wind bothered them, but they put on brave faces and entered their home. While I admit this was rather intrusive of me, I sat down under their front window so that I could hear what they were saying.

Injud raised his voice to his partner. "I like the house across the lane! Why can't our house be more like the one there?"

His partner responded, "If you like that house so much, maybe you should live in it without me!"

I was concerned about Injud and the lady. As they argued, I could feel power from the abyss drawing them into the void.

The arguing became louder and louder, and next came hammering and banging. I hoped that they were paying attention to the state of the roof and making repairs, but this was not the case. The house began to vibrate with the banging, and I made my way back to the fruit trees for safety. Pieces of wood began to fly from the house, windows were smashed, and the whole structure shook violently. Injud and his now former partner appeared and ran around the house, wildly tearing it to pieces.

Before I knew it, the house was destroyed, and as expected, the black rats returned to abscond with all of the building materials. As this all took place, the smoke from the abyss blew into the area in thick clouds. I was surprised and pleased that the smoke didn't bother me nearly as much as I had expected it would. I felt confused and frustrated with Injud and the rush to destruction I had observed, imagining what a privilege it would be to build a house with a partner of my own.

The noxious fumes did, however, bother Injud and the lady, who instinctively turned their bodies to the west, away from the smoke. With barely a word to each other, they departed, moving quickly in different directions. This time I ran after Injud both to see what he would do and to offer assistance if needed. With my sore hip, it was difficult to keep up with him; he darted this way and that, much like I have seen small birds do when they are trapped somewhere indoors. On the few occasions where I got close to him, Injud had a familiar and painful look on his face. He continued his erratic and panicked race until he bumped into another person at an empty lot.

Almost instantly, all was calm, and the new duo began discussing and planning a new house. The new partner was not a companion this time around, and I overheard talk about business and coins. I was absolutely flabbergasted, but things were beginning to make sense. In this part of Heureux, people built houses and then tore them down over and over again. The fruit of their efforts was always stolen and lost to the abyss nearby, but the builders found endless comfort in starting again.

I knew I had one more place to visit before my time in Heureux was finished: the trash repository, close to the abyss. I had felt uneasy walking by the entrance to the dump, but my confidence was buoyed by how little the smoke bothered me. I made my way back the way I had come and toward the repository. As expected, the smoke became thicker as I approached the driveway and sign. I turned straight east into the drive and approached the site itself. I could not say that the road to the dump was crowded, but neither was I alone, and there was a steady stream of individuals from Heureux walking with me. I expected them to be carrying old household goods, junk furniture, and trash to the repository, but each person carried only the clothes on his or her back. A few were trying to look at their compasses, shaking them and looking confused. I approached a middle-aged gentleman to see what was happening with this compass.

"Sir, why are you shaking your compass? Has it stopped working?"

The man looked confused and beaten. "I ... I don't know. It points this way!"

He showed me his compass, and the red mark on the needle no longer pointed to his chest; it was aimed due east, toward the landfill and the abyss. I walked with the man in silence en route to the trash repository, wondering if it would look like the facility in Ennuied. The dump there was basically a massive pile of burning rubble, but I saw nothing in the distance looming above ground level. Instead, the terrain became steeper and steeper downward, and the choking smoke, more intense. In this most unexpected place, I heard it for a moment; it was a joyful piece of music in the air punching through the grey mist into the deepest part of my being. Then suddenly it was gone.

I watched as one of the travellers tripped on something and began to fall down the slope with increasing speed. Another lady lost her balance and fell, followed by the man who had walked beside me. The revelation hit me hard that this trash repository was no garbage dump; it was a path straight to the pit that had swallowed me whole not so long ago. Every person within my line of sight fell down the slope, yet my footing remained completely secure. I tried to grab a couple of people as they fell past me, but they were moving too quickly, and I lost my grip. Occasionally, a resigned-looking young person passed by, but most of the people falling into the abyss from Heureux were at least middle-aged. Not usually so old as to be infirm but just beyond the boundless rigour of youth. It appeared to me that the magic of Heureux was most effective on the young.

I still felt steady and strong on my feet and in little danger of falling down the hill myself, but I had experienced enough of Heureux. I understood how its attractions and venues kept people pointing away from the abyss, but it was just too close by for me, and I did not hear the music at all, save that brief interlude moments before. I made my way back up the incline, away from the abyss, through Heureux, and back out the way I had entered days before. I was pleased when, once again, I was able to turn toward the south, away from Heureux and the abyss it helped to feed.

Walking in silence provided me the opportunity to reflect on my stay in this strange place. I knew that this town was not for me and I could never blend into its colours; at the same time, a twinge of jealousy rang in my heart as I thought about the pleasures and togetherness found among the people of Heureux. In many ways, there was much more companionship in that town than I had experienced in Ennuied and certainly more than I had found on my journey—which had been lonely, excluding the crystals waters, music, and of course, Khalid.

One person remained on my mind as I followed the winding path: Injud. I was in awe of his ability to relentlessly pursue pleasure and whatever he thought would bring happiness. There was resilience to this man who never gave up; part of me admired that resilience while wondering if it could land him in the abyss down the road. He truly seemed to follow the compass of Heureux and constantly looked out for his own interests. A dark, conflicted part of me, however, hated Injud and his relentless selfishness. Nourished by my disillusionment, pain, and isolation, a small seed of judgement entered my heart and took root in the fertile soil.

Chapter Twenty-Two
The Poetic Plateau

Growing up in one village and never travelling, I really had no concept of distance. A long walk for me was the forty-five minutes it took to get from the main fodder grass fields to my home. The distance I had travelled already and that which likely remained ahead might as well have traversed the entire Earth, and the days and nights passed by in a kind of rhythm borne from repetition and routine. I lived a contradiction where each day and night seemed to last a lifetime, yet looking back, I wondered where all the time had slipped away. My most basic needs were met each day by the berries, greens, seed pods, and fibrous plants, which I easily located in the wooded growth near the path and by the streams of water, which always appeared just in time. Still, what I lived each day did not approach the measure of my dreams or, for that matter, even the pleasures of Heureux.

As the days and nights rushed by, I began to wonder about the direction I was travelling. I had no doubt that my bearing remained south-westerly, toward my last memory of the beautiful music, but I had not heard the songs in a long time, and I began to doubt my course. I considered turning back and settling in Heureux, but the distance that now lay between Heureux and me made that possibility too daunting to consider. The events of this journey were nothing I could have predicted or prepared for; in fact, I seldom experienced anything when expected, and I was often surprised when something important presented itself. So too now, at a point where I would have loved to arrive at my destination, or at least hear the music afresh, I saw another road marker. It said:

Plateau of the Poetic

I reasoned that the first part of the sign made sense in that I was clearly on a plateau of some sort. When the land rose slightly and I could see ahead over the trees, the terrain in front of me was more or less flat for as far as my senses could perceive. It could be a plateau, and a massive one at that. The second part of the sign meant less to me; I certainly did not feel particularly poetic. I was learning, however, that even when I did not understand, the signs usually conveyed a true message and I best listen to this one as well. Perhaps the poetic and reflective were more important on the journey than I had realized. I tucked the message from the sign somewhere into the back of my mind and continued with the endless walking.

After many days, I noticed movement on the path ahead. I had not seen another person for some time and hoped it was a fellow traveller. To my delight, I soon discovered that it was another person, and I called out, "Greetings, fellow traveller! Do you have news of the road ahead?"

The man stopped in front of me and looked me up and down. "I have walked through without much difficulty, but I expect you will have more troubles than me."

I told the man a little about my journey with special emphasis on the most difficult parts, such as walking through the narrow path in the woods, squeezing through the gate, and emerging from the abyss. I left out the parts that showed how I always found help from others when I needed it most.

The man looked threatened for a moment. Then his self-assured demeanour returned. "Well, I am surprised you have made it this far. I notice your tattered shoes and small stature. You will not get much further."

I was angry at the man and thought of a few more stories I could tell him about just how strong I was. Instead, I dishonestly told him I wished him the best good fortune and continued walking. The exchange left me disappointed, unsettled, and disturbed. Both the man and I were on difficult journeys, and I could not help but think we could have treated each other with a little more kindness. In the evening and night-time, I continued to ponder the man I had just met and the harshness of my trek. I had looked for friendship and support as one searches for the first green shoots and coloured blossoms of spring, but what I had found were thistles and thorns. The intensity of emotion that I felt that night had to be expressed and the words poured out of my mouth:

> "The journey is long, I have come so far
> All the landmarks gone
> Looking behind, cannot see the start.
> Thought the land looked better
> Hoping for green, striving for summer
> No life at all, just rocks and dust."

The emotion of the night was still fresh within me as I set out in the morning. The air was crisp, and a moist, comforting mist hung in the air like a thick blanket, but I barely noticed, the harshness of my encounter with the stranger still on my mind. It was that morning I encountered one of the most powerful stops of my entire journey. There, on the left of the road, was the most striking rose I had ever seen.

Chapter Twenty-Three
Flowers of Love

The rose stood upright and strong—a lone blossom among the plain and ordinary rocks, dirt, and plants. I sat down to examine the flower more closely. All of the other roses I had seen had stalks covered in sharp thorns that hurt to touch. This rose plant had parts that looked like thorns, but they were soft to the skin and almost tickled my hand. I dared not touch the blossom itself, which was wound together with petals of green and red. I looked around for signs of other rose plants nearby, but I saw none. It was unbelievable that this plant grew so close to the path I travelled and that others had not picked or destroyed the lovely plant when they passed.

I returned to sit near the plant and enjoy the company of this treasure along the side of the road. I don't know how long it was that I enjoyed the companionship of the rose until I realized that I was listening to the beautiful music at the same time. The music played a melancholy tune that brought me comfort. It was as though the music itself understood me, commiserated with me, and consoled me in the difficulties of the journey. The rose itself seemed to draw the negative emotion from my heart and replace it with something peaceful and rousing.

I stayed beside the flower for a number of days, eating plants and berries and drinking water from another small stream I found nearby. I would have been content to stay there at the side of the road with my rose for a long, long time, yet

I was persistently aware that my journey must continue. I wondered if there was a way I could bring the rose with me on my travels, and I spent the next few days building a container out of wood that I could use to transport the rose. It had to be strong enough to protect the flower from damage and large enough to give it room to grow.

When the container was complete, I was more than a little pleased with myself. Considering my circumstances, I had built something that just might work. I set out to begin the process of transferring the rose to the wooden receptacle I had constructed. I began digging around the rose and found that its roots extended much further than I had anticipated and I would have to cut them to fit the rose into the wooden container. A nagging feeling of dread entered my consciousness, subtle at first, then rolling in with the strength of a breaking wave from the sea. I would not be able to take the rose with me without killing it. On further reflection, I acknowledged that it was also unlikely I could carry the container very far without help, anyway. It was just too heavy and would be too awkward to carry.

The following morning, I set out with a familiar heavy heart. I took one last look at the rose and noticed that it was beginning to wither. I surmised that this blossom was a temporary reprieve on a difficult path and set out once again for the land where the music played all the time, not just once in a while. It was after weeks more of walking alone when I caught sight of another solitary traveller on the poetic plateau. I was wary of who I might encounter and made a plan to walk by with a quick greeting. This time, the traveller reached out first with a much warmer acknowledgement. Encouraged, I responded, and a conversation ensued.

"I can see you have travelled a long time! Let me share with you some counsel," the traveller bellowed.

Hoping for some helpful advice, I replied, "Yes, tell me what you know!"

My new friend broke into a poetic song of his own:

> "Be the bestest, fastest, strongest
> Fight fatigue and travel longest
> Walk all day and walk all night
> Never stop without a fight.

> In all you do perform your best
> Never stop and never rest
> Your value comes from what you do
> Guard down one moment and you're through."

With that, the traveller bid me farewell and, with a burst of speed, launched to the northeast and his journey's end. It did not cross my mind in that moment that he was heading in the direction of the abyss. The song he had sung to me stuck in my head, inspired me, and for a time, gave new purpose to my journey. I rested less often, walked faster, and moved with purpose and dedication. Things would have continued like this for some time, had it not been for the pain in my side.

As I have said, almost all of my wounds had cleared up since my time in the abyss, but the nagging pain in my right hip stayed with me, and the harder I travelled, the worse the pain became. Eventually, the agony was too great to bear, and I was forced to stop for an extended rest. I felt great shame at not being the fastest or the strongest and worried I would never reach my destination.

At night, I fell into a deep sleep and entered the world of dreams. I floated backward in time, reversing through my journey, and back to Ennuied. I found myself in the fields of fodder grass, working and fighting to bring in the harvest, never gathering enough. Then there was Khalid, looking like he needed to speak with me, his mouth moving and me unable to decipher his words. Darkness entered my dream, and I felt the pain in my chest that drove me from Ennuied so long ago. I awoke with a start, grabbing my heart and feeling for any sign of the wounds that had plagued me for so long.

Thankfully, it had just been a dream. The wounds had not returned, but the message was clear. The wisdom of this last traveller was no better than the wisdom of Ennuied. I recalled the sign at the entrance to the forest:

> *Traveller*
> *The journey is beyond control*
> *Its paths are set and worn*
> *With strength and will, you have begun*
> *Weak and frail to come*

Still shaken by the dream about Ennuied, I sat silently until first light of dawn appeared, unaware that another remarkable experience was building. Long before I could see the sun itself, I felt light enter the place where I sat. I saw the faintest hints of colour emerge like a mirage, replacing the black and white of night. There was a flash of blue and white when I turned my head just so and looked through the corner of my eyes. As the sun progressed closer to the hidden horizon, the blue and white stood out clearly as points of light in front of me. I wondered aloud where my dreams had brought me and about whether this could be the land I sought. A wonderful sweet fragrance filled the morning air, bringing with it a sense of hope and life that I had only associated with the beautiful music and the crystal waters. I remained motionless, and the light increased. Still fearing that the scene before would fade away like the songs from that distant land, and with the blazing light of morning, I found myself in a lovely place.

What had seemed to be a barren piece of rock the night before was now covered in thin green vines, and attached to the vine was a pleasing blue-white blossom. I moved forward, and what I saw is best expressed by the words that entered my heart that night:

A flower lives in a rocky crag
One blue white blossom where nothing grows
Off the path I'm drawn by force
A few steps only up and round
Really was not hard to find
The boulders veiled, blue and white in garden
The stones are covered, nothing bare
Blue white blossoms everywhere.

The place I found myself was the most enchanting I had seen thus far on my journey. The beautiful blossoms covered the rocks and ground like a carpet. The dreams and hopes that had been stolen by trial and difficulty returned to my heart in that place, and I wished Khalid was there to share it with me. In that place, I felt alive and strong, and for a time I even forgot the pain in my hip. I felt love coming from the blossoms, and in return, I felt their need for mine. My heart was turned to verse again:

Have no others come before?
I see no footprints, camp, nor chair
Has no one stopped to see or care?

Closer now I look, beneath the flowery sea
Harsh cuts from long ago, barely can I perceive
Thicker do the flowers grow where once the blade cut so
Foolish are the traveling throng who saw
just one flower and moved along.

    I remained with the flowers and blossoms many days, lost in the softness and mutual care that I found there, but I met yet another harsh reality when the scene began to change. Harsh thorns grew up between the blossoms, and while the beauty of the place remained unmolested, I could linger no more. This was another experience of beautiful flowers on the path that I realized was temporary, perhaps a glimpse into the lands of the beautiful music. I came to believe that though the experience with the flowers was fleeting, this in no way lessened their connection to the beautiful music. The flowers also served a wonderful purpose in that they contrasted almost completely with the harsher aspects of the journey, showing me that I was still looking for a place I had not found. I returned to the path, and to my dismay I encountered still another traveller.

    He bellowed out to me, "Stranger, why are you looking so glum?"

    I did not want to respond at all and hoped the man would go away soon. "I am just fine," I replied. "I will be on my way."

    The man looked at me and then looked where I had come from, spying the rocky path and a hint of the blossoms.

    "Oh, I understand. You were in there." The traveller snorted. "Of course you have the blues. Serves you right thinking you could find peace and beauty on this path. You harvest what you plant, I always say! You harvest what you plant."

    The man continued, "What's with that limp? You walk like an old man. Toughen up, quit feeling sorry for yourself."

    The tirade went on and on, and I gradually backed away from the nasty traveller, whose voice grew fainter as I moved along. I was relieved when I could no longer hear his jarring voice in my ears. Resuming my journey, I reflected on the overwhelming absence of empathy and compassion among the travellers I had met on the poetic plateau. Competition, performance, and cruelty were not what I had expected to find from others who were in the same situation as me, trying to reach their destinations on paths fraught with difficulties and sorrows.

It seemed a great irony to be in such need of help and support from others yet unable to receive any from anyone.

Chapter Twenty-Four
The Wise Traveller

I scarcely even noticed that I had just passed by another man, different from anyone I had yet encountered. This fellow began to follow me and was in fact walking beside me for some time before I realised I was no longer alone. I was both startled and embarrassed, not knowing how many of my thoughts I had voiced aloud. This stranger was completely distinct from the others, making no effort to speak or to be spoken to. I looked him over carefully as we walked, still wary of anyone I met on this long, flat road. His shoes were worn and tattered, and I saw many scars on his skin, healed but not completely gone, and down his cheeks were the paths where many tears had flowed. He was a rather frail man, older, with greying hair and deepening wrinkles. I remained angry with the other travellers I had met, yet I found myself trusting this strange man walking beside me.

Out of the silence, he spoke. "I suspect you are beginning to question, walking this lonely path, if there is even one place free from competition and harsh words where you might feel safe, able to give and share love freely."

I nodded sombrely. "I have wondered this often of late, sir. I am not sure it is real."

"Well, this place may in fact be hidden, but if it can be found, it is well worth the toil and terror of the journey to find it."

"Sir, where do you think it is?" I replied. "Could this corner of the world exist back in Heureux? Do you know about that place? Should I have stayed there?"

I went on to describe my experiences on the journey and escape from Ennuied in detail. I told him about the forest and the pools and the lady in the woods. When I told him about the abyss and the suffering there, I noticed both a twinkle in his eye and a twitch on his forehead. I retold my escape from the abyss with Khalid and the particulars of each stop in Heureux. As I reviewed the highlights of my wanderings with the man, I relived them and experienced them again. I felt my anger rise. I had begun with a home that was not really a home, the journey had been full of pain, and now I had few rewards and many scars to show for my efforts.

The man smiled at me and said, "Mercy is really love carried out among people who are not competent with love. The hard truth is that all people love poorly."

He paused and continued, "Bitterness and thankfulness cannot exist together, since bitterness prevents us from perceiving life as a gift. Bitterness is always telling you that the journey is not providing you what you deserve. Bitterness always results in envy."

I could see that I was talking to a very learned man, yet he frustrated me because there were no direct answers to my questions in his words, only the suggestion that I carefully nurture the orientation of my heart to the world. I did not know if the old stranger was providing me fine wisdom or profound-sounding advice that would lead to my ruin.

He spoke to me one more time. "The intrigues of one life are far too vast and complex, immense and profound, to be explained by another."

And with that, this startling stranger nodded his head toward me, smiled warmly, and turned away to walk in a different direction, straight through the trees. His final words echoed in my mind and would frame the next part of my journey, the steep climb and my exit from the poetic plateau.

For better or worse, I chose to listen to this traveller, and I took his words to heart. I embraced the reality that the kindness and softness I looked for in my fellow travellers might be difficult to find but resolved to remain open to the possibility that it was real. I also chose to set aside the myriad of questions that inundated my mind and to be grateful for my life and experiences. After all, "The journey is beyond control; its paths are set and worn ..." I wondered about the mystery of each person's life and what it meant for me, alone again on my journey.

Chapter Twenty-Five
Speed in Weakness

As I moved along, the lengthy stretch of level ground gradually transformed into an aggressive incline. I was pleased with my progress and my speed. "Not too bad for someone with a battered hip," I thought to myself. Rounding a corner, I could see the path ahead for a great distance, observing that I was not alone and that many others shared the task of ascending this slope. The climbers who were far away looked like dots, motionless against the backdrop of the hill, while I could see some movement in the travellers nearby. The closest of the climbers was not far ahead, and I gauged it would not be long before I was in a position to overtake him. This was little comfort, as the hill ahead was exceedingly large and the path was long. I could not see the top of the hill for the clouds that obscured the upper reaches of the slope.

Walking behind the man, I noticed some interesting things about him. This man appeared as though he was built to run and climb, to conquer any obstacle. I glanced down at his calves with more than a little envy. Each of his steps seemed effortless as the muscles on his leg extended, giving a spring to his gait. I could also see the bulge of his physique peeking through his shirt, and I imagined that he would have few problems breaking branches in search of food in the woods or fighting off any creature that showed him malice. The man's head was covered in thick, dark hair with natural curls and waves extending to his shoulders. I could see that his large head was perfectly formed with a strong jawline above his thick neck.

On his long, broad shoulders, this traveller wore some kind of satchel that seemed built to fit his exact shape. It was bursting with provisions like bread and meat (which I had not even tasted myself since Heureux). I imagined that the climb might be much easier with proper food instead of the forest plants and berries that had been my staple diet. In his right hand, the man carried a large skin of water that seemed ready to burst with refreshing liquid. He also held something in his left hand—books, I guessed. Walking very close to him, I could make out the titles on some of the books. They included *The Complete Map of Wandering Paths*, *The Top of the Hill*, *Friends and Companionship on the Journey*, and *Abyss Escape Manual*. I was in awe of the collection of information that this man carried lightly in just his left hand! I wanted badly to read these books and wondered how much trouble I could have saved myself had I possessed them.

I made two more salient observations of this man whom I was coming to see as the perfect traveller. He wore something over his eyes, a device that allowed him to see farther and more clearly than I surmised I was able. The mechanism resembled spectacles but had large framed lenses that the man could lower in front of his eyes as needed. I noted that he used the special lenses to look far ahead along the path as well as to scan the surrounding woods for danger. My final observation of this traveller was his name, which he wore on a large badge on his chest. *Clovis*. His name was instantly familiar to me, as though I had heard it many times before. The beauty of the badge with his name made it clear that Clovis was not from the ranks of ordinary people like me.

As I passed Clovis on the path up the hill, he looked at me with confusion in his eyes and quickened his pace. He was unable to match my speed and fell behind. I observed Clovis to be the best equipped traveller I had ever seen, possessing strength, vision, knowledge, and beauty as well as all the resources needed to travel the paths of this world. This brought me to an obvious and startling question: why was I overtaking this man on the road heading up such a steep hill? Smaller in stature with worn shoes, tattered clothing, and several scars, I should not have been able to walk faster and longer than Clovis. Even more extraordinary was how this was happening. When I stepped with my strong left leg, I observed that I did not move any further past Clovis; however, when I stepped with my weak and painful right leg, I always moved further up the path than him. I shook my head at this incredulous observation, wondering afresh about just how this forest world worked.

Needless to say, I was feeling pretty good about myself and my abilities when I heard sounds coming from somewhere behind me on the path. It was the quick shuffle of another fellow traveller poised to overtake me in his climb. If there could have been an opposite of Clovis, this man would fit the description. He was slim as a twig, lacking in the physical prowess needed to climb the enormous slope we faced. His clothes were simple, and he carried only a small sack over his bony back.

As he passed by me, I called, "Traveller! What is your name, and how can you move so quickly?"

The man answered, "Hello, sir! My name is Kareem, but I don't know what you mean about moving quickly."

"Well," I replied, "you just passed a well-equipped traveller moving as swiftly as he can, and now you are about to overtake me."

Kareem responded, "I do not know this word *passed*. What does it mean? I see someone ahead who is in trouble. He looks hungry and tired, and I plan to share my bread with him."

Unsatisfied with his answer, I pressed the matter further, questions falling out of my mouth. "Do you always move so quickly? Where are you heading, anyway? I am in search of the land with beautiful music."

"Music, ah, yes. I hear music all of the time."

"But how do you move so fast? Where are you going?" I repeated.

"I am too busy to think much about those kinds of things. I see the fellow ahead, and I really must share my bread with him. And I am concerned that there are wounds to his body and soul requiring my attention. Good day, sir."

And with that, the man surged forward up the hill at speeds I could only imagine attaining. I was more than a little incredulous at the situation and wished I could make better progress on my journey to the land of beautiful music; however, I was comforted by the knowledge that there were some walking the paths who tended to the needs and wounds of others. I turned my mind and body back to the journey and climbed up the winding slope as quickly as I could. Yet again, I was interrupted by a sound coming from behind me. It was a squeaking sound, a very uncomfortable noise, and I wondered if it came from an injured animal. With fear growing in my heart, I tried to walk swiftly, but the sounds kept getting closer. It was no use. I stopped and turned to face whatever it was that approached me from the rear.

I saw it coming at me from the lower reaches of the slope. It was smaller than a man, faster, and much louder. Whatever creature this was, it was not worried about stealth. I was perplexed to discover that the animal appeared to have the head of a human being but was much lower to the ground, and it glided in a smooth way with almost no movement from the legs at all. I found some stones and a large stick to the side of the path, which I planned to use to defend myself. The creature closed the distance between us rapidly and was upon me in what seemed like seconds. I was dumbfounded when I saw the creature up close. It was, in fact, not an animal at all but a person, an elderly lady who was propelling herself up the hill in a squeaky old chair with wheels fastened to the side.

Flabbergasted, I gave the woman my usual greeting, albeit much more softly than normal. "Greetings, dear old lady on this chair with wheels." I cleared my throat. "How are you this day?"

"Hello there, sonny! It is a wonderful day. I hear the most lovely music, and I am off to see what it is all about!"

The old lady paused and looked at me. "You are a fine-looking youngster, but you look thirsty and tired. There is tea in a flask behind my chair. Let's have refreshments together. I have biscuits as well."

As we shared hot tea and cookies, the old lady asked me many questions about my journey. I looked into her eyes and found there a softness and kindness that invited me to share my deepest struggles. She was very sparing in offering advice, but in her quiet listening, I found comfort and strength.

The kind old lady spoke to me again. "Oh, sonny, I am a little sore sitting in my chair. Could you fetch me the pillow from my bag?"

I retrieved the pillow for the lady and complied with a few more of her requests, feeling great warmth inside that I could help her. She showed no shame whatsoever about receiving my assistance, and then, without further delay, the lady returned to her climb up the steep slope toward her music. Her feeble arms grasped the handles that were fastened to the chair's wheels and turned them with astounding speed. The tires turned with such velocity that bits of dirt and gravel were hurled toward me, causing me to raise my hands to my face to protect my eyes. Within a few short moments, I could no longer see the old lady in the wheeled chair, but I did hear more reverberations from somewhere lower on the slope. I no longer feared these sounds, but I did roll my eyes at the knowledge that yet another traveller was poised to overtake me, though I was walking as fast as I could.

I did not bother to look back at the next traveller as he approached; instead, I focused on keeping my own feet moving. However, when he caught up to me, he called out a greeting, and I realized that I knew this man. It was Injud, the dedicated citizen of Heureux, committed to experiencing every pleasure possible. The last time I had met Injud, he certainly did not seem interested in journeys, and I was perturbed that he now walked the paths with greater speed and grace than I could muster.

Chapter Twenty-Six
A New Friend

Injud called to me, "Hello there, traveller. Do you remember me? It is great to see you here on our journey!"

"Yes, Injud, I remember you. The last time I saw you in Heureux, you were busy with your women and pleasures while I walked alone."

Injud looked down for a moment, but his excitement about this new journey could not be contained. "Yes, that was me. But a few days ago, I was with some friends talking late into the night. We heard the strangest, most wonderful music coming from the south and the west. In that moment, our fun in Heureux lost some of its appeal, and we set out to find the music together. I have become separated from my group and hope I am going the right way. Can you help me?"

I told Injud a little about the journey and the path ahead. I assured him that as far as I knew, he was on the path that led to the beautiful music. Though I doubted he would be content with them, I told Injud how to find and harvest berries and where he was likely to find streams nearby in the woods. Injud listened carefully to everything I said, looking grateful for the help.

Inwardly, though, I burned. How could Injud be so advanced on his journey when I had seen him revelling in every indulgence of Heureux just a short time ago? My own journey seemed so much more tumultuous—the wounds, the pain, the narrow escapes—and now this man who feasted on everything that I had sacrificed was about to overtake me. It seemed unjust. I remembered then my commitment at the abyss. Leaving that dreadful place, I had resolved on the hill that if I ever had the opportunity, I would assist anyone and everyone to avoid its clutches. In that moment, I felt something tickle my belly, as though rubbed with the lightest of feathers. I am not sure if in my head or heart, but I heard something snap. It sounded like the cracking of a dry branch, yet it came from inside me.

As I child I had heard stories about faraway lands, where water gushed from the earth into towering fountains. Much like these stories from long ago, laughter began to rise within me. I felt silly at first when the chuckles began to pour from my mouth; nonetheless, the giggles quickly turned to bellows of laughter coming from somewhere deep within. With the laughter came the realization that none of my petty concerns about rank and order on the journey mattered at all. The journey was beyond my control. Its paths were set and worn.

When I came to my senses, I found that Injud was still with me and laughing as well. We resumed our conversation about the journey, and I told him everything I had learned and even included the stories about my own weaknesses. Injud nodded eagerly as I shared, understanding that honesty and humility were more valuable than strength and power. He looked deathly serious when I spoke of the abyss, and he almost fell off the rock he sat on when I told him about the crystal waters and my experience of the music. When I finally stopped speaking, I noticed that Injud had tears in his eyes—happy tears, and thankful tears that I had shared my heart with him. Too exhausted to stay awake, and in spite of the hard ground and pesky tree roots, we both drifted into the most wonderful sleep.

In the morning, still feeling the warmth of the experience, I said my goodbyes to Injud, who, armed with the new wisdom I had provided in the night, lunged forward faster than ever on his journey up the steep hill. Try as I might, there was absolutely no way I could keep up with his pace. I felt the angry emotions try to return, but I was able to keep them at bay by reliving the laughter, and I had a growing feeling that I would meet Injud again one day. It now sounded completely normal to hear more sounds coming from the path below as yet another group approached me from the rear. This time, the voices that I heard were young and happy. Soon I was surrounded by dozens of young boys and girls, most of whom I guessed were under the age of twelve. The children were full of joy and excitement. They were dancing and singing, and I suspected that they heard the music as well. I asked a few of the children about whether they heard the music and what it sounded like. Without exception, they looked at me as though I had asked them something very strange.

One of the young girls' eyes dawned with understanding, and she replied, "I think I understand, sir. You don't hear it, do you? We hear the music all of the time!"

I shared my collection of the sweetest, juiciest berries with the children, who squealed with delight for the treat. Soon afterward, the children disappeared ahead of me, their voices blending into the sounds of the woods. The breeze blew in the trees over my head, and I heard the sound of birds calling to each in other in the distance. I recalled the words of the wise old man I had encountered on the plateau: "The intrigues of one life are far too vast and complex, immense and profound, to be explained by another."

My time in this part of the forest was making this lesson all too real for me. The idea that it was even possible to judge the journey of one human being against another was losing its grip on my imagination. For certain, it seemed to me that the very act of comparison resulted in a slower pace on the journey. I also recalled the second part of the sign that welcomed me to the forest in the beginning: "With strength and will you have begun, weak and frail to come." Maybe this cryptic message was simply an indication that when the forest is permitted to teach, a completely new and different way of thinking about strength and will emerges.

On this hill, strength seemed to be found in humility, service, and childish laughter. I shook my head again and chuckled to myself in awe of this new wisdom. I was coming to understand that success on this journey was about love, and it was about lowness, the willingness to be honest about who I was and to cease trying to put myself above any other.

On the long trek up the slope, I met one more set of travellers. I had come very far already and was entering the misty regions that I hoped signalled the end of the climb. This time, the noises I heard came from the path in front of me. There was clanging and rattling, the kind of noises that made me think of chains and shackles. Turning a corner, I saw a blaze of colour on the road ahead, almost stationary; it was a man and woman dressed in bright purple, red, and yellow. The man wore a golden crown with eleven arches. He was dressed in expensive robes and carried scrolls in one hand and a large stick in the other. The woman by his side was stunning in beauty, her blonde hair flowing down the entire length of her back. The noises that sounded like chains and shackles were in fact the sound of the travellers' heavy jewellery bumping and grinding together as they slowly moved.

As I approached the couple, the woman heard me and turned around, alerting the man in the process.

The man spoke to me at once in a booming voice. "Attention, vassal! Share with me your food and supplies."

The man spoke with a peculiar power, not the authority of the music and the crystal waters but something bound with the forests. I was instantly compelled to give him the meagre supply of berries that I carried with me and a tiny pillow that I used to cushion my head at night.

The woman called, "Give me your shoes! I require them for my journey."

Once again, I was compelled to obey and gave the woman my tattered footwear. She examined them carefully but with disdain and threw them on a pile with many other pairs of shoes. The man and the woman issued many more commands to me, and each time, I was compelled to obey as though some invisible force controlled my choices.

The man with the crown then bellowed, "Stop your journey and remain with us!"

This time, I felt no need the follow the man's command. I kept right on walking and turned away from the majestic couple. I watched frustration and rage burn in the eyes of the man and the woman. They tried to follow me up the hill, but each step they attempted forward sent them back down the hill by at least two. It was not long before I lost sight of them, and I reflected that they had not really hindered my progress at all. It was true that I had lost my shoes and a few berries, but there were more berries and forest foods to be found, and my feet were now almost as tough as my shoes from all of the walking.

The royal figures had the power to force upon me a level of superficial obedience, but the forest denied them authority over my journey. With a spring in my step and lightness in my heart, I reached the apex of this the largest hill I had ever climbed. Others may have arrived sooner than me, but I was happy just to find myself at the top.

Chapter Twenty-Seven
The Land of the Bearded Men

I expected the top of the hill to lead to somewhere very significant; after all, what sense would it make to climb that hard and for that long not to arrive at an important destination? The land where I now walked was different from the hill and the plateau before; it was unlike Heureux and not the least bit similar to the abyss. It was, however, startlingly similar to the forest I had first entered after Ennuied. The trees were tall with lush undergrowth, and there was limited visibility ahead.

It felt as though I were beginning my journey afresh, though without most of the devastating wounds I had carried early on. I lay down that night beneath a large tree and made myself as comfortable as I could. I slept well, and when I awoke, I found a small but comfortable pillow tucked under my head. I was covered with a light blanket, there were new shoes on my feet, and there, close by, lay Khalid, fast asleep himself.

I was so happy to see Khalid that my eyes filled with tears. Though he remained asleep, the mere presence of this friend and ally on the journey, the one person whom I had known my whole life, allowed me to feel the depths of emotion I had experienced on the plateau, along with hope for the future. Watching him sleep, I thought about my travelling companion. Slim, small in stature, and dressed in that same simple jacket, he was a most unsuspecting hero, yet his mere presence beside me filled me with confidence. I sat in the semi-light of dawn, content to rest under the warmth of my blanket, listening to the sounds of the forest change from night-time rustling to full-on daytime activity. Eventually, Khalid awoke and greeted me with a smile.

"Hello, stranger," he said with a cheeky smile. "I see you were in need of my supplies again."

There was no angst in Khalid's voice, and in jest I assured him that I did not need his supplies in the slightest. He grinned widely, knowing that behind my banter, I was deeply grateful for the help. I brought Khalid up to speed on the events of my journey through Heureux, the plateau, and the hill. He did not share as many details with me about his whereabouts, but he did let me know that he had climbed the same hill as I did and that he was delayed with the man and the woman dressed in fine clothes. Khalid mentioned something about helping them up with hill with nothing but the clothes on their backs. There was a sparkle in his eyes as he spoke, and I wondered how he could ever have found a way to convince this man and woman to leave their treasures behind. They struck me as two people who only understood the language of force. It did not seem proper to ask Khalid further questions, and I let the matter rest.

"What do you make of this land, Khalid? It is so much like the forest with the pools."

"Agreed, it is a land of great wisdom and many threats to the journey. We will do well to tread carefully. Things may not be as they seem."

We set off together, walking on a path of dark, packed soils in reds and browns. The route led us through stands of massive trees, many streams, and a plentiful supply of excellent berries. After a long day of walking, Khalid and I built a fire and sat down to rest for the night. While we discussed the sights of the day in the firelight, an elderly bearded man approached our camp and sat down with us. This would have struck me as odd during my life in Ennuied; however, I was long accustomed to strange events in the forests. The man said nothing at first but watched us as we talked. He appeared to listen carefully and looked at us as though analysing every detail. Khalid was the smartest man I knew and the best friend I had ever had, but occasionally I wondered if there were others who could better guide me on my journey. He seemed to come and go according to his own mind and was more interested in my heart and health than which path to take. I wondered if perhaps this odd-looking fellow was a guide.

The old man wore a robe with fine embroidery forming mysterious symbols. He carried himself as one accustomed to speaking and performing valued ceremonies in front of many. He carried a crooked cane in one hand and a long, thin stick in the other. The elder's skin was pale, as though he did not see a lot of sunlight, and his hands were smooth and clean. His face itself was wrinkled in such a way as to give the impression that he had spent his lifetime thinking about serious and weighty things. His eyes were filled with an energy that I could not define. It was not the joyful ease of Khalid's sparkle or the dead energy of the mayor of Heureux. A thought flashed through my mind that I was looking into the crazed eyes of someone whose mind had cracked under tremendous strain. When I heard the man speak, though, I quickly dismissed that idea as foolish and felt bad for thinking it.

With the crackle of the fire in the background, the old man spoke. "Who are you with, travellers?"

Puzzled, I responded, "We are on a journey walking together. We are with each other."

In the man's face, I saw a small flash of anger that was quickly replaced with a more serene expression. The man proceeded to ask us many more questions.

"In which town did you begin your journey?

"Do you like or dislike the citizens of Heureux?

"Do you believe the music comes from one place, or that it moves from location to location?

"When you hear the music, do you remove your hat?"

He asked many more questions, and I shared with him some of the stories of my journey. After some time, the wrinkled old man asked for my opinion on whether the fodder nut lovers of Ennuied should have been allowed to grow the nuts within the village. I was dumbfounded with this question because I was more than confident that I had not told the man that part of my story. The questions continued, and while they seemed strange, unusual, and completely unrelated to what we were learning on the journey, we did our best to answer each one. With each response we provided, the man took the thin stick in his left hand and swung it either to the left or to the right. Most of our responses resulted in the swinging of his stick to the left and a barely perceptible twitch above his left eye. When our response warranted a swinging of the stick to the right, there was no twitch and a faint smile appeared.

The interrogation continued like this until the man asked us, "The fellow travellers you meet, what will become of them on their journey?"

I was taken aback by the question. How was I supposed to know where others' journeys would lead them? He pressed me for my opinion, and so I explained to him what I had learned on the way up the hill and told him what the wise man on the plateau had said about the mystery of each person's journey. The robed old man grimaced when I mentioned the wise fellow I had met on the plateau. As I talked about what I had learned so far, the man's stick continued to move from the right to the left and back and forth many times. He appeared to grow anxious, and the crazed look in his eyes became more pronounced. Unable to decide whether some of my comments warranted a right or left wave of the stick, the man changed the subject and excused himself. He walked off into the night, leaving Khalid and me alone with the fire once again. I probed Khalid for his thoughts on the man with the stick, but Khalid just rolled his eyes, said goodnight, and drifted off to sleep.

Chapter Twenty-Eight
The Sorters of the Forest

I reasoned that this man must live somewhere nearby, and I wondered what else we would discover as we continued on our trek. Before setting out in the morning, I climbed the tallest tree I could find and took a look ahead. The path appeared to wind through the foliage for some distance before entering a part of the forest where the trees were smaller. I saw smoke coming from this area, and when I looked very carefully, I observed what seemed to be the movement of people on the paths. I climbed down the tree and excitedly told Khalid what I had seen. Khalid was also eager to see what lay ahead on the road, though he cautioned me to remember that in this type of forest, there were both wonderful things and grave dangers.

Khalid and I made our way through the winding paths I had seen from atop the tree. We enjoyed a plentiful supply of the most wonderful berries, tender seed pods that were not bitter, and some fresh, clear water. Exiting the winding paths and approaching the stand of smaller trees, Khalid and I saw someone on the road ahead. Initially, I was sure we were approaching the same man who had visited us at the fire the night before. This bearded old man wore a similar style of robe and also carried a thick staff in his left hand. In his right hand, the old man carried a large basket. As he walked through the forest, the bearded man picked up material from the forest floor, and after careful examination, he either placed what he found in the basket or threw it on the ground in disgust.

Once we were very close to the man, I realized that it was definitely not the man from the night before, and I attempted to introduce myself to him. The man looked me in the eye for the briefest of moments before looking me up and down carefully. Hope arose within me that the old man was observing my needs and pain and intended to offer me some kind of assistance on my quest. Rather, the man did the strangest thing; he bent down to examine my shoes and located a pebble that must have met some kind of criteria that only his kind understood. He retrieved the pebble from my shoe with glee and placed it in his basket, showing no further interest in Khalid or me.

Too stunned to speak, I stood in silence and listened to the sounds of movement all around me. Khalid and I located one of many fallen trees in this area and sat down to see what would happen next. Through the undergrowth, I sighted two women working close by, one older and the other barely an adult. The women were dressed alike, wearing simple long dresses that were the same colour as the old man's robe. The elder lady was vigorously examining the trees, placing tags on certain branches and hacking off others, some dead and more living. It was difficult to discern how the older lady chose which branches to tag and which to cleave. After watching for an hour, the best I could figure was that she tagged only the branches with foliage of a particular faded shade of green.

The older lady frequently discussed what she had read in a precious book and, far more often, what one of the bearded men had said in a meeting of some kind. The young lady, who did not share the same enthusiasm for branch hacking, stopped frequently to daydream and gaze to the south and to the west. My heart was drawn to the younger, and I pondered inviting her to join Khalid and me on our journey. This business of identifying branches to destroy and discard seemed to me a form of insanity. Cutting out the deadwood made some sense (though the forest was more than capable of taking care of this task on its own), but cutting off green life nurtured by the sun and the music because it was a different shade of green was, to me, unfathomably foolish.

We saw many others at work in the forest, all dressed in the same drab colours, busy with one kind of task or another, always sorting, accepting or rejecting—usually the latter. There were little boys dressed in small robes scanning the ground for this and that with unsmiling faces. There were young robed men using their great strength to move giant rocks into piles and to cut down majestic trees that were the wrong shade of green. The whole scene eerily reminded me of the lady who had tried to organize me alongside the abyss.

I could no longer hold myself back, and I approached one of the strong young men and asked him, "What on earth are you doing? Why are you rearranging the forest? What is so important that you have forgotten about everything else to do this work?"

The man looked at me with irritation and more than a little condescension. "We are busy at the most important work. We are getting it right, finally!"

I responded with an alarming degree of arrogance. "I have heard the most beautiful music, and I seek to find the source."

The man looked stunned, and then his face contorted with rage. "You have never heard the real music! How could you? Look at your clothes! You have no robe! Nothing about you is right! We sort and separate, search and find, divide and decide because we have long known that when we get it right, the music will come to us and we will revel in its beauty. You, you are nothing but a vagabond and a drifter. You have no dedication to this important work!"

I did not back down, but I did begin to calm down, filled with compassion for this man who seemed to me trapped in meaningless toil, and I explained to him what I had learned about the music. I described how I had indeed heard the music and that it was too wonderful to fully describe. I explained that music always came to me at my weakest moments, not when I had it right, and how it always seemed like more of a surprise than something I had figured out. I told him about how I looked to the south and the west when I felt shattered inside, and the music seemed to enter through the cracks in my heart, not every time but often enough for me to keep looking. I went on to describe what I had discovered on the hill just below the land we stood upon now, how it was the old and the weakened, those that cared for the broken, and the children who heard the music most clearly. The man looked unsettled as I shared with him the raw and real events of my journey, but when I came to the part about the children and the music, he guffawed out loud.

"Children! Now I know that you are out of your mind. They don't know or understand anything. Why, I have seen children who could not sort a rock from a branch, and you say they can hear the music. Get out of here!"

Khalid and I decided to walk away from this man and leave him to his toil. We followed the path a little further and came to two mysterious buildings; the first appeared to be a majestic home, and the second looked like a store front, closed and secured with heavy chains and giant locks. Peeking in the window, Khalid and I saw that the shop was filled with all the supplies anyone on a journey could want or need. There were medical kits, blankets, satchels, books, maps, and small containers for storing food, water skins, and much more. Sitting on a simple chair outside the door of the home was the bearded old fellow from the fire the night before. Unexpectedly, the man looked happy to see us, perhaps having forgotten his frustrating work with the stick.

"Hello again, travellers. Come and see my delightful and pleasing home. We have built this home for travellers like you!"

Khalid and I approached the strange old man, and I thought now was a good time to make a better impression. "This is a striking home. You must be very happy to live here."

The man looked taken aback by my statement. "Oh, I see. Yes, it is a remarkable home, but it is not for any of us to live in. It is for the people of Heureux and people like you to see!"

Without further ado, the old man ushered us inside for a tour of the grand residence. He talked without stopping for the next hour or so as we walked through each room. We began in an entryway that was, in fact, the largest room in the house. It was filled with ornate furnishings and decorated with great care and attention. There were chairs and benches to sit on, all covered in thick red velvet. From the entryway, we made our way to the front sitting room, which was also well-furnished with deep sofas, wood framed chairs, and delicate looking tables for tea. Blocking the wide entryway to the room were a number of posts with a padded rope running between them.

When I attempted to step over the rope into the room, the old man gave me a harsh swat with the heavy walking stick he carried in his right hand. It stung, but I was used to much worse pains in the forest, and I paid little attention. Soon we were off to see the bedrooms. There were many chambers, all furnished in much the same way with single beds covered with stylish bedding and beautiful wooden furniture. Here again, the rooms were closed off with padded ropes, and outside each bedroom was a simple cot with faded sheets and blankets with holes in them. I asked the man what the cots were for, and looking at me as though I were a child, he replied that they were used for sleeping. The bathing rooms were among the strangest rooms in the house, surrounded by windows. I made a mental note never to ask to use the commode while near this place. The old man was especially proud to show us a kitchen that was filled with fancy cooking tools and large storerooms. He allowed us to explore the magnificent supply rooms, which were well-stocked with great quantities of simple bread and water.

After completing the tour, the old man stated that after seeing the wonders of this house, the citizens of Heureux would be sure to rush to join his folk. While it was not a very nice thing to say, I could not resist adding a heartfelt, "I don't think so."

Chapter Twenty-Nine
Magdala

Still watching and waiting near the building, Khalid and I saw another traveller come from the winding path into this strange section of the forest. He looked desperately poor and in great need of care and attention. His shoes were missing, and his feet were bloodied from rocks and sticks on the path; dirt, sweat, and blood mixed together, making it difficult to tell the colour of the traveller's skin. The man's pants were ripped in many places, and a knotted string held them up at the waist. His shirt was no better, but what bothered me the most was the lost look in the man's eyes, as though he had reached the end of his strength some time ago.

I found the old man and asked him to help the poor traveller. He ran into the street, using his walking stick to propel him quickly, and looked the man over, carefully poking and prodding him with the other stick that remained in his left hand.

"Well, he has pants of the correct colour. Poor traveller! What is the difference between beach bark disease and canker? If constructing a foundation for a building of high tonnage, would you use a basanite or a granophyre?"

The old man waited for some response from the man, who could only muster, "I am th-th-thirsty."

The old man looked genuinely sad when he explained, "This man knows nothing of the forest, and I cannot help him. The stores for the journey will remain chained under lock and key."

Khalid, the most calm and kind person I had ever known, was incensed. He took a stone and threw it at the locked store front with mind-numbing speed. The rock pierced the front window of the building and appeared to exit the back of the structure. He kept on throwing the rocks until the inside of the building was filled with dust and debris. With no fear whatsoever for consequence, Khalid beckoned the poor traveller and me to continue on the path. Once we were well away from the buildings, we shared our berries and water with the young man, who continued to appear confused but consumed the food and drink eagerly.

Now a trio, the three of us walked further down the path. I took the lead while Khalid hung back with our new friend, who managed to say that his name was Magdala and that he had left some village or another a long, long time ago. I suspected that Magdala's mind had snapped completely and I was relieved that Khalid was walking with him.

The surrounding woods were interesting in that the trees themselves appeared younger and less established than others we had seen, but the land itself felt old. There were hills and mounds that looked unnatural, and I suspected that they were the remnants of ancient sites, perhaps the location of solemn events that took place long ago. While I could not see any people other than our little entourage, I felt as though a million souls had passed by, and each had left a small part of him- or herself behind for others to feel and sense.

The trees thinned out somewhat, and I could see that the land was indeed covered in mounds that were not a function of natural geology. Most of the small hills were concealed with grass and shrubs, and large trees grew out of many. A few of the mounds looked exposed and were surrounded by fencing and signage. I led the group toward one of these mounds. Taller than any of us and around six paces across, the mound appeared to be constructed of heavy rocks filled with clay and soil. On the fence hung a sign made of wood, much cleaner than most of the road signs I had seen on my journey. It said:

Here, long ago, lived Thomas Tweedsmore

The music played in the fall season and was
heard by many, beautiful and strong

Thomas wore black slacks and a white
shirt, a lover of eggs and chicken

For hundreds of years the faithful have gathered at this spot

Eggs and chicken freely given, black slacks
and white shirts worn by all

I chuckled aloud as I read the sign. I turned to Khalid to ask if he also found the sign funny. Khalid explained to me that the sign was not intended as humour but to encourage people that if they did these things, they would hear the music just like Thomas Tweedsmore. I was a little startled to hear this, and disappointed. What possible value could the music hold if it came and went based on what one wore and which foods were eaten? Those things were all superficial and had nothing to do with the kinds of painful events on my journey. I thought to myself that clothing dresses the outside of the body and food simply goes in and out. As for days and seasons, I was quite sure that the music I was hearing had nothing to do with that. Being honest with myself, I realized that I was not actually certain what day and month it was anymore. In Ennuied, I had been very concerned with such things. I looked beside me toward Magdala, knowing that if we told him to wear black and white and eat eggs and chicken, he certainly would, but I was more than certain that those things would not help him to hear the music he needed so badly.

When I reread the sign, I still found it amusing, but one look at Khalid's grim face blew the fun out of me like the blowing of the great fire bellows at the fodder grass festivals. We walked away from the fenced mound silently. There were many similar hillocks nearby, and I guessed a lot more that I could not see.

I was about to ask Khalid for more of his thoughts, but he was already ahead of me with Magdala, heading toward a building up the path. This building was large and old looking; greying pillars towered above the large entryway. At the doorway stood six bearded men in robes, different people from any we had met to this point but with a similar look and feel about them. I caught up and walked ahead of Khalid and Magdala, who had slowed to a saunter, and approached the robed men.

Chapter Thirty
The Ancient Writings

I walked beneath a grand archway and into a small esplanade. There I greeted the bearded men and expressed interest about what was inside the grand structure. One of the men in a robe some shade of brown answered me. "Here are found the ancient scrolls and writings from the walkers of the paths who came before us."

I looked back at Khalid with a glint in my eye again. "Khalid," I whispered, "this bearded one says that you can find out about the paths in some old books. Let's move along; we know that books can't teach us the lessons of the road."

Khalid looked at me with the same look as he had at the mound and corrected me. "These writings from the past are valuable beyond measure; we would be wise to enter this building and learn from those who have gone before us."

It was all too apparent that Khalid was much cleverer than me, but I did not mind because he never gloated or made me feel small or stupid. I did wonder if I would be better off walking behind Khalid rather than taking the lead as often as I did, yet again, Khalid did not seem perturbed either way.

We approached another of the bearded old men at the door, and I spoke up. "We wish to look at the books in this magnificent library. May we go in?"

"Of course, young ones. Please enter and freely explore the thoughts and writings of the ancients. Please freely browse the texts in sections eighteen and sixty only. Ah, yes, please freely avoid all other sections. And one more thing: please keep the texts in the baskets in which you find them. Oh, and I will come with you for certain."

The man had that crazed look in his eyes that I had seen in the grey-robed man by the fire the other night. I noticed that it was not a hateful or sinister look, but it reminded me of the strain a child might feel if asked to move a boulder twice his size but who felt compelled by his parents to try.

Another of the old robed men approached us and motioned for us to walk away from the man we had spoken with. "Don't listen to that one. He thinks he has the writings figured out." Then the old man broke into a raging tirade. "He is misled! Stay away from that foolish man! We who are truly learned know that section ten contains the writings that matter. Come with me, and I will show you. Or better yet, let me just explain it to you myself!"

There was absolutely no way I wanted to go with this man. He sounded like the men of the council in Ennuied defending the supremacy of fodder grass. Sitting away from the group was another man, as old as the others but smaller and dressed in simple clothes; he reminded me of the wonderful fellow I had met on the plateau. This man smiled toward us knowingly and did not so much invite us to speak with him as assume we would come to him after the others.

"If you seek a look inside, you go right ahead. In this land, there are many wonders—and dangers as well, but I suspect you know that very well already."

Thinking I was being especially shrewd and testing the man, I asked, "Are there any sections we should avoid?"

The man simply replied, "You are in good company." He nodded toward Khalid and pointed to the library door.

As we walked toward the entrance, the old men in robes tried to block our way but were ultimately unable to stop us. We opened the doors and were greeted by the pleasant and inviting yet dusty smell of printed books. The building was cavernous in size, mysteriously much bigger on the inside than seemed possible by looking at the outside of the structure.

"Khalid, where should we look and explore? There is so much to read!"

Khalid replied, "I want to find something for Magdala, just what he needs. I suggest you find out if you are as alone on your journey as you feel most of the time."

I had not talked to Khalid about my feelings of isolation and loneliness, because I did not feel that way very often when he was around, and I was surprised at his intuition. I walked around for quite a while without stopping in any one location. The library contained literally hundreds of numbered sections but was divided roughly equally between the eastern and western sides of the building with some overlap in the middle. A few of the books had been piled in baskets that looked out of place in these halls. The art on the walls, the lighting, and the general feel of the library was quite distinct between the eastern and western halves of the cavernous space.

A strange thing happened to me at this point; I began to feel an intense hunger inside me, not to eat but to read. I had certainly never felt this way about any of the readings on fodder grass lore in Ennuied. I began to read parts of certain books. I discovered that in this place, I was able to read with incredible speed, much faster than I imagined possible. I moved from book stack to book stack, reading parts of some texts and others in their entirety; from east to west and in between, I explored.

I don't know precisely how long this continued, but without question, many cycles of dark and light passed, and all the while I had no interest in food or drink. Still immersed in my books, I realized I was no longer alone. Khalid and Magdala, or someone who looked a little like Magdala, were sitting next to me.

"How long have you been with me?" I asked. "I am sorry I was so captivated by my reading that I did not even notice."

Khalid smiled at me warmly. "Oh, we have been here awhile."

I could not believe the look of Magdala, who had transformed from a forlorn, broken human being into a powerful and not unattractive young man. Clean-looking hair hung past his neck and into his face. A strong chin and piercing eyes, combined with a fit body no longer hunched in pain, gave him the look that many men seek in vain. I asked them what they had been reading that could have brought about such changes. Magdala opened his mouth and spoke with a deep and thoughtful tone. He told me how he had sat on a balcony looking out to the south and west. All the while he sat, Khalid brought him books to read, some simple and some complex. Without a hint of shame, Magdala confessed that he enjoyed the children's books the best. Magdala paused as if there was more to say but he was not sure he should share it with another person.

"And I heard the music as I sat and read. I don't know how to explain this, but the music had colour. It was blue and green, and while I heard it with my ears, I saw it with my eyes. I felt strength enter my bones, and where I was broken, I began to feel whole."

I was happy for Magdala, wistful yet lacking the jealousy that might have consumed me earlier in my journey. Khalid and Magdala were inquisitive and wondered what I had been reading about. I explained that I had read more accounts than I had thought possible of others on the journey. In the narratives, I had found that many had walked a similar path to me—some from the east, others in the west, and even a few in between. It was not where the story came from that drew me; it was the accounts of tremendous strength visiting the inadequate and rectitude within bankruptcy that kept me reading and gave me hope that the land of the beautiful music was in fact somewhere for people like me. Of course, there were many other stories of power and greed and arrogance, and endless tales about judgement, being right, and punishment, but these were much less compelling to me. While I knew for certain those types of things were a real part of the forests, they were not the driving force behind much of anything on my journey. In the ancient writings, there was frequent discussion of rules and regulations, reminding me of the bearded men and their sorting. I noticed that these rules brought life or death to many; those based in love and lowness alone held the power to build rather than destroy.

Chapter Thirty-One
A Secret Garden for All

Our trio left the ancient library and continued on the path; food and drink were now on our minds. The plants in this part of the woods were a lot like those in the forest by the pools. Berries and forest foods were plentiful, and I thought they were in fact even easier to find and tastier than those in that first tall forest. There were also trees with blossoms and fruits that I had never seen before. Some of the beautiful looking fruits had a foul smell to them, so we stuck with berries and fruits that were familiar and pleasant. The path we followed led to a wooden bridge spanning a large creek with clean, swiftly moving water. There were fences around the stream itself, but with some effort we breached them and enjoyed some of the coolest, freshest water of the journey. Shortly after crossing the stream, we climbed for a while and were met with a stunning vista of the lands ahead.

We saw what looked like many communities and developments nestled within the forest. Just beyond these lands was what looked like a deep blue mountain range towering over the scene. As I looked far ahead, I saw flashes of bright light in the mountains and noticed that they were constantly changing shape and size. I realized then that this was not a mountain range but the edge of a massive weather system. With a sense of foreboding like one might feel reading a book about a war or disaster from the safety and comfort of the sitting room, we set off once again through this pleasant country.

The path we followed wound back and forth, taking us downward at a safe and amiable speed. The sweet smell of blossoms, water, and green plants became stronger as we sauntered along. The trees on the sides of the path became still more diverse with unfamiliar types and varieties, and further within the forest there were green plants and flowers. I noticed roses, yellow jasmine, the largest gardenia I had ever seen, and many unusual blossoms that smelled wonderful. After we had walked a few minutes, the trees began to return to the normal varieties that comprised most of this section of the woods, and we could no longer see any flowers. I stopped to look back for a moment and caught a glimpse of movement in the corner of my eye.

I motioned for the others to stop, and we made our way back to the location of the movement and peered carefully into the woods and through the flowers. We all noticed a rustling in the trees beyond what the lovely breeze could have caused. My mind turned back to the dogs I had seen in the trees early in my journey, and I was satisfied to let them be and continue on our way. Magdala, the changed man he was, voiced his opinion that we really better take a look into the forest because perhaps someone needed our assistance.

Reluctantly, I followed Magdala and Khalid into the woods. There was no path here at all; we made our way by wandering around trees and pushing through bushes, instinctively trying to avoid disturbing the flowers. It was tough going, and though our progress was at first slow, the trees soon thinned out and we found ourselves walking on finely manicured grass of deep green in a world of blinding colour and wonderful fragrances. Near the grass were pathways intricately constructed from fine stones placed together so tightly they resembled a single slab of marble.

On a cosy bench beside the path sat an older lady, gazing thoughtfully at a patch of yellow-red blanket flowers. She turned and looked at us without a hint of surprise or malice.

"Hello, young ones," she chimed. "Welcome to our gardens. Enjoy and listen carefully, for the music plays here often."

Khalid and Magdala were occupied looking around and sniffing at this flower and that. Only I seemed left with curiosity and questions: "Who built this place? Do you live here? Are there others?"

In spite of my flurry of questions, the old lady remained calm and relaxed. "Many have laboured in these gardens, and I suppose I have done my part. All who wish to come are welcomed here, big and small, old and young."

I continued to converse with this pleasant woman for a long time. I asked her to tell me who else was in the gardens, and I asked why there were no entrances to the gardens from the road.

"Oh, sonny, we have tried to make paths and signs many times because all are welcome, but, you see, true paths are made by the feet of many, and far too few visit this garden."

"Who does visit here? It must take many of you to maintain this beautiful place."

"Oh, young one, I do like you! But you must understand the garden shapes us far more than we shape the garden. The roots of the trees, the plants and flowers—well, they date from times before the oldest scroll in the library, and while many of the books point to this place, people can find this garden without a book. As for who comes here now, well, not as many as could, that is for sure. Mostly women and children it is, and many very old ones like me."

"What about the robed men, the ones with the beards?"

The old lady actually looked cross for a moment. "They seldom notice this place, and once they do, they often lose their robes and beards. But enough unhappy talk; eat the fruit of the trees! You will find nothing here that hurts your stomach. Drink from the waters, and most of all, listen for the music which, as I said, plays here often."

With that, the lady slowly rose from the bench where she sat, picked up a well-worn cane, and walked leisurely into the trees. I could not see Khalid or Magdala, and I was very eager to explore the gardens myself. There was something magical about this garden off the path, this strange place found in the midst of the lands of the robed and bearded men. Once we entered this particular garden, it seemed that there was no one path to follow but rather a myriad of choices and opportunities that seemed to be made just for me. As I explored, I found the kinds of trees that made me feel safe and secure and scents that brought peace to my travel-weary heart. I was also struck by the most profound sense of déjà vu; everything looked familiar. The trees became taller, and the plants, a deeper green. Ahead I observed a glimmer of light coming from the ground level, and I ran forward, disbelieving what my eyes were telling me. I found myself staring at the crystal pool I had found in the forest early in my journey, or at least one that looked precisely the same. The light shimmered from the surface, showing a smaller, leaner, happier, and much healthier reflection.

I wasted no time and jumped straight into the wonderful water, diving deeply. The water felt refreshingly cool yet warmed me on the inside. As I swam, I felt sadness for the people I had treated harshly on the journey, even those who had mistreated me, and I felt grateful that Magdala had joined us. The music followed almost at once, mingling with the waters, and it was very different from any other time. As beautiful as ever, the music was more urgent and even disquieting. It did not make me feel anxious *per se*, yet it left me with a profound sense of foreboding, and my thoughts were turned to the storm cloud I had seen from atop the hill. There was something in the mountainous clouds that was set against me—or set against the music; I was not sure which. I had long felt that I was somehow resisted in my journey.

Reflecting on my paths out of Ennuied, it was as though I had walked against the flow of an invisible river or fought a raging wind at every moment. Most of those I met on my journey did not seem to face this resistance, and I did not know if it was that we were heading in different directions or that perhaps many more experienced the resistance but could not identify what it was, that force that left them feeling alone in their struggle to do the right thing. In an instant, in the depths of that crystal pool, I knew that I would face tremendous resistance from the storm that lay ahead and that the music in me would be a tremendous force for what is good.

I left the pool feeling an uneasy confidence about what was to come. I found the others, and we made our way out of the gardens, through the trees, and back to the path. None of us were inclined to talk very much about what we had each experienced in the garden, but it was clear we had all undergone something profound and heard the music. I felt wonderful about travelling in a group after spending so much time by myself, and I suggested to the others that we consider trying to join one of the communities up ahead. Khalid and Magdala agreed that travelling in groups was a good idea, though Magdala was much more enthused than Khalid about joining any of the nearby communities.

Chapter Thirty-Two
The Spring Green Community

The communities we had seen from the hilltop were now much closer. They looked oddly similar to one another but with distinct differences. Each community seemed to be comprised of buildings with their own colour, and what looked like large boxes surrounded each building. We discovered that these boxes—*bins*, really—were used to sort the forest materials much like the bearded folk we had met earlier had done. Some of the community colours were very different from the others, such as the Orange Community and the Deep Blue Community, and others were similar with only slight differences in the shade of their colours.

We spent some time walking among the communities, exploring and entering a number of them. The residents seemed very happy to have us search the outer portions of their lands, and many encouraged us to come join them with broad smiles. Disturbingly, each of the communities appeared to be led by a man with a beard, and we hoped to have a better experience than we had had with bearded men thus far.

We noticed that some of the communities appeared to be in disarray with their work. They had expanded close to each other's borders, leading to disruptions in what I called their *bin-management procedures*. Members of the Green Community had begun to explore lands traditionally controlled by the Red Community, bringing new items to sort into their green bins. We noticed that there was quite a bit of arguing about which of the established green bins should be used to store the new materials. Some advocated one bin or another, while others suggested that new green bins be developed. As I listened, I heard one lady suggest borrowing one of the red group's bins. This suggestion led to a tremendous ruckus and many arguments.

Being so close together, the red and green communities sometimes watched each other work. I noticed another problem develop when someone observed that an item from the green bin marked *Do Not Touch —Danger* was freely placed in normal bins by the Red Community. The suggestion that this item may in fact not be dangerous brought about tremendous dissension within the green group, who had invested their time and energy into the design of platforms, fences, gates, and supervision surrounding this bin. From the sounds of the arguments on both sides, I suspected that the green group would not reach a decision on this topic for some time.

Privately, I wondered if it was really necessary for these people to sort every single thing they found into a bin. By their very nature, objects were bound to fit into many overlapping categories. Also, most groups seemed to equate their bin systems with getting things right in order to hear the music. My journey and encounters with the music seemed so different from this. It was not that the items of the forest were all the same—of course they were not—but the act of separating and sorting seemed to me an effort to control the forest when the very mind of the forest seemed set against control. I shared these thoughts quietly with Khalid, concerned that he would think I was very mistaken.

Khalid was thoughtful and replied to me, "The music often asks us to make difficult decisions. When we listen to the music, we are repeatedly required to make choices, even counterintuitive choices, in the name of love." He looked me dead in the eye. "These choices we make in the dance with the music are often painful, seldom without a cost, and always based on purposeful love. It is this dance with the music and the tough choices that follow that are so easily confused with this business of sorting."

Though I often thought of myself as clever and wise, I realized afresh that Khalid was miles ahead of me in that department; the way he worded things always helped me to understand. The decisions I had made about this or that when hearing the music were about love, not about satisfying the music with my great abilities to order the forest into categories of right and wrong, big and small, helpful and hurtful.

Foolishly, I came out of the trees and approached a Green Community member with a small beard to tell him what I had learned. Whereas I had felt welcome to join every community prior to this one, the man made it clear I was no longer welcome. With a look of both pride and pity, he suggested that his group was far too serious about the music to listen to my whimsical ramblings.

I returned to Khalid and Magdala, and we continued to search for a community that we could join. We found one group that looked promising near the edge of this part of the forest. This group, too, had a colour of its own: a light green, much like the colour of the first green shoots of spring. They, too, had bins of the same colour but fewer of them, and they had decorated a large part of their land with benches and flowers, and many were gathered trying to hear the music. The smell of smoke hung in the air, not exactly like the smoke that hung over the abyss and blew into Heureux, but not altogether different, either. It was the odour of destruction, yet it also smelled a little of the kind of fire that keeps one warm during the cold winter.

We approached a man who looked like a leader in this group. Dressed in light green, he seemed a little younger than the other robed men, and his beard looked partially shaven, as though he had tried without complete success to remove it. The man was very glad to see us and took a particular interest in Magdala. We discovered that this fellow with the partial beard was named Lucrecio. He invited us to join his group, and we sat together at dusk eating fine bread and drinking wine, listening for the music in the spring green meadow. Lucrecio spoke to us compellingly about how the music was not really about the sorting of this or that into the bins. He was not sure what it was about, but he intended to listen and find out. I was moved by the words he spoke and thought that perhaps, finally, I had found a community to journey with me.

The three of us slept peacefully that night with full stomachs, stars in our eyes, and the smell of wood burning smoke. After an early morning bite to eat with the community, we asked how we could help out. Lucrecio assigned us a job building a stylish gazebo in the meadow where we had listened for the music the night before. Many of us laboured together, and soon our work was finished. I noticed that instead of using the gazebo, the members of the community left the meadow in the direction of a part of the lands I had not yet seen. Khalid remained at the gazebo while I followed the group, and Magdala walked off in a completely different direction.

The group of men and women who had left the meadow walked calmly, as though leaving at midday were the most normal thing in the world. We re-entered the forest following a winding path and soon arrived at yet another field. It was similar to the meadow we had just left, except that there were no benches or gazebos. Rather, there was a collection of ten spring-green bins. While this was a smaller number of bins than I had seen at any of the other communities, the group was just as zealous about sorting the contents as any other community. I asked them why they were doing all of this sorting rather than listening in the other meadow, but they looked at me as though I had lost my mind and continued their work.

Feeling disappointed but not surprised, I exited the meadow with the bins; I was becoming accustomed to the powerful human desire to sort, perhaps better described as the need to control, to be the master of the forest. I returned to the meadow with the benches and gazebo and sat awhile, thinking by myself. Khalid joined me, and we remained together for some time, listening for the music without any need to talk.

Khalid interrupted the silence. "We should find Magdala. I feel uneasy."

Chapter Thirty-Three
The Music as Fire

We left in search of our friend, checking the nearby fields and some of the buildings we had seen earlier. We observed a gathering taking place toward the main road and heard what sounded like a tremendous ruckus there. Khalid and I looked at each other with alarm and made our way toward the disturbance at a running pace. On account of my persistent limp and the pain in my right hip, I could not keep up with Khalid, who ran like the wind itself.

I arrived to find Magdala and Khalid in the midst of an intense argument with the members of the Spring Green Community. Many in the group were yelling at Magdala, accusing him of breaking an age-old tradition of the forest; apparently, he had become too close to the wrong member of the community and invited this person to a moonlit walk in the meadows.

We discovered that in all of the communities, meadow walks were closely supervised and that there were rules about who could walk in the meadow together and when this was appropriate. I raised my voice as loud as I could, explaining that Magdala would have had no way of knowing this rule and asking whether this was even a good rule to begin with, but I could scarcely hear my own speech above the screams and chants of the Spring Green Community. Khalid seemed to feel no need to explain Magdala's actions and instead placed himself between Magdala and the mob, receiving many blows in the process. The crowds of the community pressed in against Khalid and Magdala, and a sick feeling entered my heart; I knew this would not end well.

I looked around the crowd, searching for the half-bearded leader, Lucrecio. I spied him sitting on the ground by himself, away from the fire and the battle, lost as though deep in thought.

I ran toward him yelling, "Lucrecio! Lucrecio! I think they are going to kill Magdala. Come quickly!"

Lucrecio heard my words clearly and came to attention as if exiting a trance. He hesitated for a moment, indecision on his face, and with the determination of a mountain climber on his final ascent, Lucrecio walked toward the chanting crowd with a powerful stride and a strength and determination in his eyes that I had not noticed before.

Lucrecio entered the foray and spoke with tremendous volume. "Silence!"

Most of the crowd settled down to listen to Lucrecio, while some paid no attention whatsoever and continued heckling Magdala and Khalid alike.

Lucrecio spoke to the people. "Is not this desire to punish contrary to everything we have learned in the Spring Green Community? Why do you want to hurt this man? This man is on a journey and has come so far already."

A few of the people nodded in agreement at Lucrecio's words, but the majority of the crowd continued to demand justice.

One fellow stood up to confront Lucrecio. "It is all fine to speak in platitudes and nice-sounding sayings, but we have sorted right and wrong for generations, and this man is an affront to the categories. What service are we to the forests if we allow this deed to go unpunished?"

There were many murmurs of agreement from young and old. Lucrecio stood tall in the midst of the tension as a peaceful look of resignation appeared on his face. Before he even spoke, the smell of wood-burning smoke became strong, almost chokingly so, and I was sure I heard the crackling of fire in the wind. With an awe and wonder that brought goose bumps and tears to my eyes, I realized the sounds of crackling and fire were the beginnings of the most awesome hearing of the music I had yet encountered. The song I heard was both beautiful and grave. There were bass sounds that felt like they arose from the centre of the earth, and the crackling sound of flames entered my ears and my heart.

Perfectly attuned with the music, Lucrecio spoke. "For generations we have spent our time and treasure sorting the goods of the forest, and we have thought this was the work of the music. We have been mistaken! I know now with certainty that many of our groupings are fundamentally flawed; moreover, this is but a destitute and ruinous imitation of the work of the music, which comes to all who listen. Enough of the bins and rules. Free this man to hear the music and to drink the crystal waters! Do this, or know well that you have set yourself against the heartbeat of the music itself!"

As Lucrecio spoke, the strangest thing happened. The smallest whiff of smoke appeared around his mouth, and I wondered for a moment if he was somehow breathing fire. Shortly, I noticed that the smoke was not in fact coming from his mouth but from the side of his face with the beard. Small flames appeared in the beard and quickly consumed what was left of his facial hair. Lucrecio was now beardless with just a few painful looking burn marks where his half-beard had been moments before. The small flames that Lucrecio endured were negligible compared to what was coming in the wind. The glow of fire appeared in the woods nearby, and fuelled by the wind, it was not long until a raging firestorm was unleashed on the lands of the Spring Green Community. The flames devoured everything in their path; buildings, trees, and grass were consumed.

With the advancing flames, I thought it unwise to seek shelter in anything flammable, so I stayed where I was. The crowd dispersed, running this way and that, but Lucrecio, Khalid, Magdala, and I, along with some others, stayed where we were. The fire roared and burned, and a hot wind breathed on us with such intensity that I thought it was the fire itself, yet because there was nothing near us that could fuel the fire, we were spared destruction, escaping with singed hair and a few small burns.

As quickly as it came, the fire disappeared, and our little posse set out to explore the damage to the Spring Green Community. The destruction was both awesome and perplexing. The field with the gazebo where the people sat to hear the music was virtually unscathed, though the structure itself and the benches were destroyed. We followed the paths to the field with the sorting bins. Here the devastation was more substantial. The fire consumed the grass and many of the trees as well as all of the bins, save one. This one bin was completely untouched by the fire and was not hot to touch. In print on the side of the bin was one unfamiliar word, *Liebe*. We left the fields and scoured the land for the buildings that had once provided shelter and for the fences that had kept the people in and what was undesirable out of the Spring Green Community, but nothing remained.

We returned to the field of listening and stood together, wondering what to do next. The bank of storm clouds I had seen in the distance was closer now, and I noted the movement of powerful winds and currents churning the blue-grey vapours; some of the clouds were so dark as to be closer to black than blue. I felt oddly comforted by the ragtag group of people standing with me in the field. How we must have looked, scarred and burned, and none of us the people we once were, yet together standing tall. We talked for some time about what our next step should be. Should we try to rebuild the Spring Green Community before the storm clouds were upon us, or should we leave this place? The notion of rebuilding the Spring Green Community caused me to feel nauseous, and I thought for a moment I heard the crackle of fire once more in the distance; I was relieved when the subject changed.

It was decided, eventually, that we would leave the lands together in search of the musical lands. In Heureux, the guiding compass had pointed to self. We decided that our compass, so to speak, would be to follow the beautiful music, to take care of each other, and also to support anyone we found in their journey without further thought of the pointless bins. We left the lands of the bearded men and the garden and headed once again to the south and to the west, from where the music came. We walked straight toward the clouds and darkness, the temperature falling noticeably. I felt more hope than ever before that the lands of the beautiful music were within reach, and I was pleased to travel with this group. I had the sense that something wonderful was at work within me and among my new travelling friends.

I walked alongside Khalid and asked him for his thoughts on the lands we now left behind. Looking calm and thoughtful, Khalid replied, "This land is a land of disparities, of hidden treasures and snares, benevolence and despotism. The riches of this land are the greatest of anywhere in this world, short of the land of the music, but its wealth is hidden from sight by man's drive for the abyss, clothed in fine robes and futile toil."

Chapter Thirty-Four
Powerful Stories

The path we travelled away from the lands of the bearded men took us in a westerly direction; it was a wide and spacious road, and I was under the impression that many people had left this land before us. It was not long before we came to an exit from the path almost as wide as the road we followed, and we slowed our pace to consider both routes. Taking a few steps into the broad roadway, I immediately noted a familiar smell; it was the smoke of the abyss wafting up from below.

It was beyond my understanding how the abyss could remain so close after I had travelled so far, but nevertheless, the abyss was undoubtedly below. Others with us ventured onto the path and noticed the smell as well, and frighteningly, they seemed powerless to keep from slipping down the slope. Though the incline of the new path was not steep at all, more than one in the group slipped and fell on the loose rocks and began tumbling away from us. Khalid and I were able to reach them and pull them back onto the road safely, and the decision was quickly made that we would stay on the now narrowing road to the west and avoid the smoke-filled path to our left. This was the first time I realized that, like me, Khalid was not drawn toward the abyss himself. Perhaps he, too, had been stuck in a dreadful hole for a few days at some point along his journey. I came to understand that the abyss was always nearby and that small decisions to walk away from destructive choices and follow the music held great power to avoid its gravity.

As we walked along, I told my new friends about my experiences in the abyss and urged them never to go anywhere near that dreadful place. Many in the group listened intently, and others looked at me with the type of disbelief that is not so much borne of antagonism as from having limited experiences and imagination. What my story did accomplish was to uncork a flurry of tales from the other travellers. While the others shared, I noticed that my listening had the most interesting effect. When I focused on what the travellers were saying, suspended all judgement, and listened for the music, the one speaking grew strikingly stronger. I treasured this startling influence as a secret pearl shared between myself and the music.

It was a surreal time in my journey, for while we shared our stories, laughing and shedding tears with one another, above us, ahead and in our way, loomed the most dreadful, towering storm clouds I had ever seen. As far as I could see above me, the soaring mass of angry grey and blue rose into the heights; below the towering plumes, it looked as dark as night. Intuitively, I knew that what I saw of the storm was merely its outer reaches, its true source of power veiled and hidden from sight.

In spite of the ominous setting, the stories continued, beginning with Lucrecio, who shared how he had been born in the lands of the bearded men; was the child of man with an exceeding long beard and his wife; and was a master of sorting, knowledgeable in hundreds of categories. He described his childhood with words like *stable, predictable, orderly,* and *safe*. When he depicted the lands, structures, and sights of his childhood, I was struck by the realization that the lands of the bearded men were almost identical now to what they had been in the past. Almost nothing had changed. As a young adult, Lucrecio had been overwhelmed by a need to travel and experience adventure, to know pleasures not easily found in the lands of the bearded men. Without his father's permission, Lucrecio left the land of his youth and wandered the paths. His journey was different from mine in that he had not experienced the terrors of The Darkness as I had in

Ennuied and that he had not yet heard the music, but, like me, he had spent a lot of time walking.

Lucrecio followed the paths and found himself in a town called Contumacious, a place with many of the same sights and opportunities as Heureux yet very different as well. Many of the citizens in Contumacious had come from places a lot like the land of the bearded men and were angry about all the revelry they had missed and the harsh treatment they had so often known at home. Lucrecio told us that while they did not use a compass like the people of Heureux, they received their direction from a mysterious map. This selective map did not show all of the geographic features. Rather, it only contained locations that were very different from the owner's homelands; the locations that were most opposite were printed darkly on the map.

Lucrecio spent some time in Contumacious but tired of the anger and left in search of something different and better. Feeling lost and alone, he stumbled along the paths for a long time in search of a healthier place to live, meeting many people along the way, eventually returning home to the land of the bearded men, which no longer felt like home at all. His stern father seemed to draw the life right out of him, and his mother's relentless efforts to control and categorize became too much to bear. By this time, Lucrecio had grown a sizeable beard himself, and after much thought and agonizing, he chose to break ties with his family in the most powerful way he could imagine. Lucrecio shaved off his beard—half of his beard, that is—and it was then that he heard the music from that wonderful hidden land for the very first time. In one of his ears, he heard a sound like violins and a pounding beat that came from the depths of the earth and the air all at the same time. The music did something inside Lucrecio, and after listening, he no longer felt the rage against his long-bearded father and his constantly sorting mother; perhaps even greater, he no longer noticed the self-loathing thoughts that had crippled him for so many years. He tried many times to explain his experience with the music to his mother, but it was as though she could not understand the words he used; she constantly urged him to return to the business of sorting and disregarded the music as a meaningless pursuit for the very young. Lucrecio had nowhere to go, no guides to show him the way, so he travelled to the very edges of the lands of the bearded men and started Spring Green Community.

As Lucrecio spoke on, the day grew darker. The temperature outside actually grew warmer, but the weather had an uneasy energy to it, and I felt the weight of warm, moist air pressing on my skin. A young lady in our entourage, Letha, spoke up next.

"I don't really understand what you both have been talking about." She giggled. "In fact, I don't even know how I got here. I was walking around my house where I was creating a wonderful life, and I found myself with all of you."

The rest of us were dumbfounded; we wondered how this woman had ended up with us without anyone noticing, and while some speculated that she had been part of the Spring Green Community, no one remembered seeing her before. Khalid, calm and thoughtful as always, asked Letha to share her story, which she was more than happy to do; in fact, I was under the impression that she thought her story should be heard by everyone. It turned out that Letha had been born into a town unlike any I had experienced on my journey. It sounded like a very large settlement with many citizens, and Letha assured us that there were many other towns just like hers. The town itself was nestled in a high mountain valley with roads connecting it to other valleys with same kind of villages. In fact, Letha was quite certain that these roads led exclusively to other towns just like hers. She told us that the homes all looked much the same, beautiful on the outside with bricks of red and bright coloured trim. Brilliant colours were reserved for the outside of the buildings, and shades of brown decorated everything within. Letha described beautiful forested parks of incredibly small size, far too small to allow much of a walk at all but nice to look at. Letha's family raised her to keep her mind open to all things and, above all, to follow her belly. A few of us snickered when she mentioned following her belly, but it turned out that among her people, following the belly meant doing what seemed and felt best in the moment, something we could all relate to at some level.

Magdala, whose confidence was returning after the events of the fire, interrupted with some questions for Letha. "How does your belly know the way, and does it tell you to walk against the wind?"

Letha looked irritated by Magdala's interjection and continued with her story, though she did add an interesting detail. It turned out that in addition to following their belly, each family had a set of secret pottery that they usually kept in a place of honour in the home. Her family's collection was kept in their sitting room beside their best furniture; they covered the ceramics in fine blankets and placed all kind of knickknacks on top as decorations. The family rarely spoke of the pottery, but her mother often stared at it when displeased with a decision Letha was making, and more than once, late at night, Letha had caught her mother sorting household items into the pottery jars. When the townsfolk were confronted about owning and using the pottery collections for sorting, it was customary to deny possessing such things and make references about the need for everyone to follow his or her belly.

Letha grew up doing what she thought was best. She worked hard at school, made friends, and got into her share of trouble doing the kinds of things that adolescents everywhere seem to love. Letha claimed that she remembered being guided by her belly from her youth; she had a keen ability to discern whether people were safe or dangerous, kind or malevolent, and she felt compassion for those who were bullied and picked on by others. As she grew older, Letha continued to follow her belly and sought to build her dream life. She chose romantic partners and made moral decisions based on how she felt in her belly; she even chose for her friend a career and a house, based on the feelings that came from her belly.

With some pride, Letha described how she had built a wonderful situation for herself, a dream life, and how others wished they were able to live like her. In her town, the people had a special way of sharing and comparing themselves to each other; they would draw pictures and write short passages about their wonderful lives and post them on the fences and dividers that stood between their houses. Then they pretended to love one another's descriptions of the ideal life they had achieved by following their bellies.

Magdala continued to break into Letha's storytelling, this time asking her why her belly had led her to the life she chose, which did not seem so wondrous to him. "How do you know," he reproved, "that the life you have chosen and spent yourself upon is what is truly good and right?" He continued, "To follow the music is like swimming against the tides of the sea itself or building a lighthouse in the middle of the pounding surf. Your story has no inspiration for me."

Letha was indignant with Magdala and began to argue with him that all the most recent books and stories showed that her life was exactly what everyone should seek to create. Khalid had been listening silently but stepped forward to speak. I agreed with Magdala that following the music felt a lot like walking against a powerful wind that blew relentlessly, and I could not help but take another look up at the storm growing larger ahead. Still, I wondered what Khalid would have to say.

He began, "I hear Letha's story very differently from you, Magdala, and I am quite certain that this lady has heard the music in her belly already because it can only be the music that speaks the language of love."

Khalid seemed scandalously unconcerned about correcting Letha on her view of the world and welcomed her warmly to our ragtag group; the two were becoming fast friends. I felt that Letha's town was a little too close to the Heureux lifestyle for my comfort, but then I wondered why that bothered me at all; I had not seen a town yet that looked and felt like the music, and the music itself was shrouded in mystery.

Chapter Thirty-Five
Suhruda

Though much of my journey had been spent making individual decisions and coping with solitude, there were many advantages to travelling in a group. The search for food, for example, was comparatively undemanding. Two or three of our party seemed to love searching the woods for fresh berries; a few of the younger men and women thought running ahead to look for sources of fresh water was tremendous fun. There were, of course, frequent conflicts and disagreements. Some of the younger travellers quarrelled about which streams had the best water. Two even came to blows over the matter, hitting one another in the face and causing a major uproar. They were so swollen that neither could drink from either stream for days. This was a great example of the power petty conflicts had to disrupt the journey. Overall, though, I believe it was our experience with the long-bearded sorters and the ensuing fires that kept us from being too inflexible with one another.

For the first time since I had experienced the crystal waters and the beautiful flowers on the plateau, I felt deeply connected to the world and people around me. I would have enjoyed this part of the journey much more were it not for what I saw developing in the atmosphere above. Now that my inner world was transforming into a delightful place, it seemed that I would face greater resistance from outside forces. Our steady forward progress had placed us under the first fragments of storm clouds. Where we walked, the weather remained warm and calm, though electricity seemed to fill the air. I stopped frequently to stare into the sky above, and what I saw filled me with awe and dread. The dark grey clouds were on the move far above us, swirling and twisting and surging upward and downward, reminding me of some of the stories that were presented in Heureux for entertainment, but this was no tale. Few in our group took note of the changes in the weather—too engrossed in sharing their own stories, I suppose—but I noticed, and Khalid watched me notice.

Members of our troop kept right on talking, oblivious of the impending weather changes. A rather interesting narrative came from a young man in his thirties named Suhruda, another person who had joined our group and the search for the beautiful music seemingly by accident. Suhruda had grown up in a place much like the land of the bearded men, a place where there were rumours of another country with the most beautiful melodies and where those with authority loved to give the people strict rules that were supposed to lead to the music. The entire town, Suhruda shared, was decorated in black and white; the whiter the white and blacker the black, the better. Suhruda shared with us some of the rules, and I was not sure if he was smirking or grimacing while he spoke. Apparently there were rules about learning and knowledge. The chiefs of the lands said that the forest was theirs to explore and discover, but only within limits, and they chose a set of men to produce guidelines for learning.

Here, Suhruda did break into an ironic grin as he explained that those chosen to make the rules were all older farm hands—not that he had anything against agriculture, he assured us, but the chosen men knew only the fields and little else about the forests. One of the farmers, he shared, believed that the forest had begun in his field of grain and that people should only eat red-feathered fowl. As Suhruda spoke, I was reminded of the men of Ennuied and their love of fodder grass, which consumed their thoughts to the exclusion of all other things. Suhruda, an inquisitive boy who lived to test and experiment, was bothered by these limitations to his learning and determined that only these farm hands could invent such a silly idea as the land of melodies—in his mind, a very dull and boring-sounding place. Based on the observations of his town, Suhruda concluded that the quest for facts and knowledge was incompatible with the land of beautiful music. He would continue to hold this conviction for a shockingly short period of time.

This was just the beginning of Suhruda's story, for the land of his birth was not a kind place. The rulers of the land were a tight-knit family who kept much of the wealth and prosperity to themselves. Whenever someone got the notion that the rules could be changed and something a little fairer, considered, the authorities were quick to use their powers to keep the regular folk quiet. One rule that made Suhruda particularly angry was called the "stressor-busy rule," which stated that when the authorities felt the community structure was under stress, they increased the number of events and activities that the people were to attend. The resulting distraction and fatigue served to keep people calm and quiet, ensuring that the status quo would prevail.

Suhruda gave us a toothy grin as he described his resistance, which began by arriving late to events, followed by skipping them, then actively disrupting the goings-on. One time, he told us, while an educational event was in progress, he dyed the plucked red feathers black, causing a tremendous disturbance when the guests perceived they had eaten the wrong chickens. He told us that the people became sick and began to argue and fight with one another.

Suhruda shared many stories with us, but none carried more emotion and weight than his retelling of the wars. The lands of Suhruda's birth were situated close to other lands, populated by people similar to his; competition for resources and trade was fierce, and from time to time, conflicts erupted. Suhruda had been a young teen when one of the worst battles in anyone's memory took place, The Battle of Prodigality Ridge.

The authorities began the battle by quietly sending some of the less scrupulous young men on well-armed forays into the ridge lands, which rose above a calm, wide, and deep section of the largest river in the area, crucial for the expansion of trade. The young men faced surprising resistance from the local people who had lived on the ridge for generations. These military setbacks unleashed a tremendous effort from the authorities to rally everyone in the land to support a set of massive assaults on the ridge. Special meetings were held where the people were told that they were somehow expanding the land of the beautiful melodies by destroying the Ridgelanders, a lesser people.

Suhruda was appalled that the people believed the propaganda they were hearing and set out to find out more about the Ridgelanders on his own, and what he discovered cut his heart to the core. Suhruda snuck out in the night time and set out to the Ridgeland with great care, knowing that his own people would take his life in an instant for questioning the rulers and their powers. He approached the Ridgelands and found that they were completely surrounded by the fighters from his land; no food, water, medicine, or supplies were being allowed to enter. Suhruda crept quietly up toward the ridge and was quickly stopped by the well-armed fighters enforcing the embargo.

"Greetings, Suhruda. Welcome to the front! I did not think you supported the cause. Grab a weapon and take position on the berm ahead."

Suhruda selected a weapon and marched ahead to the berm, where he promptly discarded the weapon and snuck up the hill, silently as he could. He heard yelling behind him and felt rocks and debris fly past his head; something struck him in his back, but he made it out of the range of his people's weapons and approached the Ridgelanders who were dug in ahead. At this point in the story, Suhruda became exceedingly quiet; he told us that he had expected to find a proud, resistant, and militant band of well-armed men and women, much like his own people, but instead he had walked into a cesspool of suffering. There were no soldiers present—just some youth, children really, with rocks and sticks in their hands—and Suhruda walked by with little resistance. Further into the settlement, Suhruda found children with stomachs distended from hunger, babies too malnourished to cry, and sickness and destruction everywhere. Balls of fire had been hurled at the Ridgeland settlement from below, destroying the medical clinic and food storage barns. Suhruda stayed for a time with the Ridgelanders, sharing what little food he had with him and helping where he could. He slipped away one night when he heard the Ridgelanders discussing a senseless plan to send the children down the hill into the camps of the invaders with baskets full of fire.

Suhruda sought freedom from the land of his birth and could no longer be bothered with what he called noxious rules and tales about silly musical lands far away. While he seemed to be enjoying walking with us, Suhruda could not figure out where and when he had joined our group. He cackled and giggled at us about our quest to find the land of the beautiful music; I decided not to remind him that he was also walking with us toward this land, whether he knew it or not. Magdala and some others of the more hot-headed travellers argued with Suhruda endlessly about certainty and guidelines for all travellers, and this brought out the fire in Suhruda, who, being reminded of the ghastly lands of his birth, resisted with many fine arguments.

Overhearing Magdala and the others attacking Suhruda, Khalid finally stepped in, red in the face with exasperation. He spoke to Magdala and the others. "The wisdom you speak of is ancient. It is found in the scrolls and books in the great library of the bearded men, but like the bearded men, you do not understand any of it. If you want to be wise, stop harassing this brave young man. Let your wisdom pierce your own hearts until love comes bursting from within. Then perhaps you will understand and see this astute and brave man in a different light."

I enjoyed listening Khalid chastise the others; he was the kindest person I had ever known, but he just could not abide cruelty or self-satisfied smugness. I respected my childhood friend a great deal and was pleased that I had seen this one coming and distanced myself from Suhruda's detractors. I looked at Khalid as he spoke to the travellers and understood what he saw in Suhruda: a valiant, caring person who had likely been hearing the real music all of his life without knowing or being aware. It was probably the music that drove him to inquire about the world around him and to resist the foolish notions of his elders, and it was almost certainly the music that led Suhruda to visit the Ridgelanders, sharing his food and supplies without thought for himself. I wondered if I had actually seen Suhruda pass me on that hill before the land of the bearded men. After castigating the others, Khalid walked side by side with Suhruda for some time, laughing and visiting, and a friendship was born.

I would have enjoyed the moment more were it not for the latest meteorological developments. The wide path on which we travelled remained reasonably tranquil, but the storm clouds were doing things I had never seen before.

Chapter Thirty-Six
Aganad

The surrounding forest stretched out and up on either side of the path, and I could see a few tall mountain peaks ahead of us through the clouds—the largest peaks I had ever seen. I was surprised that thick forest covered even the highest and most rugged peaks, having read that high mountains were normally rocky and barren. Whereas I had observed the turbulent weather we were approaching in the distance for a long time, I was disturbed to discover that the storm was beginning to strike the highlands on both sides of our path.

To my right, I noticed that the trees well above us were bowed, as though a great hand were moving across them from the east. I stopped where I was to let the rest of our group pass so that I could listen without any distractions. As the others disappeared ahead of me, I found myself at peace within the solitude, so much different from the loneliness I had experienced so often earlier in the journey. Listening carefully, I heard nothing at first, but with focus I came to realize that there was a soft rumble, like thunder far away that cracked continually. What I heard was the blowing of a tremendous wind above me, a wind that blew with enough force to bend the towering evergreens on the slope halfway to the ground.

On the path below, things remained calm; the odd, stiff breeze came down from above, enough to blow a hat from a head or to mess one's hair but nothing more than an inconvenience. I hoped that the winds would remain above us on the slopes, but the foreboding in my stomach told me otherwise, as did the mild discomfort I felt where my wounds had healed and the throbbing pain in my right hip.

On the left side of the path, I saw no evidence of the winds; rather, the tree-covered slopes were shrouded in thick, dark clouds which seemed to be pulsating. On the lower reaches of the mountain, I observed that each pulse of the clouds brought a tremendous burst of rain. I was concerned about what was taking place higher on the mountain, if this was happening below the bank of clouds. My chief worry was where all this water was going. The path I travelled was completely dry, but I reasoned that water must be exiting the slope somewhere and hoped that it was some place safe. I ran forward to re-join the group and warn them that the time of the storm was coming, only to find that they had moved far ahead of me and directly into the weather system.

The pain in my hip throbbed as I dashed up the path, furious with myself that I had let my friends out of my sight. As I trudged forward, my thoughts turned to the beautiful music and the crystal waters, and I felt some comfort. My body ached, but I knew I needed to warn the others. I found myself less concerned with my own well-being than ever before. I had left the land of my birth and searched the forests of the world, survived gaping wounds, the abyss, and a lack of all that I desired and craved to find. I was not sure if I was becoming stronger, harder, wiser, or simply closer to death, but my fear of the future diminished in tandem with the death of my expectations, and I felt hope of a new and far more powerful kind take root in my heart. Very quietly, almost too subtle to notice, the music had begun to play within me without ceasing, or perhaps I had begun to hear what had been playing inside my heart for some time.

I continued to run hard and almost sprinted right past the group, who were resting on some rocks just off the path. No one, save my friend Khalid, had even realized I was gone, and they were in yet another deep discussion with one of the new travellers sharing her story. Khalid saw me immediately and nodded a greeting before gazing up at the weather and then back at me.

Khalid was an intriguing communicator; his voice was generally calm and quiet, though he could bellow when necessary.

Much of Khalid's communication was through subtle body language, and if you didn't pay close attention to him, it was easy to miss. He was, without a doubt, the most observant person I had ever met and always seemed aware of what was happening around him. It took me some time to catch my breath, and when I was finally ready to share my report about the weather, Khalid approached me with his index finger to his mouth and quietly urged me to wait.

I whispered back, "Khalid, I don't think we have time. The weather is virtually upon us."

"There is always time to hear the story of another traveller," Khalid said quietly, "and I think we all need to hear this one as well."

I would not have heeded anyone else, but Khalid had shown impeccable judgement all of our lives, and I sat down on one of the rocks to listen. I gathered that the traveller who was sharing her story was named Aganad. I did not catch the very beginning of her tale, but I figured out that the town where she had been born was known for being very confident about everything and that Aganad's incessant questioning got her into considerable trouble.

The children in her village were told all kinds of stories to shape their behaviour and teach them right from wrong. They were all given a special toy on their second birthday and were told that this toy came alive as they slept at night. If they had been good and listened to their parents that day, the toy would get up in the night and help them with their chores, but if they had been naughty, the toy became a gremlin that made a mess of their rooms and got into all kinds of mischief for which the children would be blamed. All of the children were raised to believe in this mystical toy, but all came to realize the stories were fiction, made up to control their behaviour. Aganad had noticed inconsistencies in the story very early but went along with the game to please her parents.

The people in Aganad's village were preoccupied with magic and tales about mysterious lands. Before I arrived back with the group, she had, apparently, told the travellers many compelling stories from her village that seemed to support the reality of magic, and some of the accounts she told about other lands had a few group members convinced that they could be true. Aganad was not to be convinced so easily. Her village, like I was observing in almost every village, held elaborate ceremonies to celebrate their beliefs, though the true meaning of the shared events were sometimes subtle.

Aganad said that the celebrations and ceremonies in her village offered exceedingly self-assured appraisals of unknown lands and time-tested customs and rites that opened up a world of wonderful magic. It was said that the magic could lead to a wondrous life filled with happiness and success. Aganad was a clever young lady and could observe that the townsfolk who participated in these events, like all those who use magic to conjure joy, were not happier and were no more successful than others she had met. In fact, a good number of them were particularly sour and negative individuals who were not pleasant to be around. Aganad was clear to say that she did not judge the people of her town, but she could not accept the town charter and its specified beliefs with the confidence and assurance required, and she left to search the paths of the forest.

There was a great deal of murmuring among the travellers when Aganad shared her observations of the sour townsfolk, the group agreeing that it was sometimes the most committed who were the most dour. A big debate arose about why this could be true. Some concurred that it must be the fatigue associated with effort, while others suspected that some of the highly committed became unhappy because they were so focused on others, neglecting their own needs and well-being. I was not so sure about that one, thinking of the dedicated villagers in my hometown of Ennuied. I could not think of any who were models of selfless altruism. Lucrecio looked like he was about to speak when Khalid quietly asked him to wait, much like he had asked me to delay my weather alert. Instead, Suhruda stood up to speak.

"I think that, once again, the lot of you don't know what you are talking about. I have met many of these people, and I think some of them are right here with us in this group. You people who search after this music, you don't get it, do you? Do you need me to explain it to you?"

Magdala, still exceptionally fervent, responded, "We have read the texts from the great library, we have passed through the land of the bearded men and continue to walk. What will you teach us?"

I spoke up at this point, not intending to be controversial; I simply wanted to hear what Suhruda had to say. "Let him speak, Magdala," I urged. "Suhruda is a clever young man."

Suhruda looked like he was not going to share his thoughts with us, but reluctantly he did. "It is human to desire, to want, and to crave what we do not have, but this is pure destruction!"

Magdala had a look on his face of unadulterated incredulity, and many of the others were confused; some of the group became distracted by the weighty topic and stopped listening altogether. I continued to be very curious, and I noticed that Lucrecio was paying close attention as well.

Suhruda continued. "Those who are hyper-committed often want what they seek more than others, and there are only two possible outcomes to this search." Suhruda paused for effect. "They can get what they seek and find that it fails to meet their needs as expected, or they fail to secure what they seek and long for it continually and fruitlessly. Both of these outcomes lead to death and decay, and this is the reason so many are sour and bitter."

The group was silenced by Suhruda's astute observation, Aganad's head quietly nodding in agreement. I even forgot about the impending weather for a moment as I reflected on Suhruda's words. There was no more storytelling that evening, and I was pleased to sit down and catch up with Khalid. We began by talking about the weather, not a superficial discussion about the temperature and trends but a real exchange about the storm that almost encircled us; only to our rear, the direction from which we had come, was clear of the impending storm. I shared my observations with Khalid, including the wind that thundered above us on the right-hand slopes and the torrential rains high above on the left. Khalid did not look surprised—he never really did—but he was concerned. I hoped he would come up with a fantastic plan and organize the group to move to safety, but instead he stated that I should talk about the storm with the group in the morning and that I would know what to do.

Khalid appeared ready to turn in for the night, but I was desperate to ask him what he thought about Suhruda's words earlier. He turned toward me and grinned as though expecting more.

"Khalid," I asked, "what Suhruda said—if it is true, what is the point of desiring anything? Are we all destined to ruin and disappointment?"

Khalid looked at me with just a hint of impatience but with a pleasant look in his eyes. He questioned me. "When you were on that hill, the one after the plateau, and all of those people passed by you, had they lost all sense of desire?"

My memory turned to the children who had danced around me as they vaulted up the hill ahead and passed me. Certainly they were not free of desires. Actually, none of those who walked past me struck me as people who had eliminated desire from their lives.

I turned to Khalid. "Is it more that joyful people are honest with their desires? Perhaps it is that they don't manipulate or control others to see their desires met?"

Khalid nodded thoughtfully and added, "Disappointment is a tremendous sieve; it filters and breaks apart what will be broken." Before turning in for the night, Khalid asked me a final question. He queried, "What did you notice about desire when you heard the music and dove into the crystal waters?"

Khalid obviously did not intend that I share my answer with him but that I think about it. I reflected that when I heard the music and swam in the crystal waters, some of my desires seemed to die, or possibly they had died earlier and I only noticed when immersed in the pleasant waters. Feeling a little sheepish with myself, I acknowledged that my desires tended to be much less self-absorbed when I heard the music and felt the waters. I came to no final conclusions about what to do with my own desires, except to be as honest as I could and to give the desires that came with the music and crystal waters special attention.

Chapter Thirty-Seven
Cut and Run Corridor

I could not find any rest that night, and my thoughts returned to the building weather problems. I walked back on to the path and explored the area close by, employing all of my senses to find something that would help this group of travellers. In the starlight, my eyes captured something familiar, another sign partially hidden by the surrounding foliage. I brushed the plants and dirt off the sign, but it was very difficult to read in the poor lighting. On the top of the sign were some words in large print, which I was able to make out:

CUT AND RUN CORRIDOR

Beneath the large print, there was more writing which I could not read until the moon broke away from the thick clouds for a moment:

For those who have passed through the abyss
A pathway out to lands beyond

Initially I was so excited I could hardly contain myself, sure that I had found a means of escape for our group of travellers and that we would not have to pass through the stormy lands. I quickly followed the path, which led to the steepest stairway I had ever seen, cut into the rocky side of the mountain. I began climbing, telling myself I was checking out the path for the others to follow but knowing I was tempted to continue up and away from all of my troubles. It was not long before I noticed something odd about the narrow stairs I travelled. To my left, I heard something, and more than this, I felt it: something familiar and something I did not care to see in the light of day. The sound I heard was the rushing of water coming from the mountainside pouring into a deep pit; the sound of the water crashing at the bottom of the pit was starkly absent. I knew right away that there was no bottom to this hole and that I was, in fact, climbing a path parallel to the great abyss.

As before, the abyss was unable to pull me into its madness. I continued to climb for a while, but a realization set in that none of the others in the group, save Khalid, would be able to climb this way. I stopped moving and savoured the longing I felt to leave these lands for somewhere better; below was pain and suffering, and above was the potential to free myself from the endless paths. With agonizing ambivalence and regret, I turned around and made my way down the steep paths and stairs. Underestimating the angle of the slope, I lost my balance and fell hard, slipping into a near freefall. I may have banged my head during the fall, because I don't recall coming to a stop, but I came to my senses in an unfamiliar place. I could still clearly hear the waters tumbling into the abyss, though perhaps just a little bit more quietly. I stood up slowly, my head swimming and body feeling battered and bruised; looking around, I saw a trail heading downward at a devastating slope similar to the one I had climbed shortly before. I would have preferred almost any path to the steep and rocky trail before me, but I had no choice, being surrounded by even rougher terrain and high rock walls.

I made my way down what I expected was a parallel path. The downward passage seemed longer and more challenging than the upward journey, much longer, though I knew this was not logical. It took me less and less by surprise when I discovered that the rules governing the paths and forests were counterintuitive and perplexing.

I had already learned that children, the poor, and the weakest travelled the paths faster than me and that all the knowledge in the world helped very little. Early in the journey, I learned that I was to follow the paths to reach the land of the music but that I could not control the direction the paths took me. I found out that the beautiful crystal waters felt best coming through my wounds and that the music was clearest when I felt I must be farthest from it. I discovered that when horrible beasts from the forest attacked, some travellers were drawn to their destruction as to a feast. I ascertained that when I found deep holes in the ground, I should not fill them but walk around them.

Strangely, most of my wounds had been healed by simply walking around a hole, but doing so damaged my hip, which made me go faster uphill. I discovered that many of the desires common to all people secretly lead to the abyss and that compasses can point the wrong way. Recently, I came to the conclusion that some of those who studied the forest in great detail, sorting it into the finest parts, could be as set against the paths as the wild beasts themselves. Most of all, I learned that I was at my best when I listened closely to the music and made love and lowness, rather than power and self-promotion, my priority. In view of all of this, learning now that it was longer and harder to go down than up made sense to my transforming mind.

Continuing down the hill, I fell many times, and I felt hungry and tired, the kind of fatigue that seemed to stem from the bones. I felt sorry for myself and regretted my decision to return to the group and the impending storm. I imagined what would have happened if I had continued up the path—perhaps I would be nearing the top and the end of my suffering with storm clouds disappearing, yet something in me didn't feel right, even when I imagined taking that path, and at least a small part of me knew I had made the right choice. Each time I fell, I thought I must finally have made it to the bottom, but there always seemed further to go, and in the end I gave up searching for the base. I kept walking and falling as well as I could, pain throbbing in my side and the ground levelling beneath my feet without my knowing, until night had passed and I found myself on a flat, uninteresting path which I hoped led to the main road where I would find my fellow travellers and Khalid.

To my joy, I sighted the main path and quickened my pace. Close to the intersection ahead, something sparkled in the starlight. The flicker was familiar and, while dim, stood out in the plain darkness of my surroundings, filling me with an inexplicable relief. The glittering became more intense as I moved toward the main path, reflections and beams of light dancing on the ground to my left. There before me, mere feet from the main path, with a storm raging in the sky and my band of damaged travellers nearby, was a crystal pool, the third I had seen on my journey, and it dazzled in the starlight. The waters had been a sight to behold by day, but by night they were breathtaking, subtle and mysterious, deep, clear, and the most intensely pure sight I had seen. They reflected the starlight so perfectly, I was not sure if the stars actually came from the pool rather than the sky. And then there were the colours: deep blues and greens and, most of all, red. It is difficult to describe, but the red in the pool was undeniably in charge, not so much overwhelming the other colours as making them richer and deeper.

I stood at the pool's edge for some time, taking in the sensory concert before me, and then I followed what was my custom at the crystal pools: diving in, clothes and all. Though it was nighttime, the waters were not cold, and I propelled myself lower and lower into the depths. As with all other encounters at the pool, I felt comforted and serene; even my hip felt fine as I kicked my legs together, moving deeper still. I heard something like the call of a mourning dove, and the music entered me softly with an enchanting song that did not fill me hope and happiness as much as it did with strength and resolve. Images flashed through my mind as I hung in the depths, visions of pounding rain and tremendous winds, mud and water, and blood. Concern grew in my heart for my travelling companions, the people of Heureux, Ennuied, and even the men with long beards. Something deep within me knew the paths, and the storm clouded the way to liberation, though they were somehow inextricably linked to it. I saw my plans to escape and leave the difficulties of the path for what they were: egocentric efforts for control, comfort, and advantage.

I left the waters feeling refreshed from the wonderful dose of honesty and set out to re-join my group. As I backtracked along the main path, I reflected that most of my encounters with the crystal waters and the music took place after or during intense difficulties, and while I felt I should appreciate this, I knew I would resist it each and every time. When I reached my friends, I found them beginning to stir with the first light of morning.

Those still asleep awoke quickly as I bellowed, "I have found the crystal waters! They are right close by. Come and drink and swim!"

My companions were slow to move, and it took me a while to rouse them all and get them moving toward the site of the pool. I was thrilled for my friends, that they would have the chance to experience the waters, particularly Suhruda and Letha, who I expected would find the waters oddly familiar in a wonderful way. The walk to the site of the crystal pool seemed to take no time at all travelling together, and for a moment I forgot about the weather system around us and my need to warn the others. We arrived at the small fork in the road where I had climbed down from the stairs near the abyss and, to my horror, there was no sign of the pool. Panicking, I ran around the area, scouring every inch of the ground to no avail; the pool was gone. My fellow travellers gathered around me, some with mocking looks in their eyes, others with pity, and a few with confident expectation. Khalid looked my way and then to the sky with some impatience, and I realized he wanted me to speak about the weather.

Nervously, I addressed the group. "I don't know where the crystal pool has gone, friends. It was here, and I experienced it and hoped that all of you could, too." I was silent for an uncomfortable period of time. "Perhaps the pool appears a little differently to everyone." Privately, I thought of the land of the bearded men and the silly memorials with the fences. Rhetorically, I questioned whether I was just like those who made the mounds long ago, thinking that if others followed my steps and actions exactly, they too would come to the crystal pool.

I looked to the skies, took a deep breath, and continued. "I need to warn you all about what I see in the skies! Look up, everyone. We are upon the most dreadful weather system I have ever seen. On the left, pounding rains pummel the slopes as we speak, and to the right, winds blow that we cannot possibly endure. Ahead, the clouds are on the move in ways I cannot perceive, and the abyss remains close by."

As I continued to share with the travellers, some looked at me with disbelief; others looked at the skies and quickly looked away, not wanting to believe what was happening, while still others became panicked, one running away not to be seen again. To my surprise, it was Suhruda who stood up to defend me, acknowledging that what I said was true, and soon the entire group that remained was gazing into the sky in awe. The members of our entourage responded very differently to the growing reality that we were standing on the cusp of something beyond any of our experiences and, possibly, strength to endure. Suhruda was cautiously optimistic that there may be a way through, while Aganad was filled a sense of dread about what lay ahead; others were on the fence, but none in the group gave any thought to turning back, because for us, there was nothing in the lands we had left behind. It was decided we would gather what food and water we could store with us and enter the lands ahead of us, storm and all.

Early the following morning, those of us who remained set out together, doing our best to fan the flames of cautious optimism. As we approached the impending storm, I was worried for the group I travelled with. Though I did not notice it, I had lost much of the angry edge that I had felt so keenly on the poetic plateau, and I was genuinely concerned about how this new group of friends who I cared about was going to fare when the storm and inevitable pain were upon us. Though I did not understand how, I now knew that the abyss was always nearby, waiting to consume everything it could.

As we walked in the morning light, there was a crispness to the air that I had not felt for some time, and the forest smells were changing, the pines overpowering most everything else. I took some time to reflect on the stories I had heard from my travel-mates; while none had an experience just like mine in Ennuied, almost everyone on the journey had experienced agonizing turning points of some kind, making me wonder if pain was a foundational fabric of the journey itself. Not looking for pain but resigned to what may lie ahead, as I had learned long ago now, I continued, one foot in front of the other, and closer to the destiny that lay ahead.

PART THREE
Through Forces from Outside

Chapter Thirty-Eight
The Cold

Hiking into the storm was like crossing a border or climbing a fence; the lands we had walked disappeared, and we became enveloped in a very different place. We remained on a path in the forest; I had now walked the forest paths for so long that I could scarcely recall anything different, yet something had changed—I felt it. One thing was objectively clear; it was getting colder, much colder. To be certain, winters in Ennuied could be frigid, frost often forming on the windows of our house and the ground becoming solid beneath our feet. It was a moist cold, and it chilled us to the bone, defying all but the warmest sweaters and slippers.

This was a much different phenomenon, a dry life-extracting cold that lacked any humidity and the hope for life offered by moist winter winds. Though I felt content inside, it was clear that our travelling entourage was about to face circumstances where the path brought us difficult experiences over which we had little control. The trees that bordered the path also told us a story; the slighter trees were devoid of all but a few leaves or needles, and the undergrowth was a sad grey and brown. Only the largest of the trees managed to hold their foliage, and I mused that this stretch of forest was not for the faint of heart, even for plants.

Up to this point in the journey, the forest floor had usually been covered in thick green understory that was now conspicuous in its absence, exposing the forest and the path ahead in stark detail. I suspected any travellers who walked the paths of the forest long enough would know that the forest floor was like this, but it was a surprise to many in our group. The land which had appeared soft, amorous even, and certainly benign could be seen with shocking accuracy. The most glaring, previously hidden features in this rather barren landscape were the rocks. Many of the stones were partially buried in the earth, only the jagged tops showing above ground, waiting to trip any unsuspecting traveller. It was impossible to completely avoid the rocks; all of us had learned of their presence the hard way on the journey. As I was familiar with wounds and pain, the rocks were just another irritant for me, bruising my feet and causing me to stumble. For many, the cold, hard rocks were much more devastating. Lucrecio, once proud of his half-bearded good looks, had fallen many times because of the rocks, and his face had the scrapes and scars to prove it. Other rocks were scattered over the surface of the ground, and their origins were mysterious to all of us, particularly Suhruda, who studied the land in detail. These stones looked as though they had landed where they sat, thrown by some invisible hand, creating yet another hazard for those on long journeys.

As I observed the rocks scattered throughout the landscape and felt the polar cold from the front edge of the storm, I witnessed a stone fly through the air across the leafless trees. It struck Letha in her thigh, and she fell to the ground, unresponsive. Khalid rushed to her side to tend to her wound. The stone seemed to have come from nowhere, and I could think of no reason to strike Letha with a stone should some unseen enemy be aiming toward her. Though the cold was beginning to bite deeply, it was necessary to expose Letha's leg to examine and care for the wound. She shivered violently in the frigid air as Khalid removed some stone fragments from the fleshy part of her thigh and bandaged her wounds carefully.

Stopping to assist Letha afforded me the opportunity to observe the scene with a greater eye for detail, and in addition to the stones, I observed many other hazards, including potholes scattered with no apparent rhyme or reason, impossible to predict; sharp thorns, which must have been a vestige from greener days; and tree roots. I could not readily see the roots from the larger trees (perhaps they extended downward to some unseen source of sustenance), but the smaller trees with bare frozen branches sent their equally frozen roots in all directions, and they were a hazard plain to see along the path.

Had we the energy to complain, many in our group would have protested the appalling conditions growing around us. The coldness of this stormy land, its harshness and lack of anything soft or kind, exposed the lands we travelled in horrible detail. In some respects, the cold lands we now walked were more real than the green lands we came from; we could now see the underlying ground more accurately: stones, holes, roots, and all. The green plants, flowers, streams, and life had all seemed as real as the cold dry ground around me now, but I could see how easy it might be to view them as illusion, only a thin shell masking the reality below. Colder than anything I had experienced yet in my life, the temperature continued to fall. Looking up and to the left, I could see the air churning high above me, giant masses of cloud rotating rapidly, opposite to the direction of a clock, sending a cold, heavy wind downward to us.

As the icy weather steadily advanced, the tiny hairs in my nasal cavity froze when I breathed through my nose, and my chest hurt when I took a breath through my mouth; my skin stung everywhere it was exposed to the air. I found myself shivering as I walked, my heart racing and breaths coming short and shallow. I could hear my heart pounding in my ears, and yet I found myself discerning another sound at the same time: a soft and beautiful sound—the sound of music.

I looked all around me, trying to find the source of the music, thinking that perhaps there was a crystal pool nearby and straining my ears to see where the music came from, to no avail. When I stopped looking around me and listened to my pounding heart, I heard the music again: a peaceful and happy melody that put a spring in my step. The wondrous sounds faded when I looked for them outside, and they became clear when I listened for them inside me. This went on for hours of walking, and I began to realize that this form of the music might just continue forever. I noticed yet another strange phenomenon happening in my body: the more I listened to the music and my beating heart, the less I perceived the world of cold around me. To be sure, I felt the wind, but the shivering settled down and my breathing became almost as deep as usual. The paths of the forests, I discovered afresh, were a place where nothing was what it seemed and the rules of nature were turned end on end. Difficult circumstances beyond my control, regardless of the source, were unable to stifle the music from the beautiful lands that played within.

Some of my friends were not faring as well as I was in the cold, and I could see that we were in desperate need of clothing and shelter. We used just about everything we carried to try to stay warm, each of us wearing every piece of clothing we had (which was not a lot), even using carrying bags around our feet and hands. With the fading daylight, the temperature dropped rapidly, and we reached a quick consensus that progress was impossible; we required fire and shelter as soon as possible.

Khalid and I gathered the group and sat them down while we built a fire using the deadwood around us, of which there was no shortage. Together, we built a raging fire and hoped it would be enough. In direct contrast to the warmth of our fire, the cold set in deeply with the night, surpassing what I had conceived in my imagination and convincing me that it might not be possible to become colder. Suhruda, too, was with us near the fire but not close enough, and the cold sinking from the heights settled inside him. The shivering in his body became violent, his speech slurred, and his lips and fingers showed a growing bluish hue. I urged Suhruda to approach the fire and feel the warmth, but he had moved beyond reason into a world of confusion and anger, fighting attempts to bring him to the fire.

"You are going to burn me! You want to burn me—stay away!" he screamed.

Still yelling at the top of his lungs, taking in raspy breaths between his tirades, Suhruda was off into the woods and away from the protection of the fire; he would now feel the full extent of the cold. With a nod from Khalid (who understood the abilities of those in our group to survive the cold) and very little thought, I launched into the forest, following Suhruda as fast as my lame hip would carry me.

Chapter Thirty-Nine
The Rescue

The lack of green plants, leaves, and undergrowth made it easier to track Suhruda, who must have been feeling the rising toll of the cold in his body. To my dismay, even with this advantage, I failed to catch my friend who ran from me and from safety as though driven by an invisible destructive force bent on ruin and death. Pushing my tired body to its limits, I ran on, heart pounding, galloping in my ears like wild horses thundering through a grassy land, and despite the thrashing rhythm of my heart, still the music played. I heard the melody from some mysterious place within me, a despondent tune filled with sorrow—though not the sorrow of despair but a sadness waiting and expecting to be overcome by wondrous joy.

I stopped running and slowed to a stroll, matching the drumming of my heart with the rhythm of the music. My mind told me I should be running after Suhruda, and I suspected Magdala might not approve of my pace, yet another part of me knew this was not just the right thing to do but in fact the only helpful choice to make. I spotted Suhruda running through the trees in and out of the dim light of night, stumbling more and more, looking like a crazed madman yet reminding me of myself, long ago, pushing through the thorns of a greener forest.

In the cold of the night, particularly this night, waiting for a hypothermic madman to come to his senses, or tire of his delirium, seemed more than foolish, and ceasing to run myself meant that I felt the cold more keenly. The shivering returned, more violently than before, and my ears, fingers, and toes ached while my mind grew slower. As I waited alone for my friend to return, I believe that I saw the darker side of the paths more clearly than ever. Aside from the crystal waters and the music, and the love of my companions, this forest seemed devoid of life, an empty shell, a bitter reality without care for my well-being or that of any other in and of itself.

Here again, the sound of my slowly beating heart brought with it the sounds of music, completely incongruous, though at least as real as the cold, hard ground beneath me. The music now played a song of hope that warred with the cold pressing in from above. As I listened, my conclusions about the forest and the paths were unaltered, yet in the melody, I heard and felt the life of spring so strongly that I half-expected the ground to sprout green grass beneath my feet. My thoughts returned to Suhruda, and I scarcely noticed the cold in my own body, overwhelmed with concern.

Suhruda appeared to be running around me in wide circles through the trees, frequently stumbling, and I worried that a collision with a large tree could be his end in this weakened state. Waiting for him that night, I felt myself grow older, so much older than the day I had left Ennuied and entered the forests. I was learning that there was much waiting when walking the paths and that most of my time was, in fact, spent waiting. I resolved to embrace the wait, as it seemed to be woven into the very fabric of the forest and paths. As Suhruda tired, his running became more erratic than ever, but his circle route around me narrowed to the point where I seldom lost sight of him in the dark woods.

Abruptly, I could no longer hear his languished path through the trees; the intensity of the music within me grew, and I knew I had to take action immediately. As I set out to find Suhruda, my body ached, and I heard it creak and crack, letting me know something wasn't right, but I was determined to give him whatever aid I could provide. Finding Suhruda, though, was no simple task; the world had gone silent, and I heard nothing. The searching was as difficult as the waiting, and I would have walked right past Suhruda had my eye not noticed a shimmer almost beneath my feet, not unlike the sparkle that had alerted me to the crystal pool. I approached the site of the flash and found myself staring at my friend Suhruda, encased in a tomb of translucent ice.

I had no special tools to break through the ice; thus, I dug away with my numbed hands, hoping to find a rough edge that I could grab and perhaps break. The ice, however, was as smooth as the finely polished rocks you find in fast-moving streams—beautiful, really, were it not encasing my friend in a deathly embrace, completely impenetrable. I clawed away at the ice with my fingernails, blood from my fingertips quickly bonding to the surface of the ice. Not knowing how long Suhruda could possibly last under these merciless circumstances, I pounded and kicked at the ice with all of my strength, causing enormous pain in my weakened right hip but doing no damage whatsoever to the ice.

Looking around for something, *anything* to help, I was struck by my own foolishness and grabbed one of the many heavy rocks which scattered the ground, most having fallen here long ago. I tentatively dropped the rock on the ice over Suhruda, wary that it may harm him as well as the ice, but nothing happened: not even a scratch appeared on the frozen tomb. I tried dropping the rock from higher up—still nothing. I held the rock above my head and let it crash on to the ice with all of my might. The ground shuddered beneath my feet, and cracks appeared in the icy covering; it was now easy work to separate the pieces and expose Suhruda. I did so quickly, and to my delight and surprise, he was still breathing with short, shallow breaths.

To this day, I have no idea how this was possible, but somehow, despite my numb and weakened body, I was able to settle my heart, embrace the music, and hoist Suhruda over my shoulders for the walk back to the camp. After taking my first dozen or so steps, I looked back at the site of the icy tomb, the moonlight shimmering though the icy air, and there I saw the smallest patch of green grass directly where I had stood, and within the grass I was sure I saw a single white blossom reaching toward the dim light of the moon.

The walk back to the others was long, and my mind wandered to strange places, but eventually I reached the pleasant warmth of the blazing fire and set Suhruda down in a warm place. We all banded together to support Suhruda, making a spot for him as close to the fire as we dared, and Letha lay close to him, providing warmth from her body. After an hour or so, the shivering returned, and with it Suhruda regained consciousness. Warm drinks and rest gradually helped him recover his senses, and grateful for the help, Suhruda continued to progress.

In a quiet moment, he whispered something unusual to me about hearing pages fluttering, which I assumed was part of his delirium, but seeing my pity, he insisted that this was something real. He turned away from me with a slight smile and a look of concentration as he began muttering all kinds of things about philosophy and the operation of the universe that I could not really understand. Glancing at me once more, he mumbled something about how we don't need to do and try everything just because we know how. He said this repeatedly. I wondered to myself whether this was Suhruda's brain restarting or, perhaps, this was the way people like Suhruda heard what I called the *music:* through a symphony of words, knowledge, discovery, and wisdom. I chose to keep my mind open to the possibility and would watch to see if Suhruda's pages would have the same wonderful yet devastating and then divergent effect, inviting him into the world of upside-down reality and power in brokenness, as the music did within me.

By the warmth of the fire, Khalid busied himself checking and re-checking Suhruda's fingers and toes, and I found it odd that he also looked at me with concern. After we finished tending to Suhruda, Khalid and I spoke to each other about the storm and this vortex of cold around us, discussing how we could get the group to safety. Overhearing us, Suhruda mused that storms like this could not possibly develop without a heat source contrasting the extreme cold and that we should move out of this area as quickly as possible during the comparative warmth of daylight; these were not the musings of a man in delirium, and we told Suhruda we would take his plan to the others, who were now sleeping nearby.

Khalid turned his attention to me and ran his hand over his own left ear, urging me to do the same with mine, and to my shock, there was not much left of what had been my outer ear; during the forest chase, or perhaps in the transition from cold to warm, much of it had fallen off, and what remained left blood on my hand. Looking at the rest of my body, I noticed that the tips of my fingers had turned black, with an angry red colour between the black and my normal skin; most disturbing was that the skin of my entire body now tingled and hurt, just a little. Curious, I pinched myself on the arm and felt little pain until I pinched very hard; the same was true for my legs, chest, and everywhere else I checked. Similarly, when Khalid put his hand on my back in a kind gesture before he lay down, I barely felt anything at all. I pondered whether this damage was now part of me forever or whether my condition would improve or even worsen. While I had no answers to these questions, I settled close by the fire to rest a little before daylight, the music inside me playing softly, feeling that all in all, this had been one of the best days of my life.

Chapter Forty
The Forest Will Not Be Fooled

I awoke with the first light of morning, shivering, and in the haze of half sleep, I found myself back in the forest, alone, waiting for the return of my friend; the sound of my companions throwing wood on the fire escorted me back to my senses. I got up quickly and helped throw more of the plentiful deadwood on the fire, which happily began to roar, sharing its heat in a small circle where life remained possible. Suhruda was up and about, looking much better, still mumbling to himself, sometimes smiling and at others times, perplexed. There was a pounding, pulsating pain around my ear, and my fingers absolutely ached, though not at the blackened tips. My skin tingled and stung exactly as it had a few hours earlier; nevertheless, there were important things to discuss. The cold showed no signs whatsoever of abating, and though we could survive for a while where we were, ultimately we all agreed that it was time to move on, and Suhruda's plan seemed as good as any other.

We built the fire into a blaze that might have threatened the forest had it been much larger, soaking up all the heat that we could, almost forgetting the bitter chill of the world around us. At about midday and with many regrets, we put on every piece of clothing we had and ventured further down the path that led us into the cold. For the first few minutes, I thought the frigid air was really not so bad, but then the cold crept up my arms and legs and settled on my head. I noticed that, once again, the cold affected my travelling companions, save Khalid, much more than me, and I was concerned that if one gave up, despair would become a contagion spreading to each heart. I gave away some of my clothing to the others, thinking that this would perhaps see them through, but my little sacrifice was barely sufficient to dent the knife's edge of the icy wind.

Lucrecio was looking grim with one side of his face covered in bright red blotches, which became almost purple in the centre. Interestingly, the damaged side of his face was not the freshly bare part that had recently supported a beard but the part of his face that had long been shaved clean. Despite his obvious pain, Lucrecio remained alert, constantly looking for a way forward and out of the cold. It was he who saw the ice-covered sign.

> *Cold winds howl, the tempest blows*
> *The land rubbed bare to stone*
> *Traveller, if you hope to live, warm comfort you must find*
> *Look not to the winds or the sun's warm glow*
> *but find the heat in kind*

Most of the group was too cold to speak, but each thought carefully about the words in the sign, hoping for some clue about how to find warmth, and soon. Khalid and I managed to share a few words, as we usually did about the signs. I wondered aloud about the last line, suggesting that, perhaps, "in kind" meant finding some kind of warmth that was similar to that from sun or the wind, though from the look Khalid gave me, he was not so sure.

The cold left us no time to stop, and I found that keeping everyone close together and constantly moving toward our goal, a warmer place, helped a little bit. I did not have that much clothing left myself, but though my skin stung and tingled and I had lost much of the function of my senses, my core remained warm, for the music continued to play a balmy song from somewhere far inside. Letha was clearly losing strength; hence, I gave away the thin blanket I had wrapped around my chest, the warmest part of my body.

Letha smiled for a moment and said, "Did you feel that? It was a warm gust of wind!"

I assumed that Letha was beginning to lose her senses as Suhruda had the day before, and I was glad I had given her my blanket. I could not have guessed what was about to happen. Letha, a soft-hearted young lady, saw that Aganad was suffering and could no longer speak, her cheeks and ears taking on a very unhealthy shade. Letha took the rabbit skin that covered her own head and placed it on Aganad, who was too cold to even express her thanks—that is, until another gust of warm wind came and swirled around her, temporarily thawing her jaw enough for a shocked yet muted "thanks" to come from her mouth. We all felt the warm gust, and Magdala astutely connected the acts of kindness with the warm winds and the message on the sign; the warm winds, he suggested, were directly connected to the acts of kindness we shared with one another. This made sense to all of us, and in hopes of creating a strong warm wind, we began to share our clothes with each other, speaking comforting words, and even sharing morsels of our remaining reserves of food. Feeling quite good about ourselves, we expected the warm wind to begin thawing the land at any moment, but something altogether different happened instead.

All of us men felt something strange on our faces and saw that we were rapidly growing beards—every one of us other than Khalid, who watched with concern—and the wind began to blow, but it was not a warm wind; it was bitter and cold, perhaps the coldest we had yet to encounter. There was no time to even question what was happening. My heart pounded, the music rang out a thundering tune in my heart, and I jumped into action, Khalid by my side. I tore off most of my clothes and covered my friends with every stitch of warmth I could find, with Khalid far surpassing my feeble attempts and Lucrecio doing his best to join in.

We warmed each other and surrounded each other as the cold wind cut our skin like knives and literally tore the beards from our faces. I began to lose the energy needed to keep warm, and all of our movements slowed. We must have been at death's door, because I don't think we even felt the cold when it happened: a new wind came upon us—not a cold, biting wind but a wind that carried the fragrance of spring—and it blew with such force that we could barely remain in one spot. Each of us dropped to the ground and let the wind blow over us, resting in the warmth; our bodies were slowly restored by fresh breezes that seemed to carry the force of life itself.

As I lay in the winds, my body warming, I found the strength to smile inwardly. I should have known better. The paths of the world accepted nothing that was not real, and only acts of kindness bathed in love could have brought the warm winds. The words from that first sign tumbled about in my mind. *The journey is beyond control; its paths are set and worn* ... Who was I to think I could manipulate the forces of this world with my play-acting and shallow imitations of what only the music could truly bring into being? The beards which grew on our faces were a reminder that our acts of kindness had been more about control than love.

Warming up was not without its pain. The nerves in our bodies let us know they were not pleased with the events of the preceding days, and angry wounds covered much of our exposed flesh. In spite of this, our spirits were high because the cold was gone; even the forest around us was coming to life with singing birds and the sight of green plants telling us that we would be able to find food. In this precious moment of calm, I found myself reflecting on the nature of the forest and how the cold of the world revealed what was there all along: bare ground, stones, and unfriendly paths. If the music came from some land somewhere, it was not any of the forests and paths I had seen. Oddly, this conclusion brought me comfort rather than pain; I would no longer expect from the forest what it could not possibly provide. And, besides, the music was playing inside of me more clearly than ever, and I was happier than I had ever been.

Chapter Forty-One
Winds of the Sovereign

The warm winds were welcome, but the sky looked no better, and the road ahead was likely full of new dangers and perils. The clouds resumed their angry looks; dark patches of purple, almost black, swirled in front of us, twisting and turning violently and unpredictably. Had we not just left that tremendous cold behind us, we might have turned around and away from what lay ahead. Instead, after eating and resting a little, we walked onward to face whatever came next along the mysterious paths we travelled. It did not take long at all to feel the changes wrought by the turbulence in the atmosphere. Something must have changed in the air pressure, because gradually, all of our ears began to feel strange inside, and my head hurt. Worse than that was the ominous feeling that came over me. I had a very real sense that we were not alone, our group, and that there were forces unseen arrayed against us.

The trees in this part of the forest were different from others I had seen. They were bent and mostly bare, yet some of them were massive in size. I was perplexed about the way that the trees were bent—some this way, others that, and only a fraction were bent in the direction that the wind was blowing. Suhruda had been watching the trees as well, and knowing he had studied the natural world all his life, I asked him for his thoughts on this strange forest.

Suhruda had been thoughtful since his brush with death, more curious than ever and in awe of the turning pages that he continued to hear from time to time. Suhruda informed me that this forest was unquestionably very old; the limited foliage indicated harsh growing conditions, yet some of the trees had grown to fantastic sizes. He also observed that trees of a similar size and age tended to bend in the same direction, meaning that, very likely, the winds had blown from a particular direction when the trees were young and more malleable. Suhruda was more able to connect his knowledge of the natural world to the paths, and he observed sombrely that whatever winds we were facing and were about to face were ancient and had shaped the entire forest we walked.

Suhruda looked at me with a grim, knowing wisdom is his eyes, and then he spoke. "Eloy, we should not be surprised by what is about to take place. There have always been forces arrayed against the common people, winds that are sent from the powers to control all others. These winds may abate from time to time, but the history of the forest shows they always return with a vengeance, often from a completely unexpected direction."

As the winds blew stronger, strange noises filled the air; there was a vibrating hum, an extremely low sound one might expect to hear in the ocean depths where the sun's rays cease to penetrate the deep. Sometimes the low hum was interrupted by higher notes, almost musical, but not music I was interested in hearing. At some points in time, the sounds were louder than others but seemed to express a constant and unfathomable power. The reverberations that I heard affected me deeply, for they contrasted directly with the music that played inside of me, as though a pressure or weight was being applied to my body to crush the beautiful music into silence by brute force. I had the sense that there was intrigue all about, dark mysteries, malice, and dread, not the danger posed by a random force of nature but a purposeful, planned, malevolence. I felt like a helpless conscript, chosen to be a pawn in someone else's terrible war.

To my dismay, I realized that the winds had gradually increased their intensity, and virtually without our knowing, what had begun as an irritant at our backs had transformed into currents of air that seemed to drive our every step. I had experienced many types of wind in my life to this point—the moist winter winds of Ennuied; cool, dry winds on the paths;

and stormy winds from the distant sea—but this wind was different. The air seemed to carry no natural life; it was old and stale, as though sent to the earth from an unnatural place. I came to understand that this was a wind blowing to control the people of the paths, to exercise power, and to rally the power of the people to dark purposes.

I found some comfort looking at Khalid, who let the wind blow by him with a calm resolve, the sparkle in his eyes unfettered. Others of us were getting swept off our feet. The steady winds and blustery gusts seemed to work in tandem, as if driven and controlled by the unseen presence I felt but could not see. We came to a place in the forest where the paths branched in many directions. Lucrecio, who was in the lead at this time, aimed his walk at the path that seemed closest to the direction of the music, but just before he entered the path, a sharp gust of wind literally blew him into an adjacent path.

With a feeling of dread and doom, we began to feel the full force of the winds that we had seen twisting and turning in the clouds. It became very difficult to stand in the face of this gale that was taking its toll on our resolve. The noise of the wind was like the sound of a rushing waterfall or the galloping of a team of horses. Lucrecio called back to us, discouraged, and barely audible in the wind, yelling something about how we would never hear the music over the roar of these winds. I attempted to explain that this did not matter, the music also plays within us, but Lucrecio could no longer hear me. The wind was now propelling us in one direction along the path, and it was no longer possible to resist. Gusts of stale air pummelled us from the sides as well, knocking out of our hands what possessions we had, blowing through our bags, and turning our pockets inside out. The tremendous force of the wind blew away the few coins my friends carried; retrieving them was impossible. I was angry about the injustice of our situation; what need did the wind have of the measly possessions and wealth we carried?

After stripping us of our supplies and treasures, the winds did not relent, even ripping much of the clothing off of our backs. It was embarrassing and humiliating because we seemed to lack control over any of these events, as though we were victims of an assault from history-moulding forces, seemingly beyond our influence. Letha was incensed with the winds, shaking her fists and yelling out that this was not how the path was supposed to be; it was supposed to get better and be filled with happiness. Letha stretched herself into the winds as she continued her bitter tirade, and in the blink of an eye, a gust of wind picked her off the ground and sent her flying over the trees and away from us, her screams quickly fading into the drone of the wind. As the rest of us were pushed along at alarming speeds, I managed to position myself close to Khalid, and unless we spoke clearly and directly into each other's ears, it was impossible to have a conversation.

"Khalid! What has happened to Letha? Do you think she has died?"

"Eloy, it is not given to those who would follow the music to fight the winds strength-for-strength. Do you remember the strong ones on the hill? As for Letha, there are many paths to find."

Khalid's words left me deep in thought once again. I understood that the power we held had nothing to do with violence, muscle, or vengeance and that the strong ones on the path were the principled, kind, and childlike. I was not sure what Khalid meant about there being many paths to find. Perhaps he meant that there was always a way forward for every traveller, no matter what. The drone of the wind made further conversations difficult, and I doubted Khalid would explain what he meant in plain language, anyway—it was not his way. The winds carried us to a new kind of landscape, a dreary place where the blowing tempest shaped the woods into a barren order of sorts with the trees in even rows and very few green plants. The path we travelled changed from a dirt trail with rocks and tree roots to a much wider packed rocky roadway that scraped and burned us as the wind pushed us along at alarming speeds. We passed by many others on this path, how many I cannot say, but all were hard at work sweeping, cleaning, and making repairs to the grey stone walkway. The workers appeared to blow in the wind as we did but were held fast to the ground by their tools and equipment.

The speed of our transit through this land was increasing to the point of being extremely unsafe and, instinctively, each of us looked for something, anything, to grab hold of to stop or slow us down. In an uncanny coincidence, the path rushing beneath our feet became littered with long metal poles, perfect for grasping and heavy enough to bring our movement to a more reasonable speed. Each of us was able to grab a pole and, with its added weight, stand in the face of the ancient winds, knowing that should we let go, we would be hurt or even killed by the conspiring forces of the storm. With growing understanding of our plight, I realized that we were not clutching ordinary metal poles but rather heavy metal tools that we were to use to brush clean the already windswept roadway.

With the wind billowing past, I swept the paths in a futile attempt to finish my work, all the while hearing the music as clearly as ever. The song I heard kept me company while I worked, and I did not feel alone; it also filled me with a very real concern for my travelling companions and the strangers I had seen labouring on the path. Most of all, the music contrasted with my surroundings, and I felt more convinced than ever that it was my purpose to find the land where the music came from, where it played all the time for everyone. At that moment, I felt compelled to scan the orderly woods to the side of the windswept path, where I spotted another sign, not hidden under dirt and debris like the other signs but in plain sight, swept completely clean by the relentless winds.

Chapter Forty-Two
Relief from the Wind

> *The power of the tempest blast*
> *Conspiring to control*
> *Stifled life and bent brown grass*
> *And all a pigeon hole*
> *Conniving winds have failed to see*
> *A gap for one and all*
> *Selfless love and kindness free*
> *Make haste what was a crawl*

The simple verse on the sign filled me with the same sense of wonder I had experienced leaving the abyss and later felt acutely when climbing the long hill; something wonderful was at work in the forests, something exceptionally different from the pain and tragedy of the paths. The relentless winds of the storm and the music in my heart formed a paradox that demanded my full attention, the contrast making the sweet music more attractive than ever. As I reflected on this wondrous contradiction, the beat from the music inside me began to pound, and my loyalty to the music seemed to grow in concert with a warmth and love for the others on the dreary, dry, dusty stone path. The others in my group were nearby, busy sweeping and cleaning, some looking forlorn and others, at peace. The wind remained fierce, yet I wanted to visit my friends and some of the strangers working on the path. I found that if I stayed close to the ground and crawled, steel broom in hand, I could manoeuvre myself close to the others.

The first I approached was Lucrecio, who was working with a simple steel tool that cleaned the grooves between the slabs of rock. A few simple acts of kindness—wiping the dust around his eyes, adjusting the leather straps on his shoes, and providing a few encouraging words—seemed to give him the boost he needed, and I am quite certain Lucrecio heard the music on the inside from that day forward. Crawling along, the next person I found was a complete stranger, wrinkled and tired, as though he had been cleaning the paths for longer than he could remember. For him, listening to his story while we worked seemed like the finest service I could offer. He told me tales of his childhood in a very different place and about being caught in the winds that entrapped him in servitude long ago. The simple act of listening to this man while he worked seemed to set him free. I had not even mentioned the music I heard when this new friend changed before my eyes. The weary wrinkles seemed more like laugh lines now, and the sparkle in his eyes reminded me of the crystal pool.

I found Khalid next, working quietly, seeming happy as a clam. In an excited tone, he shared, "Do you realize, Eloy, how quickly we are moving toward the wonderful land? We have not moved this quickly since we fled the burning lands of the bearded men!"

I was pleased that I could offer some service to the others on the path, but I certainly did not feel I was moving quickly toward my goal of finding the land of the beautiful music—that is, until I remembered the last line of the sign: "Selfless kindness free, make haste what was a crawl." Perhaps it meant that when we manoeuvred under the influence of the music and the authority of love, the powerful winds could not in fact slow the journey at all. It was certainly true that the trees of the forest seemed to be flying by me as I patiently crawled from person to person, offering what support I could. It was not an unpleasant task, and I quite enjoyed myself, the music inside playing some wonderful and pleasant notes. Looking around, I noticed that many were doing the same as me—crawling to one another, deeply engaged in meaningful discussion, helping each other with the work—and I realized that our group had grown in size.

It was then that one of the most memorable events of my journey took place. To the south and west, a bright light broke through the stormy grey clouds, blazing yellow from the sun and the turquoise blue of a summer sky. With the wonderful sight came the music that was more powerful than the tempest but as soft and gentle as a songbird's call. It was a happy tune, full of hope, and the entire group heard it together. The music played for some time as we moved quickly along the path, continuing our work but barely noticing. Gradually, the music faded, and at the same time, the path changed, returning to dirt and rocks with intermittent patches of packed stone, and the wind settled to powerful gusts with relative calm in between.

As a larger group, we continued to treat one another well. For the first time in a long, long time, someone other than Khalid took the time to check on me. I had not been paying much attention to my body, but the kindness of a stranger brought back to mind my own condition, and I noticed the nagging pain in my hip once again; this pain had been my companion for so long that I suppose I had come to view it is a part of me. The numbness in my skin was also no better at all, and as my new friend poked and prodded, I scarcely felt a thing. The stranger pulled out the smallest vial of salve that she carried under her cloak, and though there was little left, she applied the healing unguent to my damaged fingers, cheeks, and ears. The balm took effect almost immediately, and my fingers returned to their normal undamaged colour—I assume that the result was similar on my face. It felt nice to receive care and concern; the company and togetherness were even better than the healing, yet I knew that there was little hope for my hip and numbed skin anywhere in these forests. I thought back to my lonely journey across the plateau, long ago now, with the flowers to the side of the path offering comfort and companionship that faded and died without fail. I felt a small twinge of bitterness but quickly dismissed the thought and chose to enjoy the company that was available, not the failed imaginings of the past—the dreams unattainable, shy of the musical lands.

The landscape surrounding the path continued to change as we walked along, the orderly forests giving way to woods where many young trees mixed with the old. Peculiarly, the trees larger than a certain height were all damaged, as though the rocks from the cold lands had also landed here at some point in the past, except that I could not see any stones on the forest floor. The clouds towering in the sky made me feel quite small; the edges of at least four distinct storms were visible from where I stood. The winds were relatively calm, but we all felt strange pressure changes in our ears, as though great volumes of air were surging up and down high in the atmosphere above. I had the distinct impression that the same murky forces behind the winds were at work in some deadly game of cat and mouse that had nothing to do with us but all the same posed great danger to us all.

Without warning, intense periods of rain came and went, and with them, hail and thunder. I had experienced hail growing up in Ennuied. It was a nuisance, damaging the fodder grass crops and making it unpleasant to venture outdoors. The hail that fell here was something different: large balls of ice that could seriously hurt an unsuspecting traveller. During a break between squalls, Suhruda took one of the hail stones and cut it in half, revealing layer after layer of hardened ice. He explained to all of us that these hailstones were passing up and down through the clouds, gathering tremendous strength and energy before falling on the path.

The sky darkened, the air felt alive, and we knew another storm was mustering its forces. This storm was different, more ominous than the others; at least a few of the storm clusters had converged with unpredictable consequences.

Chapter Forty-Three
Tragedy

Suhruda called out, "Take shelter, everyone! This is no ordinary thunderstorm! Quickly to the hollows in the large trees—we will wait this one out."

Most of the group moved quickly to find shelter, knowing this was not a time for reflection or discussion but for urgent action. Magdala, who had always struggled to accept Suhruda and his views on the forest, chose to stay on the path, yelling something about how he had the strength to handle anything and would journey on, alone if needed. He had barely finished his tirade when the rains began, sheets of water pouring on Magdala and the path, as though a giant lake in the skies were being tipped on its side and emptied. It was difficult to see him through the falling water, but I could tell that Magdala was having trouble seeing where he was going, walking on and off the path, slipping in the mud and falling down. Some of the travellers nearby laughed at Magdala, thinking he was getting what he deserved for being arrogant and rude. I thought differently, knowing it could well have been me at a different part of the journey, and I felt the foreboding of something terrible. Without warning, the hailstones began to fall (if you could call the oversized spheres of ice *hailstones*), the smallest of which were the size of an apricot and the largest, bigger than many an apple I had eaten.

The scene unfolding before us was no longer funny to anybody. Magdala was being hammered into the ground by the hail, calling out in pain, and I knew with certainty that should Magdala remain where he was, outside of the protection of the large trees, he would most certainly die. With very little forethought, I ran out into the hail toward Magdala, only to discover Lucrecio well ahead of me and Khalid ahead of him. Rain and hail separating us from our companions, we converged on Magdala together, grabbing him by the arms and legs and dragging him as fast as we could toward the shelter of the woods. The falling ice felt like a flurry of knives hurtled at me by an otherworldly being of tremendous strength. Even through my numbed skin, I felt the sharp blows, and a detached part of my mind wondered about the injuries my body was sustaining. When we were about halfway to the shelter of the woods, the unthinkable happened.

A particularly large chunk of ice struck Khalid between his eyes, and he dropped to the ground. Blood began to pool on the wet soil beside his head as the hail pummelled the length of his exposed body. Lucrecio and I tried to carry both Magdala and Khalid, but given the conditions, progress was very slow.

With dreadful gasps and a grievous-sounding gurgle caused by fluid in his lungs, Khalid called to Lucrecio and me. "Get him to the forest and safety! Do not delay!"

I could not believe what Khalid was asking. Were we to leave him alone and injured while we rushed Magdala to safety? Any doubt in my mind about what I was to do was settled with a final "Go!" from Khalid. We heaved and dragged Magdala toward the woods using every ounce of strength we could muster. As we approached the shelter of the large trees, my muscles ached and seemed barely able to carry my own weight; I wondered how much further I could go. I stole a look back at Khalid, who was now completely still, looking like little more than a wet pile of clothing left out in the storm. Seeing us now, a few of our traveling companions ran out from the trees and helped Lucrecio carry Magdala the rest of the way to the safety of a large tree. As for me, I turned around and went straight for Khalid as quickly as my exhausted body could carry me. The storm seemed to be dying down, and I held out hope that I could rescue him and bring him to the safety of the forest cover.

My hopes came to a crashing end when I saw Khalid up close. The pool of blood was much larger now, and his skin had taken on a deathly pallor. Like razors, the falling ice shredded Khalid's clothing, exposing bruising and wounds, the blood mixing with falling rainwater. Khalid had always been wiry and strong, but his body looked weak and utterly broken. His chest no longer rose and fell, and with a certainty that hit me in my gut, I knew Khalid was gone.

Kneeling where I was, rain pouring over my head, I began to weep for his loss and for the cruelty of the forest paths that would take the life of someone so kind and strong. The tears flowed, and with them, memories. I recalled my childhood play with Khalid, running around the paths of Ennuied, and our renewed friendship as young adults; most of all, I remembered the joy of discovering that I was not completely alone on my journey away from Ennuied. Khalid had been there for me time and time again, never asking for anything in return. I wished I had given more back to him, told him what a friend he was, and learned more about what mattered to him.

I put my hand on Khalid's bloody face to say goodbye, and as I did, something like a jolt of lightning passed through me. The beautiful music inside me became so intense and powerful that I put my hands over my ears in a futile effort lower the volume. The indescribable song travelled though my body, every part. A powerful energy and resolve to complete the journey mingled with my grief, in no way lessening its intensity. Though Khalid had passed, it was as though he were speaking to me and urging me to continue forward to the land of the beautiful music and to give myself for the benefit of those travelling with me. I thought about my journey so far, the miles I had travelled from Ennuied, and how most of my efforts had been about myself. Even when I had helped others, so much of it had been all about me.

In Khalid, I had seen something different: love with no conditions, no thought of reciprocation, only the hope of freedom and friendship. Khalid certainly had no expectations that those he loved and helped would meet any kind of social, moral, or behavioural criteria. In fact, he seemed most drawn to those in positions of weakness and failure, with no ability to repay him. How different he was from the bearded men and their obsession with categories, who sometimes began with kindness but quickly transitioned to categorizing everything according to their calculations. In Khalid, selfless love seemed so complete and pervasive that the categories lost all sense of relevance.

I felt humbled by the reality of my own selfishness, yet not in the same way that I felt the hail beating on my back. I did not feel chastised by the music or my memories of Khalid; I did feel the weight of the truth. Conflicting emotions ran around inside me, and I smiled to myself, thinking again of Khalid. He was nothing like the paths of the forests; in fact, if it were possible to operate in an opposite way to the expected rules of the forest, he did—and accordingly met a world of resistance that eventually took his life. Perhaps all those who walk like him meet resistance on the path. I had certainly felt this resistance during my discoveries along the journey, most of which Khalid had a hand in facilitating.

I suspected that it was Khalid who watched me enter the forest to begin with, knowing that the only way in was the path with the cutting branches, and it was he who encouraged me through the narrow gate with the painful red latch. I was also suspicious that it was Khalid's swift boot to my rear that had saved me from the abyss; it was certainly he who led me out. Watching and learning from Khalid probably prevented me from enjoying the pleasures of Heureux, which were not based in love. Khalid was no fan of the ways of the bearded men, and our resistance to their ways certainly cost us a lot of comfort, though I suspected that the storm would reach them in time as well. The winds of the storm itself blew in directions that Khalid never looked and that held no interest for me. It was astounding, all this pain and turmoil—all for simply believing in the music and recognizing that love is the foundation of the best decisions. What a place these forests were!

The winds, rain, and hail died down, and I discovered that I was no longer alone; the others had gathered around us, sharing in the sombre moment. Together, we carried Khalid to the woods and dug a crude grave, burying him with the sand, dirt, and rocks of the paths of the forest. We held a short ceremony where travellers who I did not even know had spoken with Khalid, shared what he had meant to them. Time and time again, I heard that the music became real through Khalid and his ceaseless patience, love, and uncompromising devotion to what is good. I felt some sense of comfort during the ceremony, but my thoughts were dark and lonely afterward. So many times, The Darkness had visited me as a passing phantom, a mist blown away by brighter dreams and the thought that something better lay behind a veil. This time, the sense of death was pervasive and complete, and though the music continued in my heart, explanations and wisdom were beyond my reach.

Chapter Forty-Four
Waiting

I sensed that it was time to move again, to continue the journey through the stormy lands to the place where the music always played. Our group of travellers had grown large in the windy lands, and the familiar faces were few, yet I felt a tremendous concern and affection for each of them. I moved amongst the trees to get everyone going and was surprised that many of them thought they had already arrived at their destination. I supposed that the trees afforded them some shelter, and being free of the stifling power of the winds must have felt like liberation. All the same, I knew that we were in dangerous lands and that we must keep moving or face a host of unknown terrors. I begged and cajoled, but it was impossible to get the group moving without using manipulation or power, both of which were completely out of character with the music and the life of my departed friend, Khalid. Instead, I did the only thing I could think of: I waited. In truth, I waited a long, long time. When I had entered this part of the forests, I was a young man, but I had long since left the days of youth when it was time to move along.

Strange and exceptional things happened in me and to me as I waited. The music played inside me the entire time, a ballad of long-suffering that taught me patience and peace, even while the first hairs of grey appeared and my skin developed a few more sags and folds. While waiting, I enjoyed the friendship of others who had become waiters: Lucrecio and

Suhruda both, as well as the transformed Magdala, no longer brash and apt to judge but quick to forgive. In a most wonderful turn of events, I found my old friend Injud had joined us and was waiting as well. Throughout this entire time, I willed my companions to move on and leave this place behind to find a better place, to join me and walk away. I knew that I could leave on my own any time that I wanted, but it just did not seem right; to have done so would have put me at discord with the music, so I stayed and remained with my companions.

After another of many nights in my simple forest dwelling, I awoke to a loud and unsettling noise, something I had dreaded for some time. It was the sound of the inevitable return of the storm, letting us know that we were not safe here. Thunder slapped the earth as though a great open hand had struck the waters of a vast ocean. Not a mile away in the woods, we saw smoke rising from where the lightning must have hit. My circumstances changed swiftly, and after waiting for so long, I was thrust into action by many travellers asking how to find the path and be on their way out of this place.

Thunder continued to rumble, sometimes in the distance and at other times, terrifyingly close. With a few of the others, I, still limping, helped rally as many as possible to travel together and find safety in numbers on the paths ahead. A few of the travellers refused to leave, worried about their safety, but we could no longer stay—the thunder a reminder of the power of the storm. Reflecting on the rapid-fire change of circumstances, I mused that the pressures of the storm were ancient and common to all; while they ebbed and flowed and appeared to abate, they always returned with a cruel reminder that the lands of the music were yet to be found.

As we reached the path, there was a flash of light indistinguishable from the crashing of thunder. I knew that it was important to keep moving to get away from this place, but some in our group became frozen with indecision, thinking fondly of their simple shelters in the woods and fearing the unknown thundering path. I let most of the group travel ahead of me down the road, and I waited with the undecided few. I had learned a lot about waiting, and while tempted for a moment to yell and berate the travellers, I knew that it was love and patience that achieved real results.

Real waiting was not idly enduring until enough time passed, but being actively present with others. Waiting was also not about saying things to make me feel better about how right I was, nor did it involve pretending people were somewhere they were not. It certainly had nothing to do with judging my fellow travellers. I had learned long ago on the steep hill that I could be eclipsed in a moment by another traveller who I had judged as lacking. The mystery of waiting was that in complete acceptance, long-suffering, and an undying expectancy about the matchless path ahead, tremendous power for good came to others.

Waiting could be a dangerous thing. The lightning and thunder continued, sometimes striking ahead on the path and at other times behind us near the forest dwellings. The travellers with me were confused about where to go, some wanting to return to what they assumed was safety in the forest dwellings.

A young lady named Jane spoke to me. "I just want to go back! Why the thunder and turmoil? I want to go back to happy and carefree."

Jane had dirty blonde hair and a smooth face with freckles. She looked like someone who belonged outside in the sunshine. Jane had lost her parents as a young girl and found herself in the forest. She made friends easily. Both endearingly and naively, Jane was the type who expected kindness from the world and shared it freely with others. As she spoke, Jane turned back, toward the forest dwellings where I had first noticed my grey; she spotted something in the trees, a sign made of wood:

> *Seeker of happy, lover of life*
> *Where is your home?*
> *Let go the shallow, seek the deep*
> *Pain, your friend; happy the mist*
> *Veritable delights unknown*

Reading the sign over Jane's shoulder, I was filled with tremendous delight, as though spring winds filled my heart with freshness. Jane, however, looked confused and asked me what I thought the sign could mean. I was filled with compassion for her and recalled the plethora of confusing signs I had seen over the course of my journey. I gently explained to Jane that perhaps the rudimentary dwelling she had made for herself while we waited in the forest was not actually her home. I caught myself before I said too much, dangerously coming close to imposing the specifics of my journey onto Jane's. The message on the sign presented her with choices that I likely understood strictly on the simplest of levels. Jane was experiencing something precious, something costly, something very good, and I did not want to damage anything through doing or saying foolish things.

I hoped that something wonderful would happen; perhaps the beautiful music would burst through the clouds and fill my new friend with joy and hope for a wonderful future ahead on the path. Instead, the lightning flashed and thunder shook the earth again and again. We could see smoke and flames coming from the patch of forest where I had waited with Jane and the others for such a long time. Any question of returning to that part of the woods literally vanished in a puff of smoke. Jane was stunned and panicked and not thinking clearly; she began to search the forest around us for new dwellings and shelter. As she did so, I felt a strange tingling on my skin followed by blinding light, vibrations that knocked me off of my feet, and ringing in my ears. After a few moments, the ringing subsided, and I heard Jane screaming in pain; the lightning had struck close by, burning her skin, and now she was stumbling about, partially blinded by the flash. My numb skin stung just a little, and I could see just fine through the smoke and dust. I was angry with the paths for treating Jane so harshly, but I knew well that walking the paths was sometimes a matter of life and death.

Jane called to me, "Help! All I see is a dark hole. It is dragging me, and I can't stop!"

Being careful not to touch her burns, I grasped Jane's hand and walked her away from what I knew was a passage to the abyss and up the path toward the others. Though the thunder continued, the dust and smoke settled, allowing us to make good time and catch up to the others. I watched with interest as Jane shared her story with the others and showed them her burns. I was disappointed that her companions took little interest in her wounds, instead showing her theirs, asking for her pity and support. Someone said to her that they heard the thunder and saw the smoke but that it looked rather small and certainly not worth all of the fuss.

It was difficult for me to watch Jane experience such a hard lesson about the reality of others on the path. I walked beside her and whispered slowly and carefully, "The scope of events on the path can only be judged by the one experiencing them or the very wise."

Jane smiled at me, and we talked for some time about the forests, the paths, and the music. The truth was that most of the others on the path did not mean to belittle Jane; they simply were not thinking about her at all, their attention consumed by the crashing thunder and their own needs and wants. In my own travels, the story was the same; other than Khalid, there were probably no fellow travellers who understood the gravity of my agonizing encounters along the path and how many times I had brushed close to death itself. While I was grateful to experience the empathy of others from time to time, the solitary mingling of pain, weakness, and the music formed a weave of tremendous strength, usually hidden from view but more real than the path itself. I would not trade it for anything in the world, and I hoped Jane would also find something wonderful veiled behind her difficult experience.

The circumstances of the journey permitted Jane and me to walk together for a while, and we enjoyed one another's company thoroughly. Jane was not able to describe the events of the journey in words as easily as I was, but I found that she intuitively understood the paths and where to place her feet in ways that I never would. Occasionally, as she walked beside me, I heard the music from the beautiful lands come through her shoes as they traversed the path. It never ceased to amaze me when this happened. While my old friends understood the pulse of the music and shared my need to serve the others, caring for them and protecting them from hidden dangers, most of the younger travellers did not think about these kinds of things.

Though Jane had journeyed far fewer cycles of night and day than I, she exuded empathy and compassion and supported me in everything. I was tempted toward bitterness when I thought of all the miles I walked without her by my side, but I remembered the lessons from the plateau and chose to remain thankful for the present.

Chapter Forty-Five
The Sea

The rolling thunder crashed, and lightning struck the forests around us; many travellers were stopped dead in their tracks by fear and confusion. Some of my old friends, Lucrecio, Magdala, Injud, and Suhruda, worked tirelessly to keep people moving. I overheard them say some things to the travellers that I was not sure were true to keep them on the go. I could not bring myself to do this, and I often found that there was nothing to be done but wait as the paths took their toll and the music did its work. I waited with quite a few until they were ready to go. Waiting continued to be taxing—the thunder and lightning were very real threats, and I felt we were not getting closer to the land of the beautiful music. So often it was the same story that I had experienced so many times myself: devastating experiences on the path showing travellers their weakness and fantastic misunderstandings about the world, and at the same time discovering a wonderful and mystical power at work for good. In spite of the challenges, I found great pleasure in supporting the readied travellers to continue their quest, so much so that I did not feel bad at all about the slowing of my own journey, if indeed it slowed at all. Many times, I was reminded of the books in the library of the bearded men, full of tales not unlike these new stories written every day all around me. I turned in for the night, most of the time, feeling tremendous satisfaction from the events of the day.

The thunder continued, and with it came great darkness—the kind of darkness that you could actually feel. The music which continued to play inside of me all of the time shielded me from many of the effects of the darkness, but my limp was worse than usual, and I certainly noticed what the dark did to my travelling companions. It goes without saying that the darkness made it more challenging to see the path, but it seemed to do more than this, causing many to believe that there was no path. I heard some talk of turning back, and I was stunned to hear others musing about a mystical place of wonder called Heureux where the light always shone. Moreover, in the dark, I noticed that the winds of the storm, though subtle now, led many people into the woods, and I never saw some of them again. Through the numbed nerves on my skin, the darkness felt vaguely uncomfortable, but for many, this experience was much more pronounced. I observed that some engaged in frenetic activity to distract themselves from the feeling and that others walked on, desperate to be done with this place. I noticed that all of those who sought the path found it, even when they became lost in the dark woods for a time.

I waited with a few more people until their discomfort was sufficiently unpleasant to get them moving. I did not enjoy watching the travellers experience these things, and no matter how philosophical I became about the potential for good through suffering, it bothered me. I recalled a conversation I had had with Suhruda where I tried to convince him that suffering was really all for good because it led us to the music and away from the places on the journey that held no future. I could tell that while Suhruda basically agreed with me, he was irritated about something. I asked him to clarify why he did not like what I said.

Suhruda explained that in his growing knowledge of the world, he had discovered that much of what happens could be explained through numbers and equations, allowing him to make predictions about the natural world with tremendous accuracy. With some agitation, he went on to explain that in spite of his relentless efforts, he could not find any type of predictable, quantifiable relationship between suffering on the path and good. In fact, he elaborated that his data sometimes failed to find any kind of benefit of suffering at all. What

Suhruda said to me that day stuck with me in a most unpleasant way, and were it not for the music playing inside me, it might have been it might have been the end of my travels.

I noticed more changes in my body as I continued to wait. Brown spots appeared on my hands and face. My skin felt a little looser all over my body, and the old injury in my hip worsened greatly. My hair began to disappear, and I could not eat or drink quite as much as I used to. I had seen these changes take place in others on the path, sometimes associated with complaining, sadness, and lethargy. As for me, the music played constantly, and I felt much stronger than I had ever felt before. Where crushing loneliness had been debilitating in the past, I now described my experience as one of content solitude, utterly lacking in the emotional trauma of my earlier days. I wondered aloud how I would fare now on that steep hill I had climbed so long ago. I also continued to enjoy the company of my friend Jane when time and circumstances permitted. It was interesting how comfort with solitude actually improved the connectedness I felt with her.

With all the waiting and intermittent movement, we managed to make slow but steady progress down the darkened path. There was a mysterious energy in the air, and I could not tell if it was good or bad; while menacing on one hand, it filled me with anticipation on the other. A new smell entered my nostrils, one that others had described to me but I had never experienced myself. The moist air tasted of salt, and the odour seemed to encompass a completely new realm of life, unfamiliar on land—I was sure it was the sea. Sure enough, as we continued along the path, I heard strange and wonderful sounds, a little like the familiar wind blowing through the treetops, which I assumed to be waves crashing against the shore ahead.

The sounds and smells of the water grew stronger ever so slowly—so slowly, in fact, that I questioned whether the sea was truly nearby. The pain in my hip was worse than it had ever been, and I truly longed for this endless path through the woods and forests to come to an end. At long last, the trees began to thin, and I noticed rocks peeking through the grasses and brush. Further along, the rocks appeared smooth. Suhruda, I was sure, would explain that the rocks were polished by ancient winds blowing onto the land from the sea. I guessed he would also begin a lengthy lecture about the power of the seas and how life on land depended on the rains, which were borne over the waters. Near the end of the day, we discussed stopping to rest and locate food and water, deciding to press on just a little further. All at once, the remaining trees gave way to a great open space, with tufts of grass between sheets of smooth stone and, well below us, the waves of the sea crashing against the rocky shore.

I was in absolute awe of the sea and wondered if perhaps I had finally reached my destination. Exhausted from the long walk, everyone wanted to set up camp for the night and rest, and while I, too, wanted to stop, I felt that the group did not understand the magnitude of our discovery. It was the sea! Were the sun not about to set, I would have certainly descended the slope to the water for a closer look. Instead, we built a fire for warmth and sat together, talking about all we knew of the ocean, which, in hindsight, was not very much. The music inside me played a song I can only describe as present and strong. I know these seem like strange descriptors for a song, but I heard what I heard, and that is how I can describe what played. I was startled to discover that others in the group were tapping their feet to the rhythm of the song and looking out across the water into the night-filled sky. The same song that played inside me now echoed outside my body, and it was coming from across the water. It appeared that some people sitting around the fire heard the music, judging by the looks of wonder in their eyes, while others continued visiting with each other as though nothing were happening. Eventually, the music faded away, and everyone in the group but me seemed to have fallen asleep, my mind racing with thoughts of the sea and the music beyond.

At some point in the night, I must have fallen asleep, because I woke up with a start. With barely a moment's thought, I clambered down the rocky slope to the beach and touched the water. Though I had not been to the sea in person, the water felt peculiarly familiar to me, as though I had been touching it for a long time. I took some time to look out across the deep black waters and, in the precise direction of the music the night before, I spotted land. Jagged mountains with green slopes rose from the depths, and something sparkled on the land in the distance. Overwhelmed with emotion, I was positive that these were the lands I had sought all of these long and weary miles.

I sat down on the rocks and stared out over the water toward the new lands for some time. I felt as though the sea were my friend, a familiar face, even a mirror expressing the perils of my journey without words. I was under no illusion that, like the forest, the sea was full of danger; more than once, the crashing breakers nearly dragged me into their frothing currents around the sharp rocks. It was the darkness of the sea that I could relate to best—the inner workings of the waters were completely sealed from view. The shore where the waters met the land was full of life: wonderful creatures on eight legs, some brightly coloured stars, and green plants washed in from some unseen garden. If this was the edge of the waters, I pondered what living wonders would be found in the depths. Perhaps the greatest marvel of the sea that day was in the dark water itself. How deep did it go? I pictured untold volumes beneath the surface and the tremendous power of the relentless currents.

I wanted very much to stay near the water and perhaps somehow reach the lands I could now see with own eyes. My thoughts turned to the group above, and reluctantly I climbed up the slope to discuss what I assumed would be our new plans. Reaching the top, I was surprised by how much time had passed by and that everyone seemed to be preparing to leave. I raised my voice and spoke to everyone and nobody in particular, asking them what they were doing. I explained that I had seen the lands of the beautiful music with my own eyes and that we should stay. Most of the crowd ignored me, even those I counted as friends, and a few travellers pointed to the path that continued around the corner close the water but away from the lands across the water. I spoke with Suhruda, my most trusted friend since Khalid's passing, and tried to convince him to stay. Though Suhruda listened to me and appeared to believe every word I shared, he explained that he had to go where the people went because that is how he heard the pages in his head.

Having gathered their things, the group began to trek down the new path and out of view. I would have been just fine to stay in the solitude of that place and find some way to the lands across the sea, but then I saw Jane walking by herself in the back of the crowd, sometimes stumbling and looking very much alone. Unexplainably, the more I thought of Suhruda's words and looked at Jane, the louder the music played inside me. With an ambivalence that bordered on torment, I followed after her and away from the lands I had sought from the first steps of my journey.

Chapter Forty-Six
The Coastal Lands

The path we now followed was different from what I was used to walking. Instead of compressed dirt, stones, and tree roots, this track was made from sea-smoothed rocks packed down by the feet of many travellers before us. I felt strange following the group, knowing that I had walked past the goals of my youth, pursuing another musical mystery. Less distracted about the final destination that I had left behind me, I found there was much more time to spend with the other travellers. While it was true that I had formed many friendships over the course of my travels and listened to countless stories, I began to experience something new. I found that I no longer had any agenda in my relationships with my fellow travellers other than to be with them and hopefully be more beneficial than harmful in all I did. I suppose that the others somehow sensed my lack of ulterior motives; even some of the intentions that I had always thought were positive had dissipated, and my relationships became much closer. After walking all of these miles, I felt less certain than ever about the details of the forests and the paths yet more aware of my purpose. The wisdom in leaving the lands with the music behind was a great secret, yet walking further and further away from my dream, I found that the music inside me played loud and clear.

The land flattened out in front of us into a lovely bay where the waves of the sea were gentle and the shore, sandy. There was a rock face far to our left, but the path was smooth and pleasant, and the group made excellent progress toward wherever it was they were going, occasionally taking breaks to eat some of the tasty shellfish. On the far side of the bay, though, the rocky wall moved much closer to the sea, and the path appeared to cut a narrow track between the rock face and the waters as it moved around a corner. Few in the group seemed to notice, but the path there looked precarious to my eyes. I knew I could turn around and return to the spot where I had spied the lands of the beautiful music, but the music playing inside me became quiet at the thought. Instead, I took some time to circulate among my new friends, checking their footwear for serious flaws and fixing them as well as I could. I lost count of the numbers who received my care and attention.

I noticed that Jane's shoes were falling apart and provided little protection from the moisture of the sea, and I was concerned that she might not make it through the rocky pass ahead. The jacket I wore had a small tear across the left side of the chest, and I found it simple to tear off a couple pieces of fabric to wrap her feet. By using parts of my own shoelaces, I found that I was able to wrap her feet quite nicely within the shards of her shoes.

I also busied myself finding firm walking sticks for as many people as I could. I looked for sticks that were thick and strong, without rot and tall enough to be used for walking and reaching into deep holes. When I suggested a walking stick for a traveller, he or she usually took it with a smile (as though I had done something cute), not realizing that I had a pretty good idea of what was coming down the path.

As we walked along, I was inexplicably drawn to the sea, knowing that my veiled destiny was wrapped up within its dark waters. I felt respect for the sea, dread of its power, and wonder at its mystery. As I had seen in the distance, the land began to narrow considerably. It became difficult to see the path, which passed over sheets of rock with large cracks and deep holes filled with seawater and animal life. As we rounded the corner, I thought we might find another bay, but instead the coastline ran ahead straight and narrow between a sea with crashing waves and an insurmountable cliff face. Stopping to survey the route ahead, I spotted a large rock to the side of the path with markings on it. Wiping away layers of salty sand, I was not surprised to see another message:

Take heed of the sea
The deep and the land are one ahead
Life and loss entwined

I missed Khalid, who could likely have explained the meaning of the sign. It was rather ominous yet fascinating, and at the same time, it sounded intuitively true. As the group set out again along a narrow way between the rocks and sea, I stayed close to Jane in the middle of the pack while observantly watching those in front. The crashing waves were close at first, soaking every one of us with cold salty spray as we walked. Some of the travellers laughed at the water and cheered when the big waves came, but I did not feel much humour about our situation, and I could tell that Jane did not either. Gradually, the waves seemed to lose some of their power, and they returned to the sea, giving us more room to walk.

I noticed that the travellers in the front of the group were slowing down and moving from side to side as much as forward. The path became very difficult to see and disappeared altogether as we gradually descended into a decidedly wet, flat land with hundreds of pools of water, as though it had been part of the sea floor itself a short time ago. Many of the rocks were covered in some kind of wet green plant that made them even more slippery than the ice I had encountered at the beginning of the stormy lands. In such a landscape, it was difficult to know which direction to go to find a way across to the other side. Many of the travellers slipped and fell. I heard a loud snap as someone nearby broke a leg in a fall between the large slippery stones. Those who had let me help them with their footwear—including Jane, whose makeshift shoes held up well—certainly did better than the others.

Eventually the lowlands narrowed again, and we came to a place where the sea was very close; waves sometimes filled the crevasses beneath us. The cracks and fissures grew wider and deeper to the point where it was difficult to find a way through without falling into the dangerous currents below. At one point, we found ourselves trapped with a wide cleft filled with frothing white water lying between us and the way forward. Some discovered that by placing their long walking sticks into the water below and wedging them between rocks, they were able to use the stick as leverage in the middle of a jump and propel themselves across the gap. I was concerned that my long-injured hip would prevent me from completing the jump and questioned myself about why I would take the risk to follow the others even further from the lands of beautiful music. Seeing Jane shakily make the passage, though, I knew that I would follow to help ensure her safety and the opportunity to get out of this place.

When it was my turn, I planted my walking stick firmly among the rocks and the bottom and lunged forward. My hand slipped badly on the wooden shaft, and I crashed into the far edge of the rock wall, scraping the side of my face and, worse, landing square on my injured right hip. My toughened skin did not hurt much, but the searing pain in my thigh caused me to black out for a moment. A man with a very familiar face that I could not quite place helped me to my feet, but when I turned around to thank him, he was no longer there.

Chapter Forty-Seven
In Khalid's Way

Limping badly, I moved as fast as I could across the rocks to catch up with Jane. I hobbled past many travellers in various states of distress and health. I would have helped any who asked, but I was focused on finding Jane. I suppose I believed that she was very close to the music but in need of my help, much like I had been when trapped in the abyss so long ago. I spied her well ahead of me and quickened my pace; ignoring the throbbing in my side, I closed the gap between us considerably. Once again, the coast was changing as we moved, and we were now traversing a narrow band of land between the sea and the sheer rock face. The walking was easy, but I could not help feeling ill at ease with the towering rock on one side and the waves on the other, as well as the green sea plants and shelled creatures I observed above my head among the rocks.

I caught up with Jane, who was very happy to see me. "Greetings!" she called out. "I have been looking for you. I have heard the music in a dream. It was playing in front of me on a long winding path, working its way up through a vast forest!"

It was delightful to see Jane, and much as I was intent on assisting her, I found myself comforted in a pleasing way when with her. Returning to my senses, I encouraged Jane by noting that it was wonderful to hear the music, but inside, I was much more concerned about our current situation, stuck in this dangerous place. I took some time to carefully observe my surroundings and the water. As though reading my thoughts, big waves arrived with every eleven swells, and each great wave drew a little closer to where we walked.

It was not long before the salty water lapped at our feet, causing quite a stir among the travellers. Worrying about the incoming water, some travellers turned back running, though I was not sure where they could possibly go, with the safety of the hill overlooking the lands of the beautiful music far away. Others tried to run forward, pushing people out of the way, even walking right over top of them, thinking they could outrun the advancing water. It was a tragic sight to watch. It was different with Jane; though she looked afraid of the water, she kept glancing upward toward the rocks, as though expecting an escape path to magically appear.

She turned to me and said, "I think I have seen this in my dreams. The way out is not back the way we came, nor is it forward. It is up, but I don't know how to get there!"

I reminded Jane that the paths toward the music sometimes didn't seem to make practical sense initially, and I walked closely beside her. In my heart, the music beat a powerful tune, and I knew with certainty that somehow I had to help her. We walked as close as we could to the rocky wall, looking for any way up, while the water lapped at our feet and showed no signs of receding. A strong wave crashed into shore, the white water almost knocking Jane off her feet, and I dreaded what might be coming eleven waves later. I was counting each wave and had reached wave five when I saw something forming in the sea, three more swells out. It appeared to be the convergence of more than one wave, and it was larger than any I had seen. I urged Jane to stay close to me no matter what happened and to keep her head above the water while waiting for the swell to recede. As I feared, the wave came in with tremendous force, slamming the two of us against the rock wall and leaving us in water much deeper than we could stand in. The water receded to our waists, and we were able to plant our feet on the ground and resist the force of the water returning to the sea. We were okay for the moment, but I knew more waves were coming soon.

Two sights held my attention: to my right, I saw the next waves converging and forming more of a swell than a wave; and well ahead, I saw a break in the rocks to my left and, just maybe, a way up. Jane saw the possibility of escape in the rocks but not the incoming wall of water. She moved quickly through the water, and I struggled to keep up, my old hip working hard against the resistance of the now waist-deep sea. We probably made it halfway to the chance of escape before the water arrived. In an instant, we were no longer walking but swimming. It was exceedingly difficult to make progress, because there was so much water, and all of it was trying to return to the sea. As I recall, a good minute of effort brought us only a few feet closer to our goal. Jane looked at back at me, at the open sea, and her strokes began to slow. I implored her to keep going, not to stop no matter the pain in her body, but she slowed to the point that I caught up with her. Jane looked at me with growing sadness and panic; she was much lower in the water, barely able to keep her head above. I was feeling the pain of fatigued muscles myself, but the music beat a steady, clear beat, and I knew it was time to act.

Swimming out in front of Jane, I called out, "Grab my feet!"

Jane did not understand, and I yelled, "Jane, you have to hold onto my feet. I will pull you there."

She seemed to understand. Jane grasped my ankles as I swam on my back toward the break in the rocks, using all my strength to stay above the surface. We made some progress, but Jane had lost her breath and, even with my help, was unable to keep her head in the air. She took in a few mouthfuls of salty seawater, gagging and choking. In her panic, Jane grabbed for any part of my body she could in an instinctual battle to survive. I knew that if I did not break away from her immediately, I would put myself in serious danger, and I almost did break free, but the music inside was so peaceful. Instead, I let Jane climb on top of me, and I sank under the depths. Despite my predicament, I found myself more focused than I had been at any time in my life. Under the water, I continued to propel myself toward the opening in the rocks, though I scarcely moved at all. I allowed myself to sink still further, pressure building in my ears until, at last, I touched the sea bottom.

Jane's feet were now scrambling for traction on my head and shoulders, driving me into sandy sea floor. While I probably should have been in a panic myself, I remained strangely calm. Closing my mouth and nose tightly, I began to walk toward the opening in the rocky wall that was pictured clearly in my mind. The weight of Jane's body gave me excellent traction, and while it was much slower than walking on land, I was able to make progress. Through the greenish hue of the water, I saw it ahead of me: a break in the rock wall, starting from the sea floor and breaking through the surface. I moved toward it as fast as I could, Jane's feet digging into my shoulders and back and hitting my head with numbing blows; the pressure in my chest and desire to take a breath of cold water were almost overwhelming. With a dreadful finality, I realized that there was no way I could make it the rest of the way. I pressed on as fast and far as I could, the music playing that same tune I had heard while covered in the fodder grass dust of Ennuied long ago.

With the end in sight, my body overcame my will to defy the laws of biology, and I took a deep breath of the salty, cold, dark water. The reaction of my body was complete panic: the pressure in my chest was such that I felt as though I were exploding. The music, however, continued to play, and with its tune pulsating through my devastated body, I used my last strength to push up and thrust Jane toward the break in the rocks. Although my vision was fading and my mind, slowing, I am nonetheless sure I saw her reach the rocks and climb away. As for me, the pain began to fade, and I felt myself drifting away, moving upward through the surface of the water and into the evening sky.

PART IV
The Wisdom of the Journey

Chapter Forty-Eight
Khalid

The smell of smoke from a fire—that was my next sensation. Also, heat on my back and something prickly on my stomach. I opened my eyes and sat up, the blazing sun and blue sky above me, the gentle poke of fresh green grass beneath me. Of all of the things I could have thought about, my mind went first to the fact that I could feel the grass at all. Since the icy winds of Suhruda's rescue, I had been unable to feel subtle pleasures on my skin. Looking back down from the sky, I was astounded to see none other than my close friend Khalid, sitting by a crackling fire with a friendly grin on his face and a twinkle in his eye.

"Khalid! How did you get here? Actually, how did I get here? Where is here, anyway?"

"Eloy, you followed me here, and it is very good. Let's eat and drink!"

Khalid gave me something wonderful he had been cooking over the fire. It was like nothing I had ever consumed before: not meat, more like bread, but it was like bread with substance. It could not have been more different from the fodder grass bread I had eaten as a child. Khalid passed me a drink in a simple white cup. The drink tasted of both fruit and grains, and it tingled in my mouth and stomach, a pleasant sensation; both calm and excitement rose to my head when I swallowed.

I asked Khalid again, "Where are we?"

He paused for a time. "You know where we are, don't you?

"I think that we are in the land of the beautiful music. I can hear it equally inside and out; it sounds like the tapping of fine crystal glasses. But, Khalid, where are we?"

Khalid smiled at me; he knew he was playing with me and enjoying it. "Do you not remember the writings in the library of the bearded men? Remember how both east and west, the men and women in the books searched for another land, a better place?"

"Khalid, do you mean to say I have found that place?"

Khalid looked at me with just a touch of impatience. "One does not find this place; one is led here. Were you not led by the music?"

I smiled at Khalid, knowing all was well. "I was led by the music, but I left the land when I saw it to take care of the others and follow after Jane. Khalid, where are we?"

"You have found the island you sought, friend. More than that, you have made it here by the only route. Consider the forests you travelled. Is not the life of the forest built on death?"

Khalid's words were more than a little overwhelming, but one thing was for sure: I did not think I had arrived at these lands by doing or being anything special at all. All of the mistakes I made on the path ... I knew that I had in no way earned my passage here. I shared my feelings with Khalid. I asked him about the others and why they could not also find this place.

I did not expect the response I got from Khalid. He began to laugh and laugh, the hysterical kind of laugher that one experiences as an adolescent and seldom ever again. "Of course the way is open to others, friend. The music plays for all who will listen, without prejudice for colour, location, shape, or size." He became suddenly serious. "But don't misunderstand me— the path to this place requires death. You might be surprised by the music and life that comes from the most unsuspecting of travellers. You will be filled with amazement and understanding about who lives here."

Not even pretending to fully understand Khalid, I asked him, "Do you know about Jane? Do you know if she made it? I would trade my place in this wonderful land to see to it that she did."

"Come!" Khalid said. "Let us climb the mountain peaks and look over the forest lands."

Khalid led me on a wonderful path that wound its way up the mountainside. The climb was steep, but I did not hurt as I climbed. It was then that I realized that the pain I had known in my hip since the abyss was completely gone. It felt strange not to feel as though I were suffering; to be honest, it felt more than a little awkward to be completely without pain. Perhaps those who have experienced a great deal of pain and suffering will understand what that means. We climbed quickly, heart pounding, lungs heaving, and enjoying every minute of it.

We scaled the mountain up and up; initially, our route took us close to the sea, but then it moved inland underneath three towering mountain peaks. While more pleasant than anywhere I thought I had been, these lands seemed familiar. Either I had been there before, or I was experiencing the most uncanny sense of déjà vu. I asked Khalid if he knew why I felt as though I recognized this place.

Khalid gave me one of his famous looks, somewhat impatient yet good humoured. "Of course you have been here before! In fact, one could say that you have been living here."

"I feel as though I have been, but it is impossible. I recall my life in Ennuied and the fodder grass; I remember the pain and the beginnings of my journey through the forests, the abyss, Heureux, and the land of the bearded men, but I am quite sure my feet have never touched this land."

Khalid replied, "There are many ways of being here, friend. I have seen you here many times. A place is so much more than somewhere your feet walk."

Chapter Forty-Nine
Overlooking the Forests

As I pondered Khalid's words, we continued to hike into a valley between two of the mountain peaks. The flora was indescribable, with all manner of flowers, shrubberies, and trees—all in groups of five. None looked as though they were planted that way on purpose; it was completely natural.

I knew better than to ask Khalid to explain what he meant with his words; it was just not his way to let anyone escape from the search for meaning. Thinking of my time with Jane, I laughed, realizing that I was the same way with her. It just would not have felt right trying to over-explain what can only be discovered. The bearded men, I thought, tried to explain far too much, describing mysteries which cannot always be stated in words and which words often sullied. I hoped that wherever it was we were going would help me find out what had happened to Jane after the trouble in the water.

We passed through the valley, by far the highest valley I had ever experienced, and then up a path that wound around the rocky slopes of the third mountain peak. Though we were now high up, it actually seemed warmer, and the wind was still calmer than down below. The music wound its way through my ears and every part of my insides. Perhaps in this land, the higher you travelled, the more pleasant things became.

The rocky path we climbed up the mountain peak wound its way from the inland side, facing the valley to the opposite side above the sea. As we made our way around the corner of the peak, I was astounded how high we had climbed with our efforts. The sea below looked a world away, though somehow I could see each wave and ripple, and across the sea, in plain sight, were the lands of my birth and journey, bustling with activity. It was so calm where we were that I might have thought myself indoors were it not for the fresh air and the stunning vista in front of us. Our path led to a large crack in the rock face that surrounded a pleasant and cosy flat space with plenty of room for walking and many spots from which to gaze upon the world below. Green grass covered the ground, and tulips, all in bloom at once, framed the edges. There was one small building constructed of simple, aged wood, with a sign on the door that read "Servant's Quarters" and another that said "Peace." I asked Khalid about the building and who lived there. He replied that this was a guest house for the most highly honoured visitors to this spot. I asked him who was staying there now, excited about what famous person I might see. He told me that those who stayed in that special house would never tell anyone that they were there. I would have liked to try the door, and though I felt no shame, for some reason, I knew that doing so would have been a tribute I dared not assume for myself.

My mind turned to Jane, and since I could perceive every detail of the sea, I wondered if I might be able to spot her on the land. I sincerely hoped she was not under the sea where I was, or had been, or however it worked. I began to scan the coastline, looking for some sign of Jane. Most of the seashore was lined with impenetrable walls of rock, and others parts were surrounded by thick fog. With some careful scanning, I was able to locate the coastal plateau where we had heard the music and I had seen the sparkle of the lands of the beautiful music.

Following the path that led from there, I found the tidal landscape that had formed the backdrop for the final leg of my journey. The part of the shoreline where the rising waters had taken my life and almost cost Jane her own was much longer than I had realized. There was absolutely no way that we could have somehow spanned the distance by swimming through the surf. I doubted that any mortal would have been capable of such a feat. The clarity by which I could observe things so far away was astounding, and I soon found what I was looking for: the small break in the sea wall. I hoped that the crack formed the beginning of a pathway that might have taken Jane to safety, and I was not disappointed.

Through the magic or miracle of this place, I could also see tremendous details on the land: trees and rocks, seashells and pebbles, and people as well. I spotted Jane emerging from the water onto the land, panting and barely able to move her body onto the rocks. Incredibly, it was as though no time had passed at all since I was with Jane; my discussions with Khalid, the food and drink, the climbing and hiking all had taken place in the blink of an eye. Jane lifted herself onto one rock ledge and then another until her entire body was out of the water. She kept climbing up, following the crack in the rock, and while I could see she was near the top and safety, I imagined she had no idea how long she would have to climb. I willed her to continue. In a few minutes, she made it to the top where green grass grew and a thin path led into the woods. After resting, she looked back toward the waters—to the spot where I could hold no longer hold my breath—and she had great sadness in her eyes, and love.

During the early parts of my journey on the paths, I had not considered the possibility that my absence might be felt by others, save my friend Khalid; it was now very clear that I had been mistaken. Jane looked up and across the waters, scanning the horizon, her gaze stopping directly at Khalid and me. I waved, and while she could not possibly have seen me, she seemed comforted and began her journey back into the woods.

From our vantage point, Khalid and I could see much. I noticed that many others found their way up and out of the rising surf. It pleased me to see that many of those climbing to safety wore shoes that I had helped repair. We could see many pathways, and I challenged myself to find any paths that ended, but I could not. Every path I followed with my eyes, no matter how treacherous or terrible it looked, had a way onward, forward or out. Not one of them ever ended. Perhaps this is what Khalid had meant when he spoke of there being many paths.

I looked into the distance until my eyes focused on the town of my birth, Ennuied. They were still growing the fodder grass, thinking it was the solution to all problems. While living there, I had not looked much at the paths leading to and away from the town, but there were many more than I had imagined. Significantly, I saw there was a large path entering the village from another place, and then it finally struck me: Ennuied was just another stop on the paths, not the beginning of all things.

From this distance far above the land, I could see that the paths could not be easily predicted from the ground. Peaceful-looking, level paths could be seen near dangerous rapids and deep holes, and some of the most uncomely paths were close to the most beautiful gardens and crystal pools. It was clearer than ever that no one on the paths had any grounds to think of themselves as on a better path than others—the layout of the paths made comparison impossible.

Seeing Ennuied brought a flood of memories back to my mind, and I wondered what had become of my mother, my father, Dalia, and the people I knew then. I thought of asking Khalid if he had any clues on their whereabouts, but the time did not feel right. Turning my attention back to my panoramic view of the forest lands, I observed that while all of the pathways were endlessly connected, none was able to span the gap between the forests and the lands of the beautiful music—I saw no evidence of a tunnel or bridge. I turned to Khalid, still beside me. "Khalid, what is the point of all of the walking and searching when none of the paths leads to the destination?"

Khalid looked at me with patience that could last a million years. "What happened to you while you walked?"

I replied that I had the opportunity to see and encounter many things and to learn much that I had not known. I was able to experience some wonderful things, though much of what happened on the paths was exceedingly difficult and painful. I shuddered just thinking of some of my experiences. I explained to Khalid that though I had searched day and night for the land of the beautiful music, none of the paths had led me to the place I sought. Was it the same for the myriads of others I could see walking the paths below?

As though speaking to a very small child, Khalid asked, "Friend, where are you standing now, and what do you hear?"

I replied that I was standing with a dear, lifelong friend, listening to the beautiful music and overlooking the forests from the most wonderful place I could imagine. I understood then that Khalid was leading me to an answer as he always did; even here, it was not his way to explain anything without asking for a search. I had arrived at the place I had sought all my days on the path.

I retorted to Khalid, "That should not count! I think I got here by dying, not by the paths."

With a finality that changed me forever, Khalid said, "The walk is both the journey and the destination, good friend. The life of the beautiful lands is found both here where we stand and within the forests. Though the paths took your life, they brought you to the music and to the ancient power of love and lowness and, therein, the land of the beautiful music."

At least for the moment, this made sense to me. These lands had seemed familiar to me for a reason. I had visited here before, many times in fact. I recalled my experience on the great hill beyond the plateau; after the power of judgement was broken and my heart filled with love, I was here often and tasted much peace and power from this place.

Each time I had swum in the crystal pools, I was here. Each time I had heard the music inside me, I was here. Perhaps most incredibly, each time love had brought me close to death, I was certainly here. How opposite the world was from what I had thought when I was young. I would never have considered that it was the mingling of love and death that would bring me to my destination, just as it would never have crossed my mind that power had so little to do with force and dominance and everything to do with gentleness and goodwill.

The bearded men knew that there was something mysterious about the ways of the forests and the music. Their ceaseless sorting and categorizing were really an attempt to see the forests correctly, and in so doing, bring the music to their land. As was the case for all who walked the forests, their best efforts led nowhere because sorting the products of the forest into complicated categories of right and wrong had nothing to do with love and lowness and were therefore a practice in futility, doomed to poor judgement and ultimate failure.

Chapter Fifty
New Sights

Lost in thought, I almost forgot about the amazing place where I stood: the secrets of life and love, hidden in plain sight; life entwined with death, and the music available to all. What a place the forests were! Though I felt as though I had walked many places on my journeys, looking down and across the waters, I realized this was not the case and that there were many unfamiliar locations among the paths. I asked Khalid whether we had to go soon or could stay awhile, looking over the forests and lands. He gave me a funny look that indicated I had just asked a very silly question, and I continued to scan the forests, looking for the unfamiliar.

I spotted something strange in the trees between Ennuied and the abyss. The tall green trees in the area were covered in brown spots that looked like some kind of blight. I looked more closely and found the spots were actually something hanging from the trees; there were more than I could possibly count. Dangling from strong branches, just a few feet above the ground, were structures of various sizes filled with people; some of the structures contained groups of people, while most carried just one. The structures themselves were very strange, with prison bars on the front and the back completely open to the air. The people inside looked forlorn and trapped, both gloomy and angry, yet any could have walked out the back of their cage at any time.

"Khalid, have you ever seen those strange structures hanging from the trees?"

"I have," he answered. "They are the bitter prisons filled with much misery. You see, there are two things that can happen in the face of suffering: you can listen for the music or go to prison."

Pretending that I understood, I made the mistake of judging the people in the bitter prisons. I told Khalid that they should simply get up and go and that their suffering couldn't have been so bad as to remove the power of common sense. I knew I had not gotten it right when I saw a tear in Khalid's right eye.

"Friend, their suffering was that bad and worse; nevertheless, you are right. Perhaps you remember the abyss—the only way out is the back door and the music. There is very little help for suffering through the reasoning mind because suffering and reason are tenuous partners on the best of days. The music rules reason and turns it on its head, showing it for what it is: a sharp tool for discerning the material world, providing scant relief for the broken-hearted."

I resolved to remember that the forests were filled with tremendous adversity for everyone, not just me. I continued scanning the forestlands, looking well beyond Ennuied for new discoveries. I spotted water in the distance, not like the sea, much smaller—perhaps it was a medium sized lake—and in the middle, there was an island. Streams of people crossed the water to the island, some using bridges, others boats, and some even swam the short distance to the land. The island itself was pretty enough with some clearly man-made gardens, walking trails, and a few open fields, though it was all rather small and cramped. Most of those who walked on the islands looked no different from anyone else in the forest, while a few who were dressed in strange bright clothes with masks and head dressings were venerated by the others. I noticed that the island had three tiny peaks on it, and I realized then that it was some kind of imitation of the lands of the beautiful music. I wondered whether I could use my ears like my eyes and hear things that were far away. Listening carefully, I was delighted to realize that I could and that there was indeed music playing all over the little island. I did not much care for the song; listening to it filled me with thoughts of self, success, and attainment; it was nothing like the music that had brought me to these lands.

Khalid noticed where I was looking and said, "The travellers are best to beware of destinations that leave their hearts untouched. The lands of the beautiful music cost much."

Feeling comfortable, and knowing I was probably wrong, I nevertheless chose to debate him. "Well, Khalid," I argued, "it seems to me that every time I heard the music, it was when I was at my worst and felt the least deserving of such things."

Khalid began to shake and for a moment, I was worried that he was angry with me. I should not have worried, because my childhood friend was laughing; tremendous heaves of laughter shook his entire body, and there were tears in both of his eyes. When he managed to take a breath, he replied, "Cost and deserving have nothing to do with each other." He broke into more laughter. "Good things don't come because they are deserved. But when the music plays, it will touch every part of you. It will cost, though in small measure to your return."

I figured it was probably better to let Khalid pick the next place to look at. I did not want to get it wrong again, though Khalid's contagious laughter left me feeling in rather good humour myself. Khalid must have sensed it was his turn, because he asked me to look deep into the south and east. I strained my eyes to see further than they had yet looked, and I was startled to see groups of travellers fighting and killing one another. It was like Suhruda's story but on a much larger scale: fruitless deaths much different from my own. It seemed that the soldiers were inventing new ways of hurting one another, but from this distance, I could not see any reason why they were doing so. The armies were not moving any closer to the land of the beautiful music, though strangely some of the injured and many of those made homeless by the fighting were walking paths leading straight toward the music.

I saw that the fighting was led by tiny men dressed as poorly as every other traveller; actually, they looked more beaten up and ill-equipped for the forests than most of the others. I asked Khalid about the short men, explaining that they did not look like any of the warriors I had heard about.

Khalid explained, "Oh, yes, I see what you are saying, but you must understand that this is how the battle leaders, the lovers of violence, look from here; what they seek has no value in the lands of the music. Remember the servant quarters, and the word *peace?* Here, those who seek to dominate others by force of will and violence are tiny indeed."

I wondered if this was the same reason the leaders at the little island looked so ridiculous from here with their costumes and masks, all expecting to be honoured.

One group of fighting travellers was in celebration, but I was having trouble figuring out why. I saw a lot of suffering: bitter prisons seemed to multiply on the trees, mothers cried, and fathers lost the sparkle in their eyes, yet the celebrations continued. Looking particularly carefully, I discerned that one of the fighting groups had taken some land from the others, yet from here it looked like a fool's celebration; the defeated were seething with such hate that I could actually see it with my eyes. Deep red smoke seemed to rise from their hearts, and nothing in me wanted to hear the song they must be hearing. I had the strong suspicion that those who were celebrating would not be for long; they would be defending themselves from an enemy regrouped, and all to conquer a small piece of the forest lands that were made for pilgrimage, not settlement.

Chapter Fifty-One
Two Towns

Next, I decided to look much closer to where we stood on our lovely meadow far above the peril below. I checked back on Jane, who had made her way up the small path away from the water and back into the woods. She walked with a limp. With my eyes, I followed the coast northward past the clearing, where I saw the lands of the beautiful music. The coast was rocky and difficult terrain; the black rocks looked as though a giant had passed over the ground with a plough able to break through the thick stone.

So camouflaged that I almost missed it was a city made of the same dark rock. I was astounded at how I could have missed seeing this large city before; it was so close to the land of the beautiful music, and I had passed it by so many times without realizing it in my travels. While the city was large, it was certainly not fancy—none of the buildings were decorated, and I saw no wealthy districts. The people of this strange city were dressed in simple clothes, many of them torn and dirty.

Khalid, who was watching beside me, said, "Do you see anyone familiar?"

In my head, I thought the question was most silly. I could see thousands of people; how could I possibly identify any of them? Nevertheless, I looked carefully at a number of the people. To my shock, the fifth person I looked at was Injud, my old friend from Heureux. He did not look like he was doing that well; he was filthy and exceedingly skinny. I turned to question Khalid about how Injud could have ended up in this dreadful city after running ahead of me so easily on the great hill and on the paths that followed.

Khalid replied, "What makes you think you are ahead of him? You may have died, but the city where he lives is closer than any other to lands of the beautiful music."

I decided that a city this important warranted a closer look. I chose to investigate the buildings, looking first at a large, flat structure with glass windows and doors that opened all by themselves. Judging by the pictures and signage, this was a repository for foodstuffs where the people could gather the supplies they needed for their families. Peeking in through the windows, I noticed that the shelves and tables were completely empty save for a few choice items that were locked in inaccessible display cases. I was looking at row on row of empty aisles; many townsfolk were passing back and forth, looking for something they could place in their baskets and finding little or nothing. In front of the building was a vast open space, and what I saw there surprised me. There those people who had managed to find something inside the building were sharing it with others who had found nothing. There was much talking and laughter among them.

I decided to examine another part of the city. Here I noticed there was smoke coming from the ground and people walking through the smoke. Even with the special vision that I seemed to have in this place, it was difficult to see where the people were coming from; they emerged from the smoke as if from nowhere. As was the case with my vision and hearing, when I tried to smell the smoke, I found that I could, and it was intimately familiar; it was straight from the abyss. This made no sense, because I could see the abyss in the distance and knew there were months of travel time between these two spots. While I watched, the smoke cleared ever so slightly, and I could see that the people were following the smoke straight out of the ground. There was no mistaking that these were people emerging from the same abyss I had encountered so many times, and somehow they had advanced toward the land of the music, reaching the coast as though it were mere steps from the pit. I observed that each person coming through the smoke walked with some kind of limp, just like me. They did not push each other but helped one another over the bumps and rubble on the street, and somehow I had the feeling I would meet these people soon.

My eyes were drawn to a park not that far away. The park was much like any other park in a city of reasonable size. There were paved paths, stands of trees, a small lake, and, of course, gardens. The gardens were filled with lush patches of green and flowers of every colour. When I took a deep breath through my nose, I was struck with the fragrance of lilacs and roses. The odd part about what I was looking at was the conspicuous absence of people. There were no family picnics that I could see, no wedding parties gathered together, and no groups of children at play on the grass. Instead, I saw the odd person walking by him- or herself, often looking around for others but finding no one. From watching the lonely travellers spread throughout the park, I realized that they initially looked for others with whom they could share the park, but after some time wandering, they stopped to look at the park itself. The look in their eyes was both peaceful and lonely; perhaps, like me, they were finding the place called *solitude*.

Khalid asked me, "Why do you think this city is so close to the waters and land of the beautiful music?"

I figured this one out by myself. I supposed it was the lack of what is needed that drew people to the music; not that the lack was a good thing, certainly not, but like a surgeon's knife, it had a way of cutting down to what was important. Strangely, it was this lack that seemed to allow people to embrace what good was available rather than pining away after what was not. Khalid listened and nodded thoughtfully, and as he looked at the great poor city, I saw tears in his eyes once more, though I could not discern whether they were tears of sadness or joy. Perhaps both. Yes, both.

I checked once more with Khalid to make sure I had the time to continue looking out over the forest lands. After another strange glance from him, I continued to look around. Somewhere between the abyss and the land of the bearded men, far from the waters, was a town I had not seen before. Looking closely at the welcome sign, I could see that the town was called Officium. I focused my eyes for a much closer look and found it to be filled with a grim and serious folk. The town itself was immaculate and clean, with everything in its place and almost no litter in the streets. I wondered to myself how a small city could possibly be so orderly.

One part of Officium seemed to contain most of the residential buildings, large houses for the most part, and full of people. The people who belonged in each house seemed to look alike, and I assumed that this was a result of some kind of family resemblance. It was fascinating to watch the family groupings as they moved around, following the older members of the household. The heads of the family often led his or her posse to walk around a cemetery in the centre of the residential district. Even more interesting was the way that the groups stayed close together; anyone who strayed was hit with sticks from the rest. I saw the discipline of the group maintain complete control even while they were walking through a local cesspool with a sidewalk nearby.

I next looked toward what must have been some kind of town hall. The winds blew stronger there, and I guessed it was colder. Here, many people were gathered in an open square, listening to someone talk to them in a dreary, drab voice. I could hear music playing in the background as well—the kind of music that one might expect to hear in a home for the elderly, or perhaps in a museum. The people in the crowd were all taking notes and looking very serious and sombre. I searched the faces of many of those gathered, and I could not find more than a handful with a smile, which might just as well have been a twisted grimace. Others, away from the crowd, walked around the hall reading many signs and plaques full of instructions and directions.

My eyes travelled northward to a pathway in the town that led to a bridge. To my amazement, the pathway and bridge led directly to the land of the bearded men. Khalid was watching me again and asked, "What have you learned, Eloy?"

I explained to Khalid that it appeared as though the people of Officium and those in the land of the bearded men were both serious about doing what is "right." I also found that the people in both of the lands were not particularly happy, and they did not seem to have a lot of fun together.

With a typical twinkle in his eyes, Khalid explained, "Yes, there is not much to enjoy about living tied up in the ropes and chains of duty, responsibility, and rightness. Women and men were not made to be fettered in this way." His eyes turned sad once again. "In the lands of the forest, just one boundary is needed. This one boundary is actually no chain at all; it leads to every opportunity that is truly good yet affects every decision one can make. Tell me, friend, what have you learned of this?"

Khalid looked at me, now with a confident vulnerability on his face, and I wanted to make sure I got this one right. I thought of the friend standing next to me, the one who had stuck with me when all others turned aside, my childhood playmate and adult companion. Khalid was literally deathly serious about living and doing what was "right," yet he was nothing like the bearded men or the folk of Officium. Khalid was both tremendous fun and uncompromising in doing what he knew was best. He was happy a lot of the time but also experienced deep sadness, as well as anger, though I had never once seen him with the dour expression of those in Officium or the bearded men doing their sorting.

I chose to speak slowly and carefully. "Khalid, the boundary you speak of is love, and it is, I think, the music. These people are so grim because, in trying to do right, they have followed a host of rules that may appear noble but have no life in them." After further thought, I added, "I am not sure if the people of Officium are any closer to the land of the beautiful music than those of Heureux."

Khalid looked relieved after I shared my thoughts with him. He said, "This, what you have learned, is worth more than all of the gold and silver in the forests."

I felt no pride about getting at least something right. In fact, it seemed to me that whenever I did manage to find something that was true and life-giving, thoughts of elevating myself above others simply had no room. I wondered to myself what the people of both Heureux and Officium would think of what I had said about the boundary of love. Likely, those in Heureux might consider what I said endearing or romantic, having a different understanding of love and little awareness of its deadly cost. On the other hand, I guessed that the citizens of Officium would think my words childish and naïve, lacking in serious commitment, blinded as they were to the futility of loveless discipline and afraid of the unknown, the unknowable, and change.

Chapter Fifty-Two
The Foggy Lands

I could see that the sun was beginning to set over the lands. Before dark set in, I was interested in looking at the first parts of the forest near Ennuied where I had seen the wild animals. With my eyes, I followed the path out of Ennuied to the borderlands, where I had watched the men make forays into the very edges of the forest. I noticed that since that time, one of the men had disappeared; likely, he would never return to that place. Others remained exactly as they had before. I said to Khalid, "I suppose it can be a long wait for some to begin their travels."

"Yes, long or short, there is always a wait," Khalid replied nonchalantly.

I looked around for the dogs who had fled from me in pursuit of the beautiful girl I had met at these frontier lands of the forest. As expected, I saw that the dogs continued to roam these parts, fighting with each other and looking for someone to harass. I looked for the lady I had met who left with a group of dogs but could not find her.

Khalid interrupted my search and informed me, "Friend, she is in the foggy lands."

I asked Khalid why the dogs seemed afraid of me and why I never saw them again on my journey. He answered, "The dogs learn that it is useless to attack some people from the front, but to be sure, the dogs followed you to the very final lands of your journey, nipping you in the night, howling in the winds, and striking fear into your travelling companions."

While there was still some light, I chose to examine the land of the abyss more closely. It was clearly a mysterious place, popping up here and there where it shouldn't be, tormenting people far and wide. I was curious how the abyss had the reach that it did; could it also rear its smoky head in these new musical lands? I asked Khalid for his thoughts. He told me, "Eloy, the abyss could never cross the deep, but you are right to question its reach, for both the music and the abyss pull at all who walk the forests."

As I looked at the abyss from these heights, I could see a steady stream of travellers falling into its clutches. Some walked directly to it as I had, while others were dropped there from other spots around the forest. There were also many people walking out of the abyss, all of them with some kind of limp or handicap from their brush with the pit. Still, many more people seemed to fall into the abyss than escaped from it, and I wondered what happened to them. Could it be that they were stuck there forever? The thought that they would remain there forever made no sense to me whatsoever, because that would mean that the draw of the music was overpowered by the magnetism of the abyss. Still, I wondered about those who fell into the pit and who I could not see come out.

Without any words spoken, I knew that I must turn to Khalid and watch him. As I looked at my friend, I saw his eyes turn from the abyss itself and wander through the forestlands to the north, to the farthest reaches we could see in the fading light. There, the clarity of my vision faded into what I can best describe as some kind of great fog; waves of grey mist clouded my sight to the point that even at these heights, I could not discern very much detail.

The haze came and went at the borderlands of the fog, and for a moment I was sure that I saw throngs of people rising, emerging from gateways in the earth. It was an incredible sight, so many people coming forth and entering the hidden lands where I could see them no longer. For a fraction of a second, my eyes focused on one who I thought looked like my mother. Though the whole scene lasted just a moment, I was sure that I heard a few bars of the beautiful music from the faraway land and the same tune that played in my heart. Then, just as quickly as the scene had appeared, it was gone, and I was left wondering what I had really seen and heard.

In the fading light, I turned to Khalid to question him but found that his gaze had shifted to the land of the bearded men. I followed his gaze and zoomed in, finding myself immersed in the conversation of two of the men with very long beards.

"How can we keep the people from talking of the foggy lands?" a man with a grey beard said. "It is as though they have not listened to us at all."

"They are just simple-minded," a slightly younger bearded man replied. "They lack our willingness to embrace the harsh reality of the forests. If the abyss leads to the foggy lands, then why would we busy ourselves with sorting this part of the forest?"

"Well said," the older one responded quickly. "These people talk of love and the music, which are just fine, of course, but they fail to see that those who have not busied themselves with the sorting of right and wrong have rejected the music and they have what is coming to them."

The younger man with a beard eagerly added, "It is the order of things! Some to live, and some to die. I would not want it any other way."

The two bearded men walked away together, taking comfort in their mutual rejection of the foggy lands. I was astounded at the conversation. It was not my place to accuse of wrongdoing, but I had the distinct impression that these bearded men would be happy to be assured that there was no hope for those stuck in the abyss. Perhaps they felt that if the foggy lands existed, then their sorting business might just be a waste of time; and if this was what they thought, I agreed with them completely. I also wondered if these bearded folk had ever actually heard the music that they spoke of with such confidence.

My experience of the music was always a complete undoing of what I had thought I knew so well—a destruction of confidence in my goodness and a union with this music that pulsed with patience and kindness for all. I knew that the path to the land of the beautiful music was filled with difficulties and choices to love that were intertwined with death itself, but it was not as if walking this path with its suffering somehow set any traveller apart from another. In fact, it was much the opposite. The more one walked the path of love, even to death, the more it was clear that the music played for all, and I could not imagine the power of this music silenced by the depths of the abyss.

I turned to Khalid and questioned, "Is it not possible that to reach these lands of beautiful music, one must walk the path of love and death, and that all will find their way?"

Khalid looked toward the foggy lands wistfully with a mysterious wonder in his own eyes and great confidence. "That is a worthwhile hope, my friend, and that you express it shows that the music has done its work. If you did not hold this hope, I would wonder if you had ever heard the music at all. Come, it is dark now and time to move onward."

I could see the lights of many fires in the forests, and the reflection from the moon and stars left my view of the forests below somewhere in the borderlands between colour and shadow. The plateau where we stood was lit by the night sky, as well as a soft light coming from the Servant's Quarters. While the glow coming from the small building was subtle, it was anything but dim, and I could see the flowers and the green of the grass as clearly as during the day.

"But, Khalid," I lamented, "I cannot not stop thinking about those in the lands across and below. What can we do? There is so much suffering; can we not help? I would happily return to the forests."

"Do you not see that when we watch those in the forests, they derive strength and courage? Did you not see your Jane climb the cliff or rocks and find her way? Our watching is no passive event."

"I suppose," I reflected. "I just wish there were more that I could do, and that I had considered the plight of others so much more while I walked in the forests. I was so worried and distracted with myself and hearing the music that I failed to see that the music playing inside me was to be heard by others through me."

Khalid nodded gravely and put his hand on my back in the acknowledgement that this was true and, I think, in gratitude that I could see it. We walked together slowly toward the path leading down from the mountain heights, with a soft breeze filled with warmth and life blowing on my cheek. I asked Khalid about how the world got this way and why there was such a divide between these wonderful lands and the forest paths. He asked me if it really mattered to know all this, and I answered that while it changed nothing, I would like to know more. To be honest, I don't recall everything he told me, and perhaps it was not intended that I should. This I do remember: that while he spoke, it was as though pages of time turned with unfathomable speed, making what I had conceived as ancient seem brand-new, yet all of it as though a mere moment.

The beginnings of the world had been filled with natural events and mysteries that I understood poorly, and I wished my old friend Suhruda were there to help me comprehend. I am embarrassed to say that I also missed what might have been the most important thing. I am not sure if Khalid said that the world was designed with the forestlands in place or whether they resulted from some terrible set of events. Regardless, virtually every traveller in the forest knew there was a journey required, and the great writers from east, west, north, and south agreed. Khalid talked about the future as well, which was as fuzzy to me as the past. I concluded that it was the *now* I understood best, and it was probably best to keep my mind and thoughts in the experience of the present.

Khalid said to me, "Continue down the path. You are at the beginning, and the way forward is bright and new. You will see me again soon enough. Your sister, Dalia, has been asking after you."

In a moment, Khalid was gone. Whether he vanished in an instant or crept away into the shadows, I cannot say. But as I stood in the night light, I was sure I heard the quiet closing of a door from the plateau behind me and the sound of soft breath blowing out a light. I was tempted to return to look, listen, and inquire but decided against this, considering that I would discover nothing I did not already know. Instead, I continued down the path, without limp or pain, in the most wonderful and joyful solitude I could ever have imagined.

Epilogue

> *The Dolor Door*
> *The Way of Humilis*
> *Gaudium Exigo*

Those simple Latin words at the beginning of *The Journey from Ennuied*—they make so much more sense to me now than they did long ago. I now understand that the doorway that has led me into a world of simple joy (so powerful that I can barely describe it) opened when I began listening to my pain and letting it do its work. So many things that I mistakenly thought were important and consumed my heart really needed to die. And the way forward from there was one of humility. I really don't think of myself as particularly humble, but I know that each choice I make to serve others, to forgive quickly, and to express the deepest love I have leads me to a power so full of wonder and beyond myself that I know it is the only path I truly want to walk. I can honestly say now that I have more happiness in my life than ever before. I live with a sense of purpose that guides me constantly.

"Jack Burchell, please return to the data console." The electronic resonances from the other room told me that I needed to attach the brain interface gear and receive the daily updates and news that would enter my mind directly—propaganda, really.

I did not allow them to replace the cochlear implant, fried years ago now, but the compromise was this daily download through the interface. My world continues to change with a speed that defies description. The interface allows me to receive information from a variety of sources, both government and private, but the message is usually the same: *Be afraid because trouble is brewing.*

There is now tremendous competition among the regions of the world for immigrants from the southern regions, who are considered crucial for survival and success. The current panic is that war—*conflict management,* they call it—is looming. The results are always the same: suffering for the people on both sides and the imposition of one will over another, creating generations of bitter feelings. I am no longer afraid of such things. It is not that they are unimportant—certainly not; it is more that I am focused on other priorities now.

I have found new uses for the data console. While it remains a tool for my work, I have found that it is also most useful for connecting with people, something which has become very important to me since reading *The Journey from Ennuied.* I have re-formed friendships and developed many new relationships. Some of these friendships are purely through digital connections, but I have been able to meet a surprisingly large number of people when able to travel and during my limited free time. I now find myself picturing every person I meet as on a journey, most of them doing their best to reach some unknown destination. Often, I find myself spotting them at a very specific part of the *The Journey from Ennuied.* I never tell them this, of course—that would be rather presumptuous of me; nonetheless, my observations seem to have an uncanny accuracy about them, and I am often startled by this glimpse into their lives. Lately, I have begun to wonder if life itself is not a journey and every single one of us is born to journey, to travel the paths. Sometimes I am tempted to call out to others, explaining that wealth, fame, beauty, and comfort, while attractive, pale before the more valuable destination of love and lowness.

Some of my friends and colleagues are comfortable talking with me in the language of journey, and we are able to discuss elements of *The Journey from Ennuied* together. I have allowed a few people to read my copy of the book. One night, this topic kept me thinking far into the reaches of the night. I seldom use the sleep acceleration rhythms, by the way, because I find that they interfere with the wonderful world of my dreams.

This night, I questioned whether it was necessary to use and understand the language of journey to be on one. As the minutes wove their way into hours, this notion appeared increasingly outlandish until I rejected it completely. A journey is comprised of a series of decisions made in response to one's circumstances, and in this sense, every single person is one who travels, whether knowingly or unknowingly. Many of the people in *The Journey from Ennuied* were completely unaware that they were travellers themselves. The knowledge that one is moving toward a destination—even one that is veiled—is, however, most helpful.

I have come to realize that to understand the complexities of another's journey, even in small part, is a tremendous honour. I used to think very differently. The medi-scan process, created during the wars of the forties, made it possible to develop a complete overview of one's health and genetic stability, and all of this information became readily available to the government and employers. Many of life's most important decisions are now based on this information, and it leads to a palpable sense of powerlessness when one receives bad news. For the longest time, I felt that there were no mysteries, only the simple combination of biology and environment resulting in destiny. I now believe that there is something else at work in the journey of each human being. To be certain, genetics and biology are very real, but there is something about traveling that is beyond this, a set of decisions and experiences that are intertwined with something greater. When I have the chance to share in the journey of another, I now know that my predictions and judgements are out of place, and instead, I choose respect.

I continue to work at the data console, but my home is much busier since I opened my doors to the non-modders. These are a group of people who have been identified with developmental and medical problems but have refused or been ineligible for genetic revision therapy. They are regarded by many as endearing and simple and by others as a nuisance or, even worse, an unnecessary drain on limited resources. I know, though, that each of them is on a journey not unlike my own, and they are quick to help me along my way. Sometimes when I help one of them with dressing or reading, I can almost feel Granddad with me, and I know that I am making good progress toward my destination. Some of the non-modders have actually joined me in my work at the data console, making contributions that everyone finds surprising. But I am not surprised. I should mention that since reading *The Journey from Ennuied,* I have written a few books of my own. I have taken on numerous positions of leadership in my company, and I suppose some might say I am doing important things. To me, all of this is of little value when compared to the simple love I share with the non-modders.

I have spent much time pondering who could have written *The Journey from Ennuied* and why I found it amongst my most treasured possessions. I still have no explanation and mark this as an experience that defies reason. I am convinced that mystery can be a wonderful part of every journey if we only take the time to look and find it. I hope that this book you have read will fill you with a sense of purpose about your own journey and the many toils and terrors you may face. As for me, the music I hear inside me is playing a wonderful tune, and I must go to where it leads me.

Tribute

I would like to give credit to Henri J. M. Nouwen as the inspiration for the kind traveller on the poetic plateau. The words of this traveller are paraphrased from Nouwen's words and his message. Nouwen's own encounters with the "abyss" and his quest for gentleness and love on the paths have impacted me greatly.

About the Author

Don Braun is an educator and psychologist from Calgary, Alberta. In his twenty-five years of work with children and families, Don has become a keen observer of the human experience. These pages arise from his work and the desire for all people to fully live their lives.

Don lives in Calgary with his wife and three teenage children.

CPSIA information can be obtained at www.ICGtesting.com
Printed in the USA
LVOW07s0902281215

468074LV00001B/16/P